A Time to Heal

DORA HIERS

Grace Legacy Publishing

A TIME TO HEAL
Copyright © 2019 by Dora Hiers
Published by Grace Legacy Publishing

Contact information: DoraHiers@gmail.com
Cover Art by German Creative
Published by Grace Legacy Publishing LLC
First Edition, 2019
Published in the United States of America
ISBN: 978-1693002557

DEDICATION

To *you*.
If the sea's threatening to swallow you whole
If the flames have you trapped, terrorizing, licking and
snarling,
when any way you turn offers no way out
Until choosing death seems infinitely less painful than
slogging through life...
Don't. Just don't.
Choose *life*.
Every day becomes a little easier.
Every sunrise dawns a little brighter.
Every sunset dims the agony.
Every day becomes a little less painful. Until one day...
You realize the despair has lifted. That life is worth the
living. That those circumstances have changed. That *you*
have changed.
Choose life. Choose God.

To the ones left behind.
Death was their choice, not yours.
You can't change your loved one's decision, but you're the
one left behind to live with the consequences. The
whispers. The pointed stares. The condemnation. The
judgment.
Every single day.
You don't have to live under that dark cloud of death.
Choose love and life. Joy and peace. Sunshine and
laughter.
Healing and freedom from the chains that shackle you.
Choose God.

PRAISE

"This story is a great way to get in the Christmas mood - or just to give yourself a shot of heartwarming, sweet romance, in case it's not Christmas time when you read it :-)" ~An Avid Reader on *Christmas on Mistletoe Mountain*

"Every now and then I will read a book that has me clocking extra miles on my treadmill and elliptical, *A Marshal's Secret* was one of those books. From the start, I was sucked into this page-turning, suspense filled book. The chemistry between Avery Derose and Marshal Trent Burdine was off the charts!" ~Jill Weatherholt, Harlequin Love Inspired and Indie author

"I enjoyed this story quite a bit! I am married to a Fire Captain, so much of the story rang true! The stress and the heartbreak on the job, the need to have someone to come home to. The camaraderie between the crew was special as well. I also understood Cammie's worries and concerns- about her job, about him, and about the importance of helping others become stronger, better people." ~Patricia on *Fully Involved*

1

"You gotta move if you want to eat, Jumbo."

Remi Lambright nudged the curious four-hundred-pound llama out of the way with her shoulder and tossed the bale of hay into the pasture at Forever Family Animal Sanctuary.

Jumbo munched on the hay, staring at her with huge chestnut colored eyes and lashes that most females would envy. At least his long ears pointed up, and he wasn't sounding his shrill alarm. Always a good sign with this cantankerous male.

"Sorry. That's it for chow, big guy." She patted his rump then made her way to the water bucket, sliding her gloves off and tucking them into the back pocket of her jeans.

She lifted the hose and turned the spigot, waiting until fresh water flowed over her hand before directing it into the trough. She shut off the water and straightened.

Five male llamas huddled together, their satisfied chomping noises breaking the early morning stillness, a cool breeze ruffling their fiber.

"Time to visit the little ladies. See you later, guys." She cranked the four-wheeler, drove into the female territory, and unloaded another bale.

As fifteen creatures lumbered her way, she scanned the crowd, searching for one particular animal. Where was Snickers?

A groan sounded from near the fence line. Ah, there she was, the shyest of her herd and the sanctuary's newest ward.

Snickers sniffed the ground then paced a few yards, dipped her long neck in a jerky motion, and moaned again. She plunked on the grass and rolled, but that didn't last long. With awkward movements, she got back on her feet and rubbed her head against the combination wood and wire fence.

Poor thing. The expectant mama couldn't get comfortable.

A bud of anticipation bloomed in Remi's tummy. This delivery would be her first experience with a cria birth.

"What's the matter, girl?" Remi spoke softly as she stepped closer to the beautiful silky.

Since Snickers had arrived just a few days ago, already several months pregnant, Remi had scoured the Internet for articles on llama births. With her degree in Veterinary Technology, she could probably handle a normal delivery on her own, but what if Snickers experienced complications?

A chilly North Carolina breeze picked up, swirling dust and bits of straw through the air. Branches of the majestic maple trees bordering the property and haphazardly dotting the lawn swayed in tune with the gentle wind, autumn's multi-colored leaves drifting to join the dance.

Remi tugged her sweater tighter against her chest, humming quietly as she inched closer. Should she try to entice Snickers to the shelter, out of the wind?

"Come on, sweet mama, you can do this."

The six-foot animal lumbered back and forth, cutting the same path across the pasture. A couple minutes passed with more moans from Snickers, growing louder and more urgent, but still no sign of the baby.

If Remi was in labor and obviously struggling, she would want a qualified professional on hand to deliver the baby.

Well, that wasn't happening anytime soon, so why would she allow her brain to wander down that lonely road?

She shook her head. She couldn't put Snickers and the cria at risk by not having a veterinarian around for the delivery.

She slid her phone out of her pocket and connected with the vet's office.

"Dr. Randolph's office."

"Hi, Judy. It's Remi Lambright. Is Corbin in this morning?" Please say yes.

"Hey, Remi. No, Doc Corbin hasn't been in yet this morning. He left word that he had an emergency over at the Whitman farm. I'm not sure when to expect him. Do you need him at your place?"

Remi grimaced. She didn't need *him*. She needed a *vet*.

She'd learned at the delicate age of ten not to depend on a man. When her father—

Jumbo lumbered over to the fence and rubbed his nose against Remi's shoulder, almost knocking the phone out of her hand. She fumbled to keep her grip while he raised his neck and bared his bottom teeth, flashing a giant llama grin.

Aww. He was trying to cheer her up, the big lug. She smiled, grateful for the sweetie, even if he was a bit of a troublemaker.

But he needed a home, a family, and that's why he was here. So he wouldn't be destroyed.

She was tucked way out in the country, far enough away from the big city of Charlotte and secluded from the public's prying eyes and insatiable appetites for gossip, for the same reason.

So she wouldn't be destroyed.

Animals didn't let you down like people did. But it sure would be nice if a man besides her brother or stepfather would show up when she needed him. Didn't look like that would happen today.

Snickers moaned again.

Remi twisted her head to glance at the back end of the

pregnant female. Still no sign of the baby yet.

"It looks like Snickers plans to have her cria today, but the little one's not cooperating. I could use a vet, Judy. Whether that's Corbin or his on-call doc, I don't care. Please just get somebody out here to the sanctuary."

Remi disconnected and headed into the barn. It wouldn't hurt to gather some supplies, just in case.

****

"Tell me again why I drove thirty minutes to the middle of nowhere on my first day off in months?" Gravel crunched under Mason Mulrennan's sneakers as he tossed his sunglasses on the dash and unfolded himself from the tiny sports car, a phone cradled against his ear.

He slid the seat forward and Goliath, his golden retriever, hopped from the back seat and scampered off to sniff the grassy yard.

"Because you're my brother and I asked you to." Exhaustion laced his sister's voice, and he almost regretted teasing her. Almost. But he knew she wouldn't be easy to live with for the next three months. Six months pregnant and already experiencing early labor signs, Angela's doctor had just ordered extended bed rest. She didn't enjoy sitting still, so how would she handle bed rest for that long?

Mason gave his head a little shake, feeling a twinge of sympathy for his brother-in-law, but easygoing Mike would take Angela's hormonal mood swings in stride. He couldn't have handpicked a better husband for his sister. She'd done well.

Much better than his choice for a lifelong partner. Look how that had turned out. He blew out a heavy sigh.

"You got me on a technicality." He glanced around for some indication that he was on the right farm. A faded sign— Forever Family Animal Sanctuary —hung on the front of a huge red barn. "What's the name of the place again?"

Computer keys clacked in the background. "Forever Family Animal Sanctuary."

"Okay. Just confirming. Looks like I'm at the right place."

His gaze lingered on the ancient dwelling not too far from the barn. An appealing name for the sanctuary, maybe, but the rough abode needed a lot of work on the outside to call it a home. Did the owner really live in a converted stable?

With arms folded and the phone cradled between his ear and shoulder, he lounged against the car, keeping an eye on the wandering dog. The animal sanctuary might be in the middle of nowhere, but at least the place had a decent-sized barn and acres of lush green pasture.

Goliath sniffed along a fence line on the far side of the barn. What were those funny looking animals in the enclosure?

Mason leaned away from the car, angling around to get a better look, squinting against the glare of the bright sunlight.

Were those llamas? Cool! In all his travels, he'd never seen a llama up close. He'd make sure to snap a picture of them before he left.

"Besides, this is your baby." His sister's voice snagged his attention again.

"Not quite, Angela," he sputtered. He knew what she meant, though. Angela handled the day-to-day operations of the Mason Mulrennan Foundation, a charitable organization he founded to raise funds dedicated to the protection of animals.

"You know I didn't mean that literally, Mason." Amusement accentuated her North Carolina drawl. "But I warned you when I first found out I was pregnant that you might have to handle the foundation's urgent needs for a time."

"Yes, you did, but—"

"Of course, when I said that I was thinking about *after* the baby was born. Not three months before delivery. But you know I'll do what I can from home." Her voice quivered.

"I know, Angela. We'll make this work. No worries. You just concentrate on staying healthy for the baby's sake. Let me take care of this."

His sister was an excellent administrator, and their arrangement worked. He left the organization's routine management up to her while she consulted him about controversial or high-ticket items. But, if something happened to him on the track, she was in charge, and he completely trusted her decisions. It was past time he showed her how much he appreciated her. That would start today, with taking care of this visit so she could cross this last item off her "must take care of before the baby" list.

"Thanks, Mason." She sniffled and blew her nose. When she continued, her voice grew stronger. "I emailed all the grant applicants to let them know about the delay, but from the sounds of this grant request, it appeared as if the need for funds was rather immediate."

"Immediate isn't in my vocabulary." He glanced sideways at the petite makeshift house again and scowled. The entire footprint would fit into his living room.

Maybe he could make an exception in this case.

"It is when you're strapped in that racecar running a hundred and eighty miles per hour and you see that black and white checkered flag waving in front of you."

"You got that right." He chuckled. "I can't deny that, Angela, but we're not talking racing. Fans place their trust in us when they donate their hard-earned money to our organization. I like to mull over these decisions, pray—"

"Well, it's about time you showed up, Doc. Let's get this party started. I don't think it will be long now." A clear voice tinkled to caress his ear. Not Angela's, and it didn't come from the phone.

His head jerked sideways, and he fumbled with the phone, almost dropping it. He hoisted himself away from the car in one swift movement.

No. That sweet angelic voice belonged to a leggy jean-clad female who emerged from the barn, long brown hair floating off her back with the gentle breeze, arms weighted down with more stuff than a woman should rightfully be toting around. Not when a man was around to handle the load.

She angled her cowgirl hat toward the fenced enclosure next to the barn, where Goliath dug his snout into the ground, sniffing. "Snickers is right over here."

"Look, Angela, I have to go. I'll call you when I'm done here." He disconnected and caught up with the cowgirl.

He bobbed his head once, acknowledging her, and held out his arms. "Let me carry that for you."

She squinted at him, an odd expression taking over her smooth ivory face, but finally surrendered the load. Why was she carting around a ton of towels and blankets? And why the strange look?

"Not too often I see a car like that out here." Cowgirl flicked her head to his sports car.

"No?" She probably didn't see too many cars out here, period, but he didn't say that.

She opened the gate and shook her head, flashing a pair of awfully cute dimples. She hitched her hat up with a slight flick of her wrist, and a glimpse of amber highlights sparkling from luscious green eyes caught him off guard.

Whoa! If he wasn't careful, he could get lost in those eyes, but he aimed to be careful. His ex-wife, Lisa, had taught him all about love and money. Mainly, that a woman loved money, not necessarily the man that came with it.

"Most everybody around here drives trucks of some sort, or rides horses, not little beauties like that."

Cowgirl crouched and stroked Goliath's soft fur around his head, her short fingernails scratching the length of the dog's neck. "What a sweetie!" she crooned.

Goliath raised his snout high in the air as a soft guttural

sound came from his throat.

A familiar longing lurched to life in Mason's gut. For someone to call him by a special name, with love shining from her eyes, instead of dollar signs. For feminine fingers to knead the tight muscles from his achy shoulders after a long day at the track.

He gritted his teeth and felt a huge lump crawl down his throat. He'd been there. Done that. And it hadn't turned out so well.

She stood and glanced at him, those dark eyebrows arched as she waited for him to follow.

He hesitated, staring into her eyes, searching, more than a little excited to see those amber flints distinctly void of dollar signs.

She cleared her throat and dipped her head, waiting for him to pass through the gate.

Which he did. Eagerly. But at least he wasn't waving his fluffy tail high in the air or grinning like Goliath.

A soft breeze drifted by, bringing with it the typical animal smells like dung and hay, but he also caught a whiff of her scent. Something spicy and floral. He liked it.

"I usually drive something else, too, but I left it at work." A smile slid across his lips. Several something else's actually.

"Oh?" She looked surprised and a little suspicious but appeared to shake it off. She hummed, the sound coming from her throat quiet and pleasant.

She gave no indication that she recognized him. Did she not know who he was? Exhilaration and anticipation took turns causing a ruckus in his gut and finally settled there.

Cowgirl stopped walking, and he sidestepped quickly to keep from running into her with his load. He backed up, adjusting the supplies in his arms. Goliath lifted his snout in the air and wandered away again. Cowgirl didn't issue any warnings, so he assumed llamas played nicely with dogs.

"Do you mind if I actually work on the delivery?" She pulled out a cloth from the middle of the stack.

"Uh—" Delivery? That earlier feeling of anticipation soured. He frowned. What was she talking about?

She flicked a towel on the ground and slid some gloves over her slender fingers. "Yeah. Snickers is fairly new here, and I don't want to frighten her any more than she already is. Besides, this is my first llama delivery."

A llama delivery?

He turned his head to the side and coughed.

His, too. For the first time in years, fear pulsed through his veins.

Yeah, he might have wanted to get close to the creatures, but crouching behind a llama's backside, waiting to grab a baby llama wasn't really what he had in mind. His head wobbled back and forth. What was he doing here?

She set a digital thermometer, some type of lubricant on the towel— and was that dental floss? —and speared him with a hopeful glance over her shoulder, her wide green eyes sparkling with excitement. "If it reassures you, I have a bachelor's degree in Vet Technology. Not that it qualifies me to deliver a cria, but, hey, you're here to step in if anything goes wrong."

A cria? Was that what they called baby llamas? He was in way over his head here.

Balancing the stack of towels with one arm, he massaged his forehead.

So he could offer moral support or lend a hand if she needed one, but that was the extent of his ability. What should he do?

Lord, I could definitely use a little help here. I deliver wins, interviews, and the occasional checks to non-profits, but llamas? They are way out of my realm of expertise.

The tall-as-he-was animal moaned. Rather loudly.

Mason jumped and nearly hurled the remaining towels into the field. His gaze locked on his car, and he mentally calculated how many steps it would take to reach. Fifteen, if they were gi—

"Aw, sweet girl, it'll be all right. This kind man and I are here to help you. Soon your little cria will be here, and you'll forget all about the pain." Her tone was sweet and soft, almost melodic. The animal's head angled toward the voice. Ultra-long lashes flickered, and the llama's posture relaxed, as if the animal actually understood Cowgirl.

Mason had never seen anything like this before. He'd award her the grant money just for the experience of witnessing a llama whisperer.

Cowgirl flashed a grin over a shoulder. "That's what they say about human births anyway. Guess it probably stands true for animals, huh?"

"What would you like me to do?" What was he saying? He should be whistling for Goliath, high tailing it back to his car and speeding down the road, heading back toward Charlotte. This was uncharted territory, out of Mason's comfort zone. Way out.

Cowgirl smiled back at him from her vantage point behind Snickers. "You can stack the rest of that stuff on the towel and keep the curious onlookers away."

He dumped the stack where she instructed and straightened. A tall fuzzy creature with the longest lashes and biggest eyes he'd ever seen closed in on him, invading his personal space.

Whoa! He staggered back. Then he realized that a fence separated them.

"Excuse me, buddy, but the lady says you'll need to move it on down the road." Exactly what he should be doing, but instead, his legs stayed rooted to the dewy grass, refusing to turn around and take him back to the car.

Mason gave the big fella, assuming it was a male, a gentle nudge with his arm.

The giant didn't budge.

"Hey, buddy. Your lady friend will be all right. We'll call you when the little one arrives." The animal's ears pressed flat, and he let out a piercing, shrill sound.

Mason squinted, getting the distinct impression the llama wasn't happy with him.

"That's Jumbo." Cowgirl glanced over her shoulder, twin vertical lines furrowing between her eyebrows. But when the pregnant llama reclaimed her attention, she resumed videoing the scene with her phone.

"Nice to meet you, Jumbo."

Jumbo didn't look like he agreed.

"Be careful. He—"

Something awful spewed from the llama's mouth and slammed Mason in the face.

"—spits."

The llama hissed. Cud blasted him again, this time on the front of his cotton shirt.

"Ohh." Did that groan come from him or the monster?

Keeping his gaze locked on the creature for another possible attack, he snatched a fresh towel and swiped his face. It took three rags before his face felt halfway back to normal.

"What does it take to get rid of this horrible odor?" He coughed, fighting the tremendous urge to retch. That, and hide his humiliation in the safety of his car.

Laughter tinkled nearby. He mopped another clean towel across his face and glanced over at Cowgirl, whose phone was aimed at him now.

"Please tell me you're not taping this," he growled. He could hear the jesting from his pit crew already. Being spit on by a llama. He shook his head. They would never let him live it down.

"I couldn't resist, but don't worry. I won't post it on the Sanctuary's website. This one's strictly for my enjoyment."

For her enjoyment? Seriously? Watching him be humiliated by a llama? The poor girl needed to get out more.

He scrubbed his shirt, but the rubbing motion only smeared the mess and did nothing to mask the hideous odor.

"Who knew there was such a thing as llama spittle?" he muttered, shaking his head.

He tossed the dirty rag on the grass and caught Cowgirl staring at him, the gentle breeze fluttering long strands of dark hair across her creamy cheeks, hiding those beautiful eyes.

She flicked the locks away then stuffed a free hand into the pocket of her jeans. The tip of her boot poked at the dirt, her focus now on studying the ground. "Thank you for being here when I needed somebody."

From the soft tone of her voice, Mason knew that meant a great deal to her. He puffed out his chest. He might not know anything about a llama's labor and delivery process, but he could be the man Cowgirl needed.

Yeah. He could do this even if Jumbo decided to spit again.

Mason glared at the tall, fuzzy creature.

He'd just make sure he moved as fast, no, faster, than his racecar.

****

The cria finally tumbled onto the grass.

Remi ceased videoing and got to work, taking the cria's temperature and attending to the umbilical cord. Satisfied that all was well, she rubbed the taut muscles on the back of her neck and smiled as Mama ministered to her baby. She shuddered out a relieved sigh, the tension sliding off her shoulders.

It looked like the pair would be fine. The vet? Now he was a different story.

"Cool, huh?" She finally allowed herself a long glance at the man who'd been her shadow for the last hour. He'd raked his fingers through his hair so much during the delivery that thick dark strands spiked up. Right now, he rubbed the heavy stubble that covered his jaws.

She'd never met a vet quite like him. He hadn't even volunteered to retrieve his medical bag during the delivery.

He'd stood close by, patiently watching the status of Mama and baby, occasionally murmuring soft words of encouragement in that deep rumble of a voice, igniting delicious shivers that rippled from the roots of her hair to her boot-covered toes.

"Yeah." His head wagged back and forth. Awe glazed his expression. Hers probably sported the same look, minus the green around the edges that showed on his. He must've had a long night on call to look so rough.

Even rough, the man was mighty good to look at. Not that she was looking.

"Do you ever get tired of it?" she asked, tipping her hat to get a better look at him. Okay. Maybe she was looking. Just a little. But she couldn't resist the alluring force that pulled her in closer, hoping to catch a better glance of the man who'd stepped in to help.

Usually, only her brother filled that role.

"Of what? Being blasted with llama crud?" Humor sparkled from the depths of his cocoa-colored eyes as he stroked the beautiful golden retriever's head.

"No." She chuckled. "I imagine that would get old fast. I meant helping with deliveries. Watching animals give birth."

"Who could ever tire of witnessing the miracle of birth? It's as if life blossoms right in front of you." He cleared his throat and reached for another clean towel.

He was a mess. She glanced down and cringed. She wasn't in any better shape, but at least she wasn't covered with the remains of Jumbo's digestive track. The least she could do was offer him a chance to clean up, right?

"I could use a cup of coffee and a break. Would you like to join me? I might even let you use my bathroom to wash up."

He smiled, and her heart did flip-flops. *Stop it right now, Remi Lambright. Just because he rescued you today doesn't mean he'll be around the next time. And it certainly doesn't give you license to get all soft inside.*

Her response to his smile didn't bode well for her weak heart muscle, but he had llama goo all over his shirt, and he stunk something fierce. It wouldn't be right not to offer the poor guy a place to clean up, and she might as well make him a cup of coffee for his trouble.

"That sounds great." He scooped the soiled items together and hoisted the load in one arm, wrinkling his nose. "Lead the way."

Remi escorted him out of the pasture, doing her best to ignore the butterflies dancing around in her tummy at the nearness of the vet as his rubber soles shuffled against the grass. Prancing beside him, the dog's plumy tail sliced through the autumn air.

She stopped at the entrance to the barn and gestured. "Just drop those in a pile there. I'll take care of everything later."

"Where do they need to end up? I don't mind helping."

"You've already been a tremendous help." He'd actually stayed for the entire labor and delivery, and his sweet words of encouragement during the labor had shattered her deep-rooted values about men.

Was he a man she could count on? Remi didn't know, but he'd shown up just when she needed him today and seemed to accept the crazy antics of her animals with good humor.

While he dumped the load where she'd pointed out, she stole another glance at him.

Kindness glimmered from his rugged, just-woke-up-and-no-time-to-shave face, and his powerful shoulders suggested he was a man who could carry any burden, no matter how heavy.

"Welcome to Forever Family Animal Sanctuary. Forgive me for not offering my name earlier. I'm Remi Lambright."

He flashed a soft look, one that spoke volumes. Past hurt? Loneliness?

Her heart stuttered.

"I'm Mason." He reached down to pat the dog's head again. "And this is Goliath."

She bent to scratch the canine's ears. When he moaned and rolled over onto his back, she gave him a belly rub, chuckling when his leg twitched spasmodically in the air. "Goliath. What a big, tough name for such a softie like you."

She rose and extended her hand. "Nice to meet you, Mason."

His hand was rough, strong. Used to a hard day's work.

She liked that. Startled, she tugged her hand away, rubbing the spot where his touch still tingled.

His gaze dipped to her hands.

Forcing herself to stop fiddling, she sauntered over to the fence and looped her forearms over the gate. Mason and his canine companion followed.

The entire female population of llamas had ambled over to welcome the caramel-colored baby and congratulate the new mama.

"You delivered the little one, so you should have the honor of naming her." Her phone vibrated. Since the sanctuary line was forwarded to this one while she worked, she needed to take the call. "Excuse me, please."

Turning away from Mason, she connected the call. "Forever Family Animal Sanctuary. This is Remi."

"Hi Remi. This is Nan Greenway with *Athletes in the News*. How are you today?"

The breath whooshed from her chest. It had been twenty years. Would the reporters never leave her and her family alone? She stalked a few yards away from Mason, forcing even breaths, in and out. "I'm fine. Thank you."

Soft steps padded the ground behind her then a moist nuzzle pressed against her fisted hand. Loosening the clenched grip, her fingertips found Goliath's head, seeking comfort in the soft fur.

"I'm glad to hear that. Listen, our magazine's planning a special golfer's anniversary edition next month, and I'm writing a special feature on your father, highlighting his career. I'd love to include some personal tidbits, like some of the things you remember about him as a father. Is there any chance we can meet for an interview?"

Some personal tidbits? What she remembered about him as a father?

Oh yeah. She had plenty of memories, but none she was willing to share with the world.

"No." Good. Her voice sounded firm, unlike the gelatin her legs had become.

"A personal segment about what a great father he was would go a long way to—"

"I'm sorry, but no. Thank you for asking, but if you'll excuse me, I have work to do." Remi disconnected and slid the phone back into her pocket. She closed her eyes and exhaled, hoping to expel the horrific memories and emotions the call invoked.

Halloween Day. Twenty years ago. Her dad had picked up Remi and her brothers to take them trick or treating.

"Are you all right?" A gentle touch landed on her arm.

Heaving a deep sigh, she swiped a sleeve across her cheeks and forced her lashes up.

Mason's concerned face was so much clearer, so much more welcome than the image forever implanted in her head. She blinked, banishing the memory to oblivion, the only way she had learned to cope over the years.

"Yeah. Sorry I zoned out." She reached into her pocket and pulled out a couple miniature candies. "Want one?"

"Sure. Thanks." He unwrapped the paper and popped the whole thing in his mouth.

She did the same with her favorite treat, savoring the fused taste of chocolate and peanut butter on her tongue, and moved back to the fence rail, resuming her stance. In seconds, the vet joined her.

The cool October breeze lifted the hair off her neck and reminded her that Mason still needed to change his shirt. What would he smell like if not the llama crud? She cleared her throat, squashing that train of thought. "So what did you decide?"

"Decide?" A dark brow hiked.

Remi flicked her head toward the cria. "Her name."

"You sure you want me to name her? My only contribution today was moral support." He rammed a hand through his thick hair. A cowlick popped up in front.

Fighting the urge to smooth it down, she pulled out more candy and shared. "Yep. You name her." She angled her body sideways and propped her boot against the rail, waiting for his response.

He bit into the candy and chewed, quietly staring at the cria and the leftover piece of chocolate before popping it in his mouth. "How about Reesie?"

She smiled. "That's perfect! Her coloring matches the inside of my favorite candy. Reesie, she is."

That settled, Remi turned and took off for the house. Halfway there, she hesitated and glanced over a shoulder, pointing at the barn. "You might want to ditch that shirt over there. You wouldn't want to corrupt that new car smell."

"Not a bad idea." His chuckle warmed her insides.

He headed toward the barn, whipping the shirt over his head and tossing it on top of the pile of soiled linens, leaving his chest bare, exposed.

"I'll get one of my brother's shirts for you and get the coffee going. You can meet me inside the house." She jerked around and resumed walking before another emotion, one she had no practice or experience with, kindled a fire she didn't want to burn.

2

Mason lathered the washcloth and scrubbed his face, feeling as invigorated as if he'd just won a race.

He reached for the clean shirt Remi had left in the bathroom and tugged it over his head. Her brother must be tall and slender. A bit snug and longer than he usually wore his shirts but at least it would work until he got home. Better than that smelly thing he discarded in the barn anyway.

He still couldn't believe that Cowgirl hadn't recognized his face or connected his name. How long would that last? He'd never told her that he was the vet, but he hadn't corrected her, either. He should set her straight on who he was, but...why? It felt nice, freeing, actually, not to be bothered with the price of fame. To be...himself.

When he opened the bathroom door, the strong smell of coffee removed any lingering trace of llama. He followed the caffeine trail, which wasn't long or far, because the converted stable didn't boast many rooms. From what he could tell, it consisted of an open great room slash kitchen, a bathroom, and what had to be a very small bedroom.

The space was rustic and rather primitive, but she'd done a great job making the interior comfortable and homey with her feminine touch.

"Feel better?" Remi's emerald orbs speared his, striking him again with their depth and beauty. They appeared to be guile free, but he'd been fooled before.

She stood at the kitchen counter, two plates stacked with sandwiches, sliced apples and chips in front of her, a spoon poised over a coffee cup.

"Much. Thank you."

"I forgot to ask how you take your coffee."

"With sweetener if you have it."

She nodded and dumped white powder from a couple packets, stirred. She tossed the spoon in the sink and handed him a plate and mug, gesturing for him to follow.

"Thank you for this." His stomach growled. How had the time gotten away from him?

"You're welcome." She settled on a worn leather couch and stretched her long legs onto an oversized ottoman. A fire glowed in the gas fireplace, chasing the unusual early fall chill from the room. Goliath had stretched out in front of the hearth, his chest lifting with soft snores.

He sank onto the other end of the couch, feeling the need to keep space between them, while breathing deep of her spicy, floral scent. *Get a grip, man. Wait until she figures out who you are. That's always a game changer.*

"Mind if I bless the food?" he asked.

"Sure." Her eyebrows lifted then her lashes fluttered closed. She lowered her head.

He offered a short heartfelt prayer, including thanks for the new cria, then took a giant bite of the sandwich. "Mmm…ham and cheese. One of my favorites."

For a little thing, she sure devoured lunch fast, finishing hers about the same time as him. They settled back with the coffee.

"At least you smell better." She took a sip. Green eyes sparkled at him from over the rim of the mug.

"You could have warned me, you know."

Her mouth gaped open, but it didn't disguise the curving of her lips. "I did warn you."

"About thirty seconds too late."

"Nah. You were just standing thirty feet too close."

So, she was a bit feisty. A grin slid across his lips, enjoying the banter. "Does Jumbo ever spit on you?"

"Not often. He's a smart one. He knows who feeds

him. Mostly he spits on his buddies when they get too close to his food, but I guess he was upset with you for trying to block his view of Snickers." Her lashes dipped for a second then flickered back up, her voice softening. "Thank you for all your help today."

Spunky, yet shy. Two traits he found extremely intriguing.

"You're welcome." He nodded and glanced around the room, cradling the warm mug, taking pleasure in the gentle company. He spent too much time around the shop with testosterone-heavy males.

"It's not much, but it works for just me."

His gaze jerked back to her. Did she think he didn't like her comfortable home? That wasn't the case at all, but he couldn't tell her what he'd really been thinking, could he?

He glanced at the slender fingers gripping the mug. No rings.

So she was single. He tried to squelch the bud of excitement from sprouting and taking shape, but it didn't work.

"Actually, I was thinking about how nice it felt in here." With you, but he left that unsaid. "It may be small, but what it lacks in size or opulence, it makes up for in coziness and livability."

So different from The Castle, the nickname he'd adopted for his house, which was much too big and formal for his liking. Why had he ever allowed Lisa to talk him into purchasing the gargantuan place?

Really, if he counted the bathroom as part of the master bedroom, he only lived in two rooms of The Castle when he was there, which wasn't often. From the looks of it, Remi used every room of her house. Much more practical.

"That's sweet of you to say, but I recognize my limitations. My brother and stepfather helped with a lot of the conversion, but they have full time jobs, too. Lives of their own."

Meaning she did much of the work herself? Impressive. "It was a stable, right?"

She nodded.

"That's pretty creative. What made you think of converting a stable into your home?"

"When I bought this property, the stable was in bad shape. There was no way I would use it to house animals as it was, but I saw the potential to transform it into a comfortable living space. It's not where I envision it yet, but without more time and money..." Her voice trailed off as she shrugged, picked up a throw pillow and hugged it to her chest.

Yeah. Everybody wanted money. Usually *his* money.

"Like I said, it works for me, and I love it just the way it is."

He angled around to see her expression, surprised to find a soft, satisfied look on her face. She obviously meant what she said. Interesting thought process, though, her taking the stable because she didn't consider it fit for the animals.

"What do you envision?" he asked, more to keep her talking than from curiosity, so captivated he was by her voice, her expression, and her caring spirit.

She flicked long dark strands behind an ear. Was her hair as smooth and silky as it looked? His fingers itched to find out. He hiked one leg over the other and pressed back against the cushion, propping one hand on his thigh and the other around the arm of the couch.

"My master plan calls for a second floor with spare bedrooms and an adjoining bath. I'd also like to add a half bath downstairs. Right now it's just one bedroom and one bath."

Hmmm...an updated kitchen with more modern appliances wasn't on her list? Was that due to lack of funds? Or because those items weren't a priority?

And why more bedrooms if it was just her? Did she hope for a family to share the space or was it more for resale value? He kept those questions to himself. "How do you handle everything here by yourself?"

"Oh, I couldn't do this on my own. My brother, Camdon, has been a huge help, along with my mom and stepfather. And a handful of volunteers."

So, her brother's name was Camdon, and she was close to her mom and stepfather. Mason filed that information away for future retrieval. If there was to be a later...he found himself wishing for one.

"Do you get many volunteers willing to drive out this far from Charlotte?"

She wrinkled that cute little nose. "Not as many as I'd like, but every person makes a difference."

Not enough volunteers. Just as he suspected. "That sounds like a politically correct answer."

Her laughter warmed his belly more than the coffee. "Maybe, but it's the truth. I couldn't manage the sanctuary without them."

He hadn't seen anyone on the ranch besides her since he'd arrived that morning. That meant she did the bulk of the work around here herself. She could use more help than she let on.

He studied her profile. High cheekbones, a cute button nose sprinkled with freckles, dimples that always seemed to be winking, long silky hair. His gaze dipped to the slender legs that stretched forever.

He wanted to get to know her better. Was she more sass than sweetness? He didn't think so. He would give up winning the next race to catch a flash of those dimples, to get a front row seat as she worked her charm on the animals, and to delve into why she turned so melancholy after that phone conversation. But how could he do that without giving away his identity?

Eventually she would figure out who he was. In the meantime, could they spend enough time together before the ridiculously exorbitant amount in his bank account became a factor?

Time was what he needed. An investment of time, rather than money, at this point. Could it work?

He rubbed the back of his neck, letting an idea percolate. Could he commit the time to volunteer regularly at the ranch?

He spent every weekend at tracks across the country. What about the rest of the week? The season was winding down, and he employed capable men and women who could run the shop, people he could depend on to get things done when he wasn't around.

Could he commit to two days a week? Three?

For so long now he'd invested everything into his racing career, and God had heaped abundant blessings on him. Maybe God was nudging him to invest time and effort into finding that special someone and less on his livelihood. He was tired of opening the door to the huge, lonely castle knowing nobody waited for him inside. He longed for love, laughter and children to fill the empty holes in his life.

What was the alternative? Ending up like his seventy-year-old buddy, Harley, a pit crew chief from Mason's early racing days, long since retired. Harley's wife had divorced him ages ago because his career involved spending so much time away from home. He'd lived alone for decades, with no family nearby, just his racing buddies who were gone most of the time.

Lisa might have divorced Mason for entirely different reasons, but the result was the same.

At thirty-two, he lived alone, no love or laughter gracing his home. But then, life with Lisa hadn't included either of those. And children hadn't been on her bucket list.

God, what should I do here? I don't want to deceive Remi, but it would be great to get to know her outside of the context of money.

She turned to face him, and he caught a glimpse of lingering pain in her expression, similar to the one he'd witnessed while she'd been talking on the phone. What was that all about?

He wanted the chance to find out.

"Count me in."

****

She coughed, her eyebrows lifting her forehead. Was this guy for real or was she in the middle of a sweet dream? First, he arrived in time to assist with her first cria delivery, and now he was offering to volunteer at the ranch?

"Count you in for what?" Surely, she'd misunderstood.

"Your volunteer ranks." His arm reached along the back of the couch, and he turned those cocoa orbs loose on her. Her pulse zapped a response that she felt all the way to her toes.

She'd just met the guy, and already a strong physical pull tugged her to him. It had to be a natural response to seeing the miracle of a cria birth, and then sharing coffee and conversation with a male other than her brother or stepfather.

Factor in relaxing in front of a glowing fire and a snoring dog, and she was toast.

Feeling an urgent need to put a little space between them, she sprang off the couch and moved to stand in front of the stone hearth. Goliath's sleepy head popped up then plopped back down on his paws with a moan.

There. She felt safer over here. Less vulnerable. Now, if she could only slow her heart rate down to normal. She rubbed moist palms along the denim of her jeans. Willed her voice not to rebel. "Really?"

"Are you trying to dissuade me?" His hand scrubbed the whiskers smattering his cheeks, but that didn't hide his boyish grin.

Was she? Trying to dissuade him?

Her gaze landed on his sculpted biceps, taut against her brother's snug shirt. His worn jeans bore the stains of demanding work on a ranch, and he looked so comfortable stretched out on her couch, as if he belonged there.

Shivers tingled along her arms, and her breath caught.

Most of her volunteers were teenagers. How would she handle a man, and not just any man, but this fine specimen, on her property for an extended period?

She gave her arms a brisk rub. She'd have to assign him chores in the farthest field or she would never get any work done. "The only reason I would ever turn down a volunteer is if they were an animal abuser."

His face darkened, and he practically growled. "Animal abusers deserve to be locked up, and the key thrown away."

His passionate words ignited similar feelings within her, but she'd become somewhat jaded over time owning the animal refuge. If law enforcement couldn't lock up the abusers, she'd settle for moving the animals to a better place, to people who would love and treat them with respect. "I agree. We procure quite a few animals who have suffered from abuse. Jumbo was one of them. That's why he misbehaves occasionally, but underneath all the craziness, he's a sweet soul, just looking for a little bit of love."

"Jumbo was abused?" From his tone and clenched fists, she gathered that he'd like to beat the abuser to a pulp.

"Yeah." She didn't want to go into the specifics, how gaunt and parasite-infested the poor animal was when he first arrived at the sanctuary. "His owner couldn't afford to take care of him and pretty much abandoned him."

Left him to starve to death. Literally.

Remi cleared her throat and swiped at her eyes to keep the tears from spilling over. Why did people do that? Procure animals as pets, only to discard them as they would trash.

"It's obvious you love them." His voice, low and husky, did weird things to her insides.

"Llamas have quickly become my favorite animals." She took in a deep cleansing breath and exhaled slowly, trying to restore her composure. She'd loved Jumbo from the minute he arrived, but her brother and Jillian always complained about his behavior. Hopefully, consistent training and loads of love would cure his unpleasant habits.

"I like Jumbo's spunk." His soft tone and gentle expression were balm to her wounds, and although he referenced the llama, Mason's gaze never wavered from her face.

She looked away as heat rushed up her neck.

He pushed off the couch and reached for his dishes. "I better get started."

Goliath bolted from his near sleep and trotted over to Mason. They were leaving already. Disappointment lodged in her chest. Over what, she didn't understand. She was used to spending days at a time alone. Well, not really alone because she had the animals around, but minus any companions of the human variety.

"I'm going to check on Reesie." His long, powerful strides took him to the sink where he rinsed his plate and cup.

She followed, until they stood side by side at the kitchen counter. He smelled clean, the rose scent from her bathroom soap hovering around him like a delicate cloud.

She smiled and stifled a chuckle at the incongruence of the floral scent coming from this totally masculine guy. What did he normally smell like? When he wasn't sporting llama crud or rose soap?

He flashed a questioning gaze as she deposited her dishes in the sink.

"Yep. Like I said. You definitely smell better."

"Like *I* said. I like spunk." He looked straight at her, a smile tugging up one corner of his mouth and warmth radiating from his eyes. "Next time I come I'll make sure to bring my own soap. Something a little more manly."

So, he planned to come again or was he just saying that? Her heart stuttered then raced, and her palms moistened just thinking about a return visit.

"Or learn to dodge Jumbo." Her voice came out quivery.

"I think I'd rather be friends." He leaned closer, still maintaining a safe distance, but close enough that she glimpsed his loneliness. Or was it merely a reflection from her eyes?

"He'd like that. He has very few male friends," she whispered. Jumbo tended to be wary around men. Just like her.

"Good." He cleared his throat and moved back.

She released the air that had backed up in her lungs.

"What would you like me to do after I check on Reesie and Snickers?" He tugged on his shoes and turned, his fingers gripping the door handle.

Huh?

"Do you have a list of chores for the volunteers?"

Did he see the startled expression on her face? The doubt?

"Are you sure you have time?" She really hadn't taken him seriously. How would a busy vet afford time away from work to help her at the sanctuary?

"I'm here. I'm all yours for right now."

His words dashed frigid water on her dreams, and her bubble crashed.

I'm all yours for right now. Yeah. How could she forget? Her dad used to spout those very words. He'd taught her life's most important lesson. One she wouldn't let go of any time soon.

"The stalls need mucking." An unpleasant task, for sure. After he finished, she needn't worry about the handsome vet showing up at Forever Family Animal Sanctuary again.

He scratched his head and nodded. "Okay. See you in a bit."

Not likely. He'd probably hang out in the barn for a few minutes, just enough time to make him look good then slink away in that fancy car of his.

The door clicked closed behind the vet and his dog.

She glanced at the clock. After one already? A ton of chores could be done outside, but she wasn't about to head to the barn now. She could work on some grant applications until he left, which wouldn't be long.

She booted up the computer and searched the Internet. After completing a grant request, she checked the time again. One hour had passed. Stretching her back and arms, she glanced out the front window.

The vet's car hadn't moved. He was still here?

Well, it had only been an hour. She sat back down and resumed her search.

Two more hours crawled by. She rose and moved to stand next to the window. Pulling the fabric back with her fingertips, she stared out the window.

His car was still there!

Remorse poked her like a stick in the belly. Maybe she hadn't given the guy enough credit. She filled two thermal mugs with coffee and scooped some oatmeal cookies into a bag, and then left for the barn. She'd bring a peace offering and let him off the hook.

She froze near the entrance to the barn. The guy was humming? While he mucked out the stalls? Shaking her head, she continued inside, catching her breath at the vision of his backside as he bent over, brushing her horse.

He must've heard her because the humming stopped. He glanced over a shoulder, pride in his expression as he patted the horse's rump. "I finished the stalls. I thought I'd introduce myself to your horses."

"Ah, I see you met Pocono." She tossed a biscuit to Goliath then held out the mug and the bag of cookies for Mason.

"Thank you." He set the brush down and took the mug and cookies from her with a wink.

How could he be so kind after she'd sent him to muck the stalls? She lowered her head, feeling awful. Her behavior wasn't any better than Jumbo's. "I'm the one who should be thanking you."

"It's all good." He flexed one arm, showing off the massive bulge under the taut sleeve. "I haven't had this good of a workout outside of a gym in ages."

The man could still joke with her? After the torture she'd put him through?

He devoured the cookies then downed the coffee and set the empty mug on a hay bale. Gripping Pocono's halter, he led the horse back to the stall. When the vet returned, a key fob dangled from his hand.

"I'll be back tomorrow." He hesitated, as if he wanted to say more, but didn't. Instead, his lips curved upwards in a delicious shy smile before he quietly issued an order to his dog. "Come, Goliath."

Back tomorrow? Sure, he would. As if she believed that.

Remi propped a hip against the stack of hay bales and slid her hands in her pockets, watching the pair.

The dog's flume of a tail curled in the air as the canine trotted alongside the vet. Then they disappeared into the tiny vehicle. The engine roared to life, and the sports car pulled away. As if the man couldn't get away fast enough.

"Thank you, Mason." Not that he could hear her now, but she felt better saying it.

Her phone vibrated against her fingers. She tugged it from her pocket, disappointment in her behavior kicking her in the belly. Why had she allowed those famous last words of her father come up to haunt her now? That so wasn't fair to a guy willing to wallow in horse manure all afternoon.

She checked the screen name before connecting. Finally. The original vet. "Hey, Corbin."

"Remi, sorry I missed your call earlier. It's been a zoo around here. Pun intended." Amusement mingled with fatigue in his tone.

She smiled but couldn't bring herself to chuckle. With

Mason's departure, the light in her day had just waned. "It's all right. We did fine without you."

"I knew you would. How's Snickers?"

"Mama and cria are great. I was worried at first, but the on-call vet showed up, and Snickers delivered shortly after that. No complications. Unless you count Jumbo's normal behavior."

Silence on the other end.

Her phone alerted her to an incoming call. Her brother.

"Listen, Corbin, I have to go. My brother is on the other line. I'll talk to you later."

****

Mason tossed the bundle of hay toward the males anxiously hovering around him, occasionally bumping and nudging his shoulder or back.

Several llamas started eating immediately. Every time he heard the occasional shrill hum, his head jerked up in a frantic effort to pinpoint Jumbo's location, and he automatically backed up a few paces. Over the last couple of days working at the sanctuary, he had discovered that these llamas usually let him know when they were alarmed, but mostly their humming was their way of telling another llama to back off.

Freshly shorn again last month, Remi had explained the various products their fibrous coats produced. Most of them were multi-colored, but Jumbo stood out among the crowd, his chestnut and black fiber shimmering in the afternoon sun. Remi had done a fantastic job nurturing the giant back to perfect health. He was…majestic. Beautiful. Even if the fella was a little mischievous. That just gave him personality.

Mason leaned on the pitchfork, smiling at the scene before him. The llamas munched contentedly, and Goliath raced back and forth across the length of the enclosure, barking.

"I can see why Remi adores the bunch of you." He ran his hand along a llama's back and turned, headed back to the barn, gripping the farm tool lightly. Goliath raced, beating him to the gate.

He could hear one of the llamas lumbering along behind him. He angled his head over a shoulder.

Jumbo.

Mason quickened his pace and unlatched the gate, stepped through the opening and deposited the pitchfork along the fence. He plopped his forearms across the rail. Goliath sat on his haunches, panting, his tongue hanging out of his mouth.

Long lashes and voluminous eyes, much bigger proportionally than the llama's face, got up close and personal. The giant stared at him, solemn and expressive, so still Mason wasn't sure how to react. Should he run or try to make friends?

His hand reached up to touch the strikingly vivid white "T" marking on the llama's face, then he allowed it to drop away. Hadn't Remi said that the llamas didn't like to be petted on the face, only the neck or back?

"Hey there, buddy. Glad to see you're in a cheerful mood today." Even so, Mason decided it wouldn't hurt to back up a bit. No sense in giving the big fella such a close target.

Tires crunched across the gravel driveway. A car pulled in and parked next to his truck.

Jumbo's chestnut-colored ears flicked down. Arching his nose in the air, he emitted a shrill, piercing sound. The other llamas jerked their heads in Jumbo's direction, naturally curious, but otherwise frozen in place.

Mason started backing away from Jumbo. That reaction couldn't be good.

The engine stopped, and a door opened and closed.

Mason considered running, but how would that look to the person in the car? He'd never live it down.

He opted to turn around and walk away slowly, as if Jumbo weren't on high alert.

A hiss was his only warning before warmth splattered

his back.

"Not again." He closed his eyes and groaned.

Hadn't he just called Jumbo cheerful? Didn't that count for something? He turned and glared at the ornery beast.

Which earned him another lashing. This time it landed on the front of his shirt.

Goliath let out a series of angry barks. At least the dog was smart enough to do it from a safe distance.

"Whoa! That's some nasty stuff." A female's voice sounded behind him. She didn't even bother hiding her disgust.

He knew that voice. Didn't have to turn around to know that Nan Greenway with *Athletes in the News* stood behind him.

And…between him and getting to know Remi.

He blew out a breath. This day tumbled from pretty decent to beyond terrible in what, sixty seconds?

So much for his plan to get to know Remi outside the context of his wallet. The few days he'd spent on the sanctuary were sweet but not nearly enough.

How had Nan tracked him down? He'd warned his staff not to give away his whereabouts to anybody.

"Yeah. It is. You'll have to excuse me for a minute while I go change." Without revealing his face to Nan, Mason took his time ambling to the barn, Goliath trotting beside him. Once inside, he tugged off his shirt and retrieved a fresh towel from the stack Remi kept for this purpose. He tossed the soiled shirt in the heap, joining the others marked for serious disinfectant. More likely, the trash.

A quick swipe with a towel and a change of shirts would have to do until he could make use of Remi's bathroom. Again. Had she noticed that he'd stashed a bar of soap in there yesterday? Something that didn't smell quite so…feminine.

He grinned, but it slipped as he considered the sports reporter waiting outside.

"Might as well face the music." Mason spoke to Goliath. Pocono slipped his head over the stall's half-door.

Mason rubbed the horse's ears then stepped outside, the still blue sky a direct contrast to the churning in his gut.

Standing next to Nan, Remi's arms were folded across her chest and a boot tapped the gravel. Nan appeared to be doing most of the talking, the woman's palms waving in the air, lips moving.

Oh, God, I had really hoped for more time with Remi. Is it possible?

Mason sighed and braced himself for the answer. He stepped over to join their conversation, situating himself next to Remi. Her subtle scent drifted his way. He took a deep breath of it. Might be the last one.

"Mason, have you met Nan Greenway? She's a reporter with *Athletes in the News*." Remi offered him a weak smile, but her narrowed eyebrows and rigid spine indicated she wasn't happy about the reporter's presence.

Now why was that? Had Nan already spilled the beans? Or did Remi have experience with the reporter who refused to take no for an answer?

Nan was a sports reporter. It wasn't likely that their paths had crossed.

An idea flitted through Mason's mind, building momentum. The animal sanctuary could use a little publicity, and Remi needed more volunteers. He could make both happen. Fame and fortune should be good for something, right?

"Yes, actually, I have." He acknowledged Nan with a nod. "I think it's awesome that you're here to do a feature on the Forever Family Animal Sanctuary."

Nan narrowed her pencil-thin eyebrows. Her severely painted red lips turned down.

"Come on. I'll show you around." He flicked his head in the direction of the llama paddock then turned back to Remi. "That is, if you don't mind."

Remi's arms had dropped to hang limply along her too slim hips. He couldn't read the unidentifiable emotion that glazed her face. Relief? Pain? Fear?

He stepped close and peered under the cowgirl hat.

Amber specks shimmered with dampness.

Anger had him clenching his fists and he forced his voice low, but it still came out stronger than he would have liked. "Did the reporter say something to upset you?"

Remi gulped but shook her head.

Well, it was only him and Nan on the ranch. What had Remi so rattled that she was near tears?

He nudged Remi's chin up with his thumb. "Are you okay?"

"Yeah. I'm good." She blinked a couple times, but the tears never fell. She cleared her throat. "I'll catch up with you when you're done."

"Count on it." And he meant it. He wouldn't leave the ranch until he found out why she was so upset. He turned and took a couple steps, intent on catching up with Nan.

"Mason?"

He stopped and angled a questioning glance over his shoulder.

Remi looked so dejected and lonely, as if it was just her against the world. A sudden urge to go back and tug her against his chest hit him with the strength of slamming into a wall at the track going a hundred and seventy miles an hour. He stuffed his hands in his pockets, fighting the temptation.

"Yeah?"

"Thank you for being here."

He shrugged. "No problem."

But wasn't it? Handling Nan for now only postponed the inevitable. He didn't like deceiving Remi. Not that he'd ever volunteered the information that he was a vet, but he really needed to tell Remi that he wasn't who she thought he was before someone else spilled the beans.

He clamped his lips together, the desire to keep quiet

and the need to confess duking it out in his head.

Would admitting who he was mark the end of the beginning?

Or would she be willing to explore a relationship?

****

A rush of cool air breezed by, bringing the familiar animal smells of manure and hay with it. Remi lifted her head and breathed deep, comforted slightly, but unable to dislodge the strange feeling rolling around in her tummy, leaving her a little unsettled.

What just happened there?

Her gaze drifted to Mason. His wide shoulders looked capable of handling large animals and heavy burdens. His boot tapped a soft rhythm on the lower fence rail, and his muscled forearms rested across the top. Occasionally, he gestured at a horse in the far pasture or a llama, his face animated as he offered information to the reporter. He pointed at Jumbo, and a grin transformed his heavily whiskered face.

Remi found her resistance weakening to his casual, comfortable, and totally at home on the ranch vibe.

He'd been a tremendous help at the sanctuary this week. She still couldn't believe he'd followed through on his word. How was his veterinary practice coping with his absence? Wasn't he anxious to get back to his work responsibilities?

Just then, he glanced over his shoulder at her, and the grin softened, turning into something gentle and tender.

Remi felt the familiar tug at her lips whenever he was around.

A camera clicked. The reporter captured Mason's tender expression for the entire sports world to see. Didn't Mason know the reporter wasn't here for the ranch? That Nan came here to interview Remi about her father?

Remi's smile shut down, abruptly extinguishing the tiny flame that his smile kindled in her heart. She mashed her hands inside the pockets of her denim jacket and stomped to the barn, away from the reporter's nosey questions, camera flashes and invasions of privacy. Away from the emotions Mason evoked, the emotional scars he made her face.

Mason was the first man —ever— to warm the icicles that encased her spirit worse than the metal bars that closed around a prison cell. He was the first man to make her question her father's legacy.

That a man didn't stick around when the going got tough.

That if her own father didn't love her, how could she expect or hope for a husband's forever love?

Thoughts and dreams of a lifetime commitment died years ago when they lowered her dad's body into the ground. They might as well have lowered the casket lid on her heart, too.

Nah. The handsome vet wouldn't stick around. Not after he found out about her father, and the publicity surrounding his suicide. Or the social phobia that had taken over her life since that horrendous day.

Mason would rev up that fancy sports car or that truck he'd taken to driving lately and leave Forever Family Animal Sanctuary in the dust of those high-performance tires.

And she wouldn't blame him. The media wasn't kind or forgiving, and they would pummel his vet practice just for associating with her. Just like the media had blasted Remi's mother, blaming Lessa for her husband's suicide, practically burning her at the stake.

No, Remi wouldn't want anybody to go through the public humiliation that her entire family suffered from the media's invasion. Especially not a sweet, gentle man like Mason.

She swiped at her wet cheeks with a denim sleeve. When she reached the barn door, she turned for one last glance at the attractive man. He'd followed her progress, the lopsided smile still on his face.

Yeah, it was probably best if she stayed clear of the vet.

3

"That should do it for this week. Thanks, Ram." Remi lifted the tailgate lid to the ancient truck and slammed it in place. The entire frame trembled.

"You'll need to be replacing this here truck before long, Ms. Remi." The owner of the animal supply store chuckled as he ripped off his work gloves. Ram tapped them on the top of the tailgate with one hand and rubbed the gray stubble lining his jaws with the other. He tugged the cap that perpetually hid the upper half of his face down.

Remi didn't mind. Somehow, not being able to see into his eyes made her feel less vulnerable around him, made her trips into town for supplies more tolerable.

"Yeah. I know." Remi stared at the dent-ridden black utility truck. How much longer could she count on the clunker to run? This afternoon she'd dig a little more into grant opportunities for vehicles. Maybe she'd find something that she missed in her research earlier this week.

She sighed. The livestock ate right through her cash flow, leaving little left for things like working vehicles or sprucing up the house. Even so, she wouldn't trade any of them for a nicer truck or house. She'd just have to make do and keep applying. "Well, I better be going. Thanks again, Ram."

"You're welcome, Ms. Remi. See you next week." The man tipped his hat, tugging it even lower on his head, and hurried back inside the store.

Remi opened the door, gripping the keys tight. Her fingers itched to crank the engine and get the truck moving toward home.

"Remi, wait!"

She closed her eyes and groaned. She'd almost made it. Who wanted to speak with her now? Could she slide into the truck quietly and slip away, pretending she didn't hear whoever called her name?

Not likely, and she didn't have it in her to be rude.

God, please, if You're alive and real like Mason believes You are, will You help me shake my social phobia? The prayer, more like a sigh, bubbled up from the depths of her soul.

God hadn't answered that prayer in nearly twenty years, and truthfully, she didn't really expect Him to. Why would she think God listened to her or cared about what she wanted? But, in some small way, addressing her thoughts to God made her feel a little less crazy, less alone in the world.

Remi forced her lashes up and turned around.

Corbin Randolph rushed toward her. His veterinary clinic was located next door to the animal supply store. He'd probably seen her through one of the exam room windows.

Now that Mason volunteered at the sanctuary so much, she no longer considered Corbin her vet, but Mason wouldn't be around forever. He had his own practice to take care of. Disappointment swelled like a balloon full to bursting, and hope deflated just as quickly. Guess she still needed to consider Corbin the sanctuary's official vet.

The least she could do was thank him for sending Mason to the sanctuary. She hiked a boot on the truck step and waited for him. "Hey, Corbin."

"Hi." Breathing hard, he slid a hand through thick blond hair while his blue eyes flashed appreciation. He'd asked her out on several occasions, but she'd rattled off one flimsy excuse after another. He just didn't seem to take the hint that she wasn't interested.

Mason's dark hair, the tiny crinkles lining his twinkling eyes, and his flirty-yet-shy smile flitted through her head. She tapped the truck with her boot, tamping back her frustration. She couldn't be interested in him, either.

"Remi, didn't you mention that an on-call vet showed up to help with your llama delivery?"

"Yeah. Thank you for sending him. He was a tremendous help." Was? Is.

"Male or female?" Corbin's sandy eyebrows knitted together.

"Male." Definitely. All. Male.

Remi's pulse kicked up a notch. She cleared her throat and lowered her boot to the ground. Tucked her hands in the pockets of her jeans.

"What did you say his name was?"

"His name?" This line of questioning was growing stranger by the minute. Didn't Corbin know the names of the vets he partnered with to handle emergency calls? How many vets were there in the small town of Harrison? Oh, maybe he utilized a veterinary service in Charlotte. Then, naturally, he wouldn't know who'd been sent to the sanctuary.

"Yeah. His name."

"Mason."

He scratched his head and frowned. "Is that a first or last name?"

Now it was her turn to be embarrassed. Mason had completed the volunteer forms, but she'd tucked them away in the file without sparing the time to review them yet. She had no idea if Mason was his first or last name. He would have mentioned if she were calling him by his last name, right?

"I think it's his first name, but I don't know for sure." She shook her head. "I can find out when I get back to the sanctuary." Suspicion moved in, replacing the embarrassment. She frowned. "Why the twenty questions?"

Red crept up Corbin's neck and covered his face in splotches. "Uh..."

"Ms. Lambright!"

At the sound of the all-too-familiar female voice, Remi jerked her head to the right. A woman dressed in stylish slacks with a silk shirt— a silk shirt in mid-October? What was she thinking? —and decked out in four-inch heels tottered toward them.

Remi dipped her head and moaned. Could the day get any worse? Why hadn't she hopped in the truck and taken off before Corbin got a hold of her?

She had parked in the back of the shopping center. How did the reporter find her? And why keep tracking Remi down after she'd refused the interview?

Remi gritted her teeth. How could she be more firm without being rude?

"I'll catch up with you later, Remi." Corbin turned, appearing anxious to leave. Apparently, the reporter had that effect on him, too.

"Sure. I'll call when I find out Mason's full name."

With a quick nod, he hustled back into his office. If only she could scurry away like that, like a rat into its hole.

Remi turned back around and watched the reporter approach. The private parking lot had erupted into grand central station this morning. Who would've guessed? She definitely needed to consider changing her schedule.

Her boot tapped a frantic rhythm, her hands clenched against her sides.

She was a mess. She took a few deep breaths and consciously locked her boot to the ground. Humming a little tune that she used with the llamas, she dug out a couple pieces of candy and popped them both in her mouth. Chocolate. Peanut butter. Mmmm. She closed her eyes, letting the flavors merge on her tongue.

There. That was better.

When crazy-high-heels-and-silk-lover was within hearing distance, Remi stopped humming.

"Good morning, Tami." The reporter beamed with triumph. What was up with that?

"Remi."

"Sorry?"

"It's Remi. Remi Lambright."

"Oh, yes. Of course. How could I forget?" No apology for the error. What did Remi expect from the reporter?

"Ms. Greenway." Dread pitted in Remi's stomach. "What can I do for you?"

"What a pleasant surprise to find Mason Mulrennan at your facility yesterday."

Mason Mulrennan. So that was his full name. Why did it sound familiar? She couldn't place it.

Unwilling to swipe her sweaty palms against her jeans and clue the woman in on her nervousness, Remi tucked them in her pockets and fingered another piece of candy, waiting for the woman to get to the point.

Nan hiked thin eyebrows and angled her neck, looking at her expectantly.

What did the reporter want from her? "Mason's been a tremendous help."

"Help?" Nan's voice erupted in a near screech, even shriller than the llamas' alarm system. What was wrong with the lady?

"He volunteers at the sanctuary," Remi offered.

"Volunteers?" Nan's jaw dropped, and Remi could have sworn the woman swayed slightly. Must be from parking those four-inch heels in gravel. If she planned to stick around town, she really needed to invest in some quality leather boots. "Ah. He volunteers at the sanctuary. I see now. That makes sense." Nan's head bobbed, a slow up and down motion that made Remi uncomfortable. "Something to do with the Mason Mulrennan Foundation, I'm sure."

The Mason Mulrennan Foundation. Now that name really rang some bells.

"Still, how does a phenomenally successful racecar driver afford time away from his shop to volunteer at a little country animal shelter? Why doesn't the man just write a check and be done with it?"

What? Mason was a racecar driver? Not a vet?

Remi reared back as if the woman had struck her in the face. Her left eyelid twitched, and her lips trembled. Her lungs lost all capability for normal function. She sniffled and jerked her hand out of her pocket. She watched the last piece of candy drop to the ground. Fitting, wasn't it?

She swiped a sleeve across her face, trying to regain her composure, but failed miserably.

Seriously?

Mason. A racecar driver?

According to the reporter, and Nan should know, Mason wasn't just any racecar driver. The man was *phenomenally successful.* So why was he volunteering at her ranch?

"I don't..." She needed time to process this information. She had to get away from the reporter, away from people, away from the hurt and humiliation that never loosened its grip on her or her family.

"Excuse me, but I need to get back to the sanctuary." Remi took a step toward the truck on unstable legs, as weak as overcooked spaghetti. She reached for the door handle to steady them then heaved herself into the truck. Without offering Nan another opportunity to plead for a personal interview, Remi cranked the engine, nodded at the reporter, and stomped on the accelerator.

The fresh breeze floating through the open windows couldn't cool her hot face or tame the tears that tracked down her cheeks. The unsullied air didn't ease the pain or erase the condemnation, the years of pointed fingers and whispered conversations behind her back.

She'd thought that by choosing a career path working with animals she could escape the vicious gossip and censure, the disapproval. But no. Twenty years later, and here she was, staring at the same mess, just a different person leading the pack.

Remi swiped a sleeve across her face and made the right turn leading toward home, her focus blurred.

"Why, God? My dad's been dead for two decades. Why can't these reporters just leave us alone? Why must they constantly hound my family?"

Her conscious pricked. Nan hadn't even brought up her father today.

"And what about Mason? Why did he even show up at the sanctuary in the first place? What does he really want?" She didn't care that she spoke the words aloud. Nobody would hear her on the long, lonely stretch of road. Especially not God.

"The first man I meet that I might be remotely interested in, ever, and he drives racecars for a living! How rich is that!" Sniffing, she plucked a tissue from the box in the center console and wiped her nose, keeping her eyes on the road.

She swiped at her eyes again, stiffening her shoulders and steeling her resolve. Mason Mulrennan had some explaining to do.

She didn't care what he did for a living—

Okay. Maybe she did. But as a volunteer working with her animals, she needed to know his motive for being there.

There. That felt better. She lifted her chin.

She'd confront him and listen to his reasoning. Then order him to leave.

An image of the man leaning against the fence, his head angled over a shoulder, sporting that tender expression on his face, stole her breath.

Why, God? Why couldn't he be the man I thought he was? And why am I talking to a God who could care less about me?

****

Mason hummed, sliding the stiff bristles of the brush along Pocono's back, the strong scents of leather, hay, and horse becoming familiar and almost as comfortable as the hand cleaner, steel, and rubber smells from the shop.

"There you go, Pocono." He unhooked the halter and led the beautiful specimen back into the stall. He secured the door with the latch and rubbed the horse's soft muzzle. "See you next week, buddy."

Where was Remi? He glanced at his phone. With a plane to catch in a few hours, he really needed to clean up and head out, but he didn't want to leave without saying goodbye and to let her know that he'd be back on Tuesday.

The conversation could wait until next week, couldn't it?

He put the brush back on the shelf and sighed. Tuesday seemed so far away.

He would miss her. Over the last week, he'd grown accustomed to her shy looks in the mornings, which had eventually warmed to sharing lunches and coffee breaks. His lips curved thinking about the occasional glimpse of cute dimples that flashed around full lips and gleaming white teeth. The laugh lines that fanned out from her eyes every time he dumped a shirt in the soiled stack.

A truck roared into the driveway, grinding to a rather abrupt stop directly outside the barn. A door opened then slammed. Boots mashed the gravel, determination in the rapid steps.

What had her all riled?

He grabbed a towel and wiped his hands.

A shadow blocked the waning sunlight from the open barn door.

Remi.

Her hands fisted against her hips. Leather boots planted firmly on the dirt. Remi's shoulders pressed back, all stiff and starch. She looked ready to pummel him. Her cowgirl hat hid most of her face, but he knew her jade eyes flashed anger, and her lips were compressed into a thin line. Angry or not, she was beautiful.

And, apparently, now she knew about him.

He ran a hand through his hair, frustration at the timing pumping through his veins, and inhaled a ragged breath. So much for waiting until next week to confess.

"Why didn't you tell me?" Her lips quivered.

Because he hadn't wanted her to judge him by how fat his wallet was, but he couldn't say that to her.

His shoulders sagged, and a disappointed sigh escaped.

Her arms dropped to her sides, but her hands still curled into tight fists. She stalked inside the barn, her steps measured and determined, her back proud and stiff, her nostrils flaring. "You're not a vet. You are not qualified to treat animals. Didn't you see how that might present a problem?"

"The thought did occur to me." Fleeting, but it had passed through his rather weak excuse for a brain once or twice.

Her eyebrows arched menacingly, and she stepped closer until her cowgirl hat almost touched him. She glanced up.

Yep. He was right. Those amber specks glittered with fury, and the cute dimples had left home.

Looked like he was in some serious trouble.

"The thought *occurred* to you?" Her incredulous tone indicated that she had a hard time believing him.

What had he been thinking?

Obviously, he'd been overwhelmed and dumbfounded because she didn't recognize him. Was that an excuse? He gave a slight shake of his head. Not one she'd accept.

She'd dazzled him with her beauty in a natural, shy, didn't-even-know it kind of way. So different from his ex-wife, Lisa, who flaunted her beauty in front of the camera every chance she was offered. Remi's beauty was refreshing and pure, pristine as a mountain spring, bubbling and inviting. He surely didn't want to admit that right now, either.

He cleared his throat and brandished an arm, encompassing the stalls and the pasture outside. "If any one of these animals had suffered—"

"If they had suffered, it would have been your fault." She jabbed a slender finger against his torso, her chest heaving.

"I would have admitted—"

"By then it might have been too late."

"—who I was." And that he wanted the opportunity to explore something between them before his added baggage of celebrity status got in the way.

"Who are you?" She took a step back and crossed her arms.

He'd rather she still poked him with her finger. She was closer that way.

"Mason Mulrennan." What was so wrong with that?

"What do you do for a living, Mason Mulrennan?" Dark eyebrows framed wide, expressive eyes, the rich, vibrant color of a grassy forest floor after a much-needed soaking rain.

She knew. He sighed, hating that he'd deceived her, but relieved that it was now out in the open.

"I'm a racecar driver." There. Now his identity, and his wallet, separated them. A huge, gaping chasm.

His gaze never left her face, never veered to the left or right, waiting and searching for her soul-deep response.

"A far cry from a vet, don't you think?" Her eyes grew fat with tears that never spilled over. She was a trooper, but the guardedness on her face was evidence that she knew disappointment on a first-name basis.

Disappointment. Wariness. Not the usual reactions he experienced from fans when they found out who he was. She didn't run for the camera or squeal with surprise. She didn't even ask for an autograph.

And she definitely hadn't shown signs that she'd recognized him before now.

He lowered his head and scrubbed the whiskers covering his cheeks, hiding his surprise at her reaction. He couldn't squelch the seed of promise, the burst of anticipation, which budded and bloomed in his gut.

He lifted his head, allowed the honesty to pour from his heart as he traced soft and gentle circles along her upper arm. "I would never have let your animals suffer, Remi. Trust me on that."

"Trust you? Why should I trust you?" She looked pointedly at his hand but didn't jerk away from his touch. That was a good sign, wasn't it?

"I love animals. I'm sure you could see that this week. And why would I bother showing up if I didn't?" He dropped his hand, and although the warmth of her skin faded quickly, the tingle from touching her resonated all the way to his new boots.

She inhaled. When she spoke again, her voice lost its fire. "Well, there is that."

He nodded and took a deep reassuring breath.

"Don't bother coming back."

He jerked back as if she'd slapped him. "What? Why not?"

"Because I will not have someone here at this sanctuary that I can't trust."

His phone shrieked with an alarm. The absolute latest for him to still make the flight on time. He wasn't ready, and he didn't want to leave her for four torturous days with this hanging over them. Dread pitted in his gut. Talk about terrible timing.

He cupped her chin and tilted her face up. She tried to turn her head away, but he held her chin in a firm yet gentle grasp, trying hard to resist the pleasure at the touch of her smooth skin against his rough hand. "Remi, please. Look at me."

He waited until her dark eyebrows lifted, revealing forest green orbs, full in equal measure of sass and charm. "I promise you that you can trust me. I'll be back on Tuesday morning."

"Don't bother." Her hands remained clenched at her sides, the tears glistening, but still refusing to fall. Tough as steel on the outside. But that gruff exterior shielded a fragile heart.

"I won't let you down, Remi. I'll be here." And he

would. Not a single volunteer had shown up this week besides him.

He would be the man that she needed. She could count on him.

****

Remi poured coffee into two cups and carried them to the back deck. She handed Camdon one.

"Thank you." He took a short sip. "Mmm. Just what I needed."

"*You're* just what I needed. Thanks for coming over tonight." She settled on one end of the wicker couch, curling her legs underneath her body, disappointment slinking into her chest and making its home there. "I just don't know what to think about him."

The sun made its final dip past the horizon and darkness blanketed the sky. With the light glowing from the fire pit, she could barely make out Camdon's dark eyebrows, furrowed in concern. Just like her big brother.

"I don't blame you, Remi. I don't know what to think, either."

"Why would he work here all week and make me believe that he was a vet when he's actually a racecar driver?"

"It doesn't make sense. Would you like me to make some phone calls and see what I can find out?" A crease lined his forehead. His almost-black hair stood up from raking his hand through it.

Camdon, such a sweet older brother. He'd always looked out for their family, forever worrying over them, especially his twin, Carson. Carson had left town years ago, his way of escaping the pain of their father's suicide, and Remi knew Camdon fretted the most about him since their mother, Lessa, had remarried.

Remi shook her head. "Nah. Mason Mulrennan won't be back."

"He said he would, didn't he?"

"Yes, but—"

"I wouldn't discount his word." Camdon's quiet tone, meant to comfort her, didn't work.

Her stomach twisted. How many knots could she have inside her belly? Remi stared at him, her jaw gaping. "Why not?"

Camdon and her stepfather, Ryan, were the only two males in the world she could depend on. Why should she believe Mason? He'd deceived her, put her animals at risk, and made her look the fool in front of the reporter. Not that Remi cared about the reporter, but she did care about her animals. Mason Mulrennan's word meant nothing.

"Well, for one, he's a public figure." Camdon held up an index finger.

"Exactly. That's another reason *not* to believe him."

Camdon cocked his head and shot her a disapproving glare.

"It's the truth," she mumbled, still not willing to concede.

"In Remi's world." Camdon's voice was soft, not condemning. Gentleness abounded in his words and expression.

True. But that's the world she was forced to live in.

"I'm a public figure." Camdon scraped the heavy evening stubble lining his jaw.

That's funny. With that gesture, Remi realized how much Mason looked like her older brother. How had she not noticed that before now?

Dark hair. Unshaven most of the time, with a few days of whiskers lining their faces. But where Camdon was serious, Mason tended to joke around. Tease. Get under her skin. And where Camdon was tall, slender and more tailored, Mason's thick athletic torso and muscled arms bulged from beneath rugged work shirts.

"Semi-public. You're the man behind the man." Camdon was a Deputy City Manager who did his best to stay behind the scenes.

Ignoring her comment, her brother leaned forward and

waved two fingers in the air. "And two, he did show up to work all week. He didn't have to. I'm sure he has a ton of other commitments." He reclined against the couch, crossing one leg over the other.

Another true statement. Remi scratched her head. She had wondered how he'd managed a busy vet practice when he wasn't in the office to treat his patients. As a racecar driver, what did he give up to be here all week?

With nervous energy, she unbuckled her legs from the settee and stepped closer to the fire pit, staring into the orange glow. She sipped the hazelnut brew, the warmth sliding down her throat not enough to thaw the chill that shrouded her heart since finding out about Mason.

"Camdon, did I tell you that Nan Greenway asked for an interview?"

"She called me, too."

She turned around to face her brother, hugging her waist with one arm. "What did you tell her?"

"No. The same thing I always tell her." He sipped his coffee then set the mug on the side table.

"Yeah. Me, too. But she actually showed up here on the property this week. Mason showed her around."

His green eyes rolled, and he wagged his head back and forth. "Nan probably thought she hit the jackpot."

"Really, I was just glad that Mason showed her around." Remi's blood pressure had escalated to the point of threatening to throw Nan off the property when Mason had taken over. He'd exercised such finesse, such smooth control with the reporter. "Not only did he get her off my back, but he really had a talent for handling her and her nosey questions."

Camdon's forehead furrowed. He leaned forward, resting his elbows on his knees and cupping his chin in his hands. "I guess there is some advantage to having the guy around then."

Yeah. There was that. Mason had accomplished the work of three of her this week, allowing her to enjoy a beautiful evening chatting with her brother in front of a radiant fire, instead of working.

But, he wouldn't show his face again. Not after she'd warned him not to come back.

Isn't that what she wanted? Remi hung her head.

Truthfully?

No.

But that's what she expected. He was probably no different from her father. Showing off a charismatic persona to the camera, but inside, he allowed a dark side, the opposite of who the world believed he was, to dwell and flourish.

"Camdon, it's been almost twenty years. Why can't I seem to move on with my life like you and Mom have?" Remi plopped back down onto the cushioned couch, the sigh she heaved coming from deep in her soul.

Camdon's Adam's apple bobbed. He reached along the wicker back and tugged her under his shoulder, snug against his side. She cuddled against her big brother, sniffling.

"You'll get there, Remi." His voice rumbled over her head.

"I don't know. It doesn't seem like Carson's gotten over it, either. He's not back yet." She shook her head, the soft cotton of her brother's shirt drying the moisture that accumulated around her eyes.

His rough chin moved up and down. "He will. Carson will come home. Just like Mason Mulrennan will show up on Tuesday. You wait and see."

Remi gulped, disillusionment warring with hope, the former winning the battle.

She craved Carson's return, longed to wrap her arms around her brother's neck to comfort him.

Mason was a different story. She wanted to wrap her fingers around his neck for a very different reason.

What would she do if he showed up on Tuesday like he said?

Tell him to take a hike?

Was Mason a man who actually stuck close to a friend through high floodwaters or did he just give up and wave the white flag, surrendering, when times got tough?

Mason had already spent several days at the sanctuary and that was after a llama spewed crud over him on multiple occasions. He'd also assisted with a messy cria delivery and mucked out the barn.

What if he proved to be a man she could depend on?

Remi shivered and looked out at the stars lighting the now black sky. Carson was out there somewhere, gazing up at the same sky.

So was Mason.

She sighed, finding warmth and comfort from her brother's arms. "I hope you're right about Carson. I can't wait to see him again."

If she never saw Mason Mulrennan again, it would be soon enough.

4

Tuesday couldn't get here soon enough. Anticipation over seeing Remi again was eating a hole in his belly.

He'd been sorely tempted to drive out to the sanctuary today, but he decided a day to heal from the bruises after yesterday's spin into the wall was probably the better choice.

And he needed to be healed and whole in case she took a few more emotional swings.

Mason stepped out of the truck, pain shooting up and down his back. Rolling his shoulders, he stretched out the kinks and moaned.

He was getting too old for this grueling schedule, the long hours jostling in a racecar every weekend, and the lingering black and blue marks.

He opened the cab's half door. "Come on, boy."

Goliath hopped out and headed for the grass, nose to the ground, ready to do business.

Mason chuckled and reached back into the cab for the coffees and sack of chicken biscuits, a favorite of his friend Harley's. With his knee, he nudged the door closed, pushed the button to lock the truck, and glanced around.

Paint flaked from the exterior walls of Harley's one-story rancher. A gutter hung at a limp angle against the house. A couple clunkers sat outside the open garage. The garage door was up, leaving the space wide open and exposed.

Mason's stomach dived.

Harley never left his garage open overnight. Expensive automotive tools would look mighty tempting for the crooks in the neighborhood, Harley always said.

Goliath's deep bark made him turn around.

A couple of teens ambled down the street, hands stuffed casually in their pockets, ogling the tools with interest. Jeans swallowed their hips and hung below their boxers. Almost men but not so old that they shouldn't be in school.

He set the breakfast sack and the to-go carrier of coffees on the hood of the truck, stalked over to the garage and yanked the door down, all the while, eyeing the wayward teens. He headed back to the truck, settling his rump against the door and crossing his arms, as they passed Harley's yard. A low rumble came from Goliath's throat, but he didn't twitch from his alert stance.

The teens glared back.

Mason held his ground, waiting.

Harley was right. Looked to be plenty of would-be crooks in the neighborhood.

They turned the corner heading west. Mason tugged his phone from his pocket and checked the time.

Ten o'clock. Wouldn't hurt to let the authorities know about the delinquents. Let the local police force follow up. He doubted they were homeschooled.

He made the call and disconnected, anxious to see his old friend and catch up. Harley, although retired years ago, still kept to the same schedule as his crew chief days. Work every day except Mondays. Mondays were the crew's only real day off, if you could call them that. They worked so many hours during the week, crew members usually spent Mondays recuperating from the hectic weekend racing schedule and catching up on chores at home.

But that couldn't be Harley's excuse anymore.

Was the old man still in bed? That wouldn't explain why Harley's garage was wide open. Unless he'd accidentally left the door up all night.

Nah. More than likely he'd already been out piddling in the garage this morning.

Mason whistled for Goliath, who scurried to his side. He scooped up the coffees and the sack and waded through grass higher than his knees to get to the front door.

What was up with the old man? He hadn't sounded sick when he talked to him on Saturday.

He'd tried, at least the last three years since Lisa left, to wheedle Harley into bunking with him in The Castle. Mason insisted he had plenty of rooms to share and an oversized garage to protect all of Harley's tools. Harley could piddle to his heart's content, and Mason could keep a watchful eye on the friend who'd done so much for him in his early racing years, but Harley had turned him down flat every time.

He knocked. No answer.

Goliath whined. Mason patted the dog's furry head. "It's okay, buddy."

He knocked again. Waited.

The old man knew he was coming this morning. What was the deal?

He leaned over the porch rail and pressed his face against the window, blocking out fall's bright morning glare with his free hand. No movement. But he couldn't see any farther than the living room. Maybe Harley was reading the paper in the kitchen and couldn't hear him knocking. More than likely since the old man was hard of hearing.

Balancing their breakfast in one hand, Mason hopped off the front stoop and trucked to the back of the house, Goliath nipping his heels. He banged sharply on the glass window inset in the door.

Still no response.

He set the bag and cup holder down and tried the door handle. Locked. Like it always was.

Goliath whined, his nose pressed to the bottom of the door, and planted a giant paw on the door. The dog grew agitated, his nails clicking against the wood frame, as if digging in the back yard.

Mason didn't like the looks of this. Something wasn't right.

Sliding his phone from his pocket, he fumbled with the buttons to connect with Harley's landline. Hearing the phone ring inside the house, he counted. Three. Four. Five.

Mason rubbed a hand across his face and squeezed his eyes closed, his heart crashing to his toenails. *Oh, God, please not Harley. Not yet. Not when he was all alone.*

Why hadn't he asked Harley for a spare key? Wait! His friend would have one stashed around here somewhere.

Mason's gaze darted around the back deck. Ceramic flowerpot, a dead stalk sticking out of the dirt. He lifted the vase. Nothing. Not that he expected Harley to hide a key in the obvious place. If Harley stashed a key somewhere, where would he hide it?

Not the garage. He kept that locked. Usually.

What about that old clunker that had been sitting next to the garage for years?

Mason scrambled to the beat up car, Goliath at his heels. He jiggled the door handles, but they were all locked.

What about underneath? He bent over, his fingers trailing the bottom of the frame until they bumped into something. Jackpot!

He tugged at the magnetic holder and raced back to the house, his fingers trembling as he slid the key into the lock.

"Harley!" The door slammed into the drywall, but he didn't care. He'd fix it for his friend later.

Goliath's legs spun out from underneath him on the wood floor. The dog finally gained traction and bolted toward the bedroom, this time Mason nipping at the golden's paws.

"Harley! Where are you, buddy?" Mason made his way down the narrow hall as Goliath turned the corner into the master bedroom, whimpered.

Not good. Mason sucked in a breath, preparing himself for the worst as he took a tentative step inside the bedroom.

The old man's limp body sprawled out on the floor just this side of the bathroom door. Goliath poked Harley in the side then cast a sorrowful gaze toward his master.

"Good boy. We'll take care of him." Sinking to his knees, Mason cradled his friend's grizzled face. "Harley! Wake up!"

Eyelids fluttered then slitted open. The old man's raspy voice barely made it past his lips. "I knew you'd make it. Waited for you. Didn't want to die alone."

****

"He died alone." The chair legs scraped the tile floor. Mason stretched and poured another cup of coffee. What was this? His fifth?

He mashed a hand through his hair then flattened his palms against the cool granite, hanging his head. Defeat crashed through his body, rolling through like violent waves.

"Not alone. You made it in time."

With a heavy sigh, he picked up the cup and turned around to face his sister, settling his hips against the counter. Her Tuscan-inspired kitchen, normally comfortable and peaceful, did little to settle his stomach. "Not when it really counted. The doctor said he could have been that way since Saturday afternoon. He suffered all that time by himself."

She nodded, her palm splaying against her protruding belly in a protective gesture. "But you were there with him at the end, Mason. Just before he slipped through Heaven's gate."

A giant clump of sorrow wedged in his throat, remorse that he hadn't been there earlier for his friend, but he finally pushed it down. "Yeah."

Because he'd had Goliath with him, Mason had followed the rescue unit in his truck. He'd stood next to the gurney in the emergency room, rehashing stories from their racing days together, until Harley's hand went limp. The doctor had pressed a Stethoscope to the old man's heart then nodded, her lips pressed together, her shoulders sagging, her lips moving in silent prayer.

"I feel so selfish." He huffed and paced the length of the kitchen, the ceramic tile chilling his feet all the way through his socks. Why had he taken off his shoes? This was Angela's house, and his ex-wife wasn't around anymore to frown over his greasy shoes.

It was about time to make some changes. Starting with wearing shoes, or boots if he wanted to, inside his own house. And Angela's.

But didn't that make him even more selfish? He swiveled and strode to the other side of the spacious room.

His sister scoffed. Her gaze tracked his movements. "Selfish? You and Mike are the most unselfish people I know."

"You don't understand, Angela." Mason rammed a hand through his hair. A longing raged through him with more ferocious intensity than a wildfire. He jerked the chair out and plopped down on it.

How did he explain how he felt without making Harley's death all about Mason? But this was his sister. She'd understand.

"I don't want to end up like Harley. Alone, with no family to stand by my side." There. He'd said it.

"What am I? Chopped liver? And what about Mom and Dad?"

"You have Mike." Mason lowered his gaze and gestured toward her belly. "And, very soon, a little one here to keep you company in your old age. If I live to be as old as Harley, I'm guessing Mom and Dad won't be around. But you know what I'm talking about."

"Yeah. I know, Mason. I'm sorry."

A sigh heaved from deep in his gut. He tapped a rhythm on the tile with his sock-covered foot. "It's all right, Angela. God is in control. I know that. It's just tough to wait on His timing."

"It's that competitive nature of yours. Always striving for the win."

He chuckled and some of the pressure loosened from around his chest. Maybe that explained part of it, but lately he longed for something more than a win.

Love. Commitment. Family.

He closed his eyes and a dark-haired beauty flitted across his vision, standing amidst colorful llamas in a lush green pasture overflowing with yellow and red wildflowers, laughing as she filmed him with her phone. The sound of her joy, clear and beautiful as the scenery.

She wasn't happy with him right now, and even though she'd told him not to come back, he sensed that she needed to know that he was a man of his word.

But what about Harley? His eyelids bolted open. "Angela, I need a huge favor."

She rolled her eyes. "What's new?"

In their teens, he would have bopped her on the head. But they were older now, and she was pregnant, so he settled for a stern look. "It's all your fault anyway, dear sister. You ordered me to the animal sanctuary in the first place."

Angela jerked. Her eyes widened as she snatched his hand and placed it on top of her belly. The baby jabbed him once, twice, then seemed to somersault under his hand.

His jaw dropped with awe. He barely mustered a whisper. As if he spoke too loudly, the little one would stop his antics. "Was that the baby?"

She threw her head back and laughed, her hand still holding his in place. "What do you think?"

Wonder exploded in his chest, but it just added fuel to the ache left by Harley's passing. Would the Lord choose to bless him with a love that transcended his celebrity status? Would he ever experience the miracle of feeling his own flesh-and-blood child grow in the womb?

But this wasn't about him. He shook away the melancholy. "With all that commotion going on inside your belly, how do you ever sleep at night?"

"It's tough sometimes. Especially when he sleeps during the day and keeps me up at night with his frolicking. I hope that switches around before he makes his grand entrance into our lives."

"You keep referring to him as a boy. I hope you're not disappointed if *he* turns out to be a *she*." Satisfied that the baby was finished with the gymnastics, Mason lifted his hand. Goliath sauntered over and nudged him. He scratched the dog's neck.

"You know me better than that. We'll be thrilled with either a boy or a girl." She smiled, her hand again resting against her abdomen. "So what's the favor? And what does it have to do with the sanctuary? You know I can't—"

"I promised Remi—" He paused. Just saying her name settled his spirit. *Are you trying to tell me something, Lord?*

"Remi?"

"The owner."

"Ah, that's right." Angela studied him over the rim of a mug of decaffeinated tea.

"I promised her that I'd be back out tomorrow."

Dark eyebrows hiked high above her bangs. The "I'm a new Mama" mug, his first gift after learning of her pregnancy, clanged down on the wood tabletop. "I'm not sure which question begs to be asked first."

"Save it." As if.

With a smile curving her lips, she wagged her head back and forth. "Oh no."

He figured as much. But he could wait her out.

"So…"

Maybe not. He really had to get to the shop and catch up on some things if he hoped to spend the next few days at the sanctuary. With Remi.

"Why do you have to go back? It should have been a

quick couple hour visit, max, just to check things out."

"A birth of a baby of any species usually takes more than two hours." He wouldn't have missed that for anything.

A confused look passed across his sister's face.

"I arrived in time to witness a llama birthing. Got roped into helping Remi deliver the baby." He shook his head. "Actually, they call llama babies 'crias.'"

Angela's jaw dropped. She clapped her hands together. "Get out! How cool was that?"

"That part was pretty special." He chuckled. "But then I had to clean up after being spit on by a prankster."

"You're talking a different language. Help me out here."

"Did you know that llamas spit?"

Her belly jiggled with laughter. "That had to be a sight."

"More like a smell."

"It stinks?"

He closed his eyes, shuddering with the memory. His eyelids flickered open again to see her staring, waiting for his response. "Worse than you could ever imagine."

"So that still doesn't explain why you have to go back." Furrows etched Angela's brow. She scratched the back of her head.

Yeah. He knew she wouldn't give up.

"She didn't know who I was." Wonder seeped through to his voice again.

She gasped. "For real?"

He nodded.

"Not just faking it?"

"Not a clue." How did she find out? The reporter?

He sipped his coffee. It didn't matter how Remi found out his identity. What was important was repairing the damage and showing her that he was a man she could trust.

"So let me guess. You want me to handle the funeral

arrangements?"

He knew he could count on his sister. Just like Remi could count on him to be there at the sanctuary tomorrow.

He rinsed out his cup and walked over to the back door to slide his feet into his boots. Clomping over to where she sat, he curled his hands around her shoulders. "Yes, please, and keep me in the loop."

She covered his hands with her own and angled her face to accept his peck on her cheek. "You've got it. Any budgetary restrictions?"

He shook his head. "He gave his best for me. Let's do the same for him."

****

Remi shoveled the scrambled eggs onto two plates next to the blackberry-jelly slathered toast.

"That's plenty for me, Remi. They smell divine." Jillian Sutthill, her best friend since kindergarten, stood with her rump against the counter, her palms resting against the surface. She lifted her nose and took a deep breath. Wisps of blonde hair brushed across her ivory cheeks.

"You sure? There's plenty more." Remi held the skillet poised above the plates.

"Save it for your breakfast tomorrow." Jillian turned and lifted the decanter, poured coffee into two mugs.

Remi slid the skillet back onto the stove and carried the warm plates to the table. Jillian met her with the coffee.

Her friend offered a quick blessing over the food, and they dug in.

"Sorry I've been so out of touch lately. Things were rather hectic gearing up for the fire department's open house. Now that it's over, I feel like I have so much time on my hands." Jillian scooped some eggs onto her fork.

"How did it go?" She wished she could have been there, but Jillian understood her reluctance to mingle with hundreds of people.

Having survived a natural gas explosion and burns claiming thirty percent of her body, Jillian was used to stares, so she didn't much like being in the public eye, either, but she tolerated it better than Remi.

"It went well. We probably had over five hundred people this year. More kids come out every year, and that's always a good thing."

"That's wonderful." Remi took a bite of toast, but she really didn't have an appetite. She'd cooked mostly for her friend.

"So catch me up with what's been happening here."

"Snickers had her cria." Remi sipped her coffee.

"She did?" Jillian's face lit up. "What did she have?"

"A girl. We named her Reesie."

"We?" Jillian gaped. Her fork clanged against the plate.

Remi's slip of the tongue would cost her in the form of information. Information she wasn't sure she was ready to share yet. If ever. Why bother? She didn't expect Mason to show up at the sanctuary again.

"I had a helper with the delivery."

"Really? Corbin made it all the way out here in time?"

Remi scoffed and shook her head, idly pushing her fork through the food on her plate. "Ha! No. Not Corbin."

"Your mom? Camdon?" Shadows darkened Jillian's expression before she dipped her head, her blonde bangs draping her eyes.

Remi covered her friend's hand with her own. "Hey, it's okay. Carson will be back."

Remi knew Jillian missed Camdon's identical twin. Not only had they all grown up hanging out with each other, but Carson and Jillian had dated during high school. Then, right after graduation, with Jillian's heart set on the altar, Carson had deserted her. Walked away from all of them without a backward glance.

"Maybe. Maybe not. But it doesn't matter anymore."

Yes, it did, and Remi knew her friend still ached for her brother to return. Wait until she got her hands on Carson. She didn't know whether she'd hug him because she missed him so much or shake him for making her best friend so sad.

"Mason Mulrennan was here."

Jillian twitched then squinted, her eyes flashing from brown to gold in seconds. "Mason Mulrennan? The racecar driver Mason Mulrennan?"

"How does everybody know who the guy is but me?"

"Because you don't watch sports."

"Is racecar driving actually considered a sport?" Remi mulled that around in her head.

"What do you mean he was here?"

"Here. At the sanctuary."

Jillian cocked her head. "Doing what exactly?"

That was a good question. Why had the man shown up when he did? She gave her head a slight shake. It didn't matter. She wouldn't hear from him again. "He helped deliver Reesie."

Jillian leaned back against the chair, her head wagging from side to side as if in slow motion, the eggs on her plate forgotten. "Mason Mulrennan. Here at the sanctuary. Delivering your little cria. Unbelievable."

Yeah. She still had a hard time wrapping her brain around it. She took a bite of toast, the blackberry goodness suddenly bitter on her tongue.

A heavy duty motor revved into the driveway then cut off. Who could that be? She wasn't expecting anyone besides Jillian this morning.

Unless—

Surely it wasn't—

No!

She stood up so fast the chair fell backward. She tugged it upright, but the toast caught midway down her throat. She coughed, her eyes tearing.

Jillian thumped her on the back. "You okay?"

"Uh, yes, thanks." Remi finally caught her breath, her palm covering her chest to slow the beating of her heart.

She marched to the window and lifted the fabric, fear and hope duking it out in the vicinity of her chest.

"He's here." The words came out on a whisper. He'd said he would come, and he did.

"Who's here?"

"Mason Mulrennan."

"Really?" Wooden chair legs scraped back from the table and leather boot soles slapped the floor behind her. Jillian's breath blew against the back of Remi's neck as her friend peered out the window behind her. "Is he as hunky looking as he is on the television? All brown eyes and heart-stopping gorgeous?"

Remi twisted and glared at her friend.

Jillian's eyebrows arched. "What? I'm just asking. It's not every day you get to see a celebrity."

Remi heaved a sigh and allowed the fabric to fall back in place. "Yeah. Well, I'd rather not see a celebrity, today or any other day. I told him not to come back."

"You did what?" Jillian almost squealed.

Remi turned around and faced her friend. "You heard me."

Jillian stared at her for a moment then nodded, slow and thoughtful. "Okay. I get why you wouldn't want to see him."

"Good. I knew you'd see it my way."

"But if you told him not to come back, why is he here?"

Why indeed. She intended to find out. Now if she could only get her heart to slow down and cooperate. Must be from the adrenaline, the anger that the obstinate man disregarded her wishes so blatantly.

She tugged her denim jacket off the hook by the door and shoved her arms through the sleeves then reached for the doorknob. "I'll have to catch you up on things later, Jillian. Right now I'm going to find out what he's doing here."

"Do you need backup?" A glint of some kind flickered across Jillian's face.

Remi wasn't quite sure what to make of it. She frowned

and shook her head. "Nah. I'm good."

"Well, then, I'll leave you to it. Call me if you need help putting out any fires." A teasing smile lifted the corners of Jillian's mouth.

What did she mean by that? Remi didn't wait to find out. She flung the door open and stomped to the barn, her racing heart and weak legs betraying the signals her brain pulsed.

Jillian followed. She untied and mounted her horse. With a quick flick of her blonde head and another impish smile, she urged Lightning toward her house, just down the road a bit.

Cardinals flitted from tree to tree, and robins pranced around in the still lush blanket of grass. The dazzling autumn sunlight mocked her as she tromped to the barn. Why wasn't the day gloomy and gray to match the turmoil roiling around in her tummy?

Heavy boots thumped across the dirt inside the barn. A horse's lead clicked to the post hook. The low, deep voice, fraught with anguish and pain, echoed from inside the cavernous space, slowing her steps. "Okay, Angela. That'll work. I'll swing by the funeral home this evening on my way back home to sign the paperwork."

Silence.

Who was Angela? A girlfriend?

Remi pinched her eyebrows. That didn't matter. What mattered was that someone he knew had died.

This conversation wasn't meant for her, and she didn't intend to listen. She took a step away.

"Whatever it costs is fine. Harley deserves it." He sniffled then cleared his throat. His voice sounded rough, as if he hadn't gotten sleep in days.

Remi hesitated, recognizing pain and loss. Maybe she should offer him a steaming cup of hot chocolate. A sympathetic ear. She would have liked those things herself when her father died.

Instead, she'd gotten the cold shoulder, whispers and

stares.

Remi retraced her steps to the kitchen and prepped some to-go cups of hot chocolate. She doubted Mason would appreciate a shoulder to cry on, but she could at least listen. Figuring out why he was here could wait. A few minutes, anyway.

She grabbed a couple napkins and headed back to the barn, balancing the cups. When she reached the open door, she coughed to let the poor guy know she was around before she invaded his personal zone.

She stepped into the barn, the musty hay and animal smells wrapping around her like a warm blanket. She breathed deep of the reminders that her animals loved and accepted her unconditionally, no strings attached.

She put the mugs down, cuddled Pocono's neck and planted a kiss on his forehead. Ah, so the big guy was hiding in Pocono's stall.

Goliath padded out to greet her, his tail wagging in such big circles that his rump actually moved with it.

"Hey, there, sweet boy." She squatted and buried her face in his fur. "I'm so glad you came to see me today."

Moaning, he plopped down on the ground and rolled over. She complied with the requested belly rub. "I'm going to visit with your daddy. You might want to stay out here. It's not going to be a pretty sight."

Goliath stretched out and plopped his head on the straw as if he understood. She rose and scooped up the mugs. Straw crunched under her boots as she made her way to Pocono's stall.

She was wrong.

It was a pretty sight.

Correction. He was. Not pretty. But take-her-breath-away good looking.

Strong arms hoisted the pitchfork midair, poised to heave soiled straw into the wheelbarrow. Why was he here mucking out her stalls again?

Who was this man?

He looked up, and she caught a glimpse of pain flash across his face. Sorrow glazed his eyes before he blinked it away.

"Good morning, sunshine." He dumped the load and continued digging.

All brown eyes and heart-stopping gorgeous. Jillian was right.

Remi almost dropped the cups. She fumbled with her grip then held out a trembling hand, offering him one. "Hot chocolate."

He stretched, those incredibly muscular legs looking too powerful, too good, in his well-worn jeans. He'd shed his jacket, and the long-sleeved shirt strained against his bulky chest.

She averted her head, just enough so she wouldn't wish for something that she couldn't have.

Like love. A man to share her dreams, to comfort her over her failures, to celebrate her successes. A marriage like her mom's, melded around faith and shared values. Family.

All off limits.

Especially the faith. That spark had flickered out a long time ago.

And a racecar driver?

Definitely a red light.

"Thanks." His fingers wrapped around hers, warm and comforting.

How was that? She'd meant to comfort him. She cleared her throat and pulled her hand back when she was sure his fingers gripped the cup.

He sipped then licked whipped cream from his upper lip. When her heart raced in response, she stared down at the tip of her boots.

"This is wonderful. Thank you, Remi."

"You're welcome." So why are you here?

"I told you I would be here today."

Her head jerked back up. The man was dangerous if he

could peek into her thoughts like that. What else could he see? "And I told you not to come."

"That you did, but you also stated very emphatically that you didn't want anybody here that you couldn't trust. I want you to know that you can trust me, Remi. I'm a man of my word."

"Appears that way." For now.

"It's not just an act. It's who I am." He took another sip of the hot chocolate then set it on the ledge of the stall's open half door, spearing her with a soulful glance before he picked up the pronged fork again.

Mercy! Did she have to wipe her brain clean so that he couldn't see straight through to what she was thinking?

"I might have overheard a conversation that I wasn't meant—"

"One of my good friends died yesterday." The pitchfork stilled with its prongs hidden in the straw. His gaze focused at the ground.

"Oh, Mason, I'm so sorry."

His chest lifted then fell. Jillian could have heard his sigh all the way inside her house.

"Is there anything I can do?"

Slowly, his gaze made its way from the ground to her face. Longing, pain, heartache. She saw it all. Not just the lines on his face, but in the slight sag of his powerful shoulders and the way he hung his head.

"Yeah. There is. You can come with me to the funeral."

She jerked back as if he'd slapped her. "Come with you to the funeral?"

"Yeah. I'd like you to be there."

"Why?"

"He was someone special to me."

Did that mean she was someone special because he'd asked her to go with him? She gulped. Again, in her head, that flashing red light strobed.

"We've—" he coughed and cleared his throat, started

again. "Harley was my first pit crew chief. He worked with me until he retired a few years back."

"You've known each other a long time then."

He nodded. "I was seventeen, when the racing bug bit me."

Goliath padded into the stall and plunked down next to Mason with a huff. The mighty man knelt, one knee braced against the straw, and stroked the dog's neck. Goliath moaned and stretched, closing his eyes in ecstasy.

"I found him yesterday. All alone." Mason stood. His fingers tracked through his own hair, leaving a cowlick sticking up in front.

Her hand ached with the desire to smooth it out for him. She was in dangerous territory now. "I'm sorry, but—"

Mason's dark head dipped for a few seconds. Except for Goliath's soft snuffle, the space was charged with an agonizing silence.

How could the dog sleep while his master suffered? But then, she knew all about death. It was a mystery of life. How loved ones could die, yet people went about their daily business. Working. Playing. Laughing.

"I understand if you'd rather not. I was just hoping..." His husky voice trailed off. When he raised his head, their gazes collided. His unshaven jaw clenched before he dragged his attention back to the floor and sighed.

Her heart pinched. That was so sweet of him, but she hadn't been to a funeral since her dad's service, and she surely hadn't wanted to go back then. "I don't think it's a good idea."

Brown eyes as warm as the hot chocolate she just drank bore into hers. She shifted, uncomfortable with how they made her feel. Whole. Desirable. Accepted.

"I think it's the best idea I've had in years." And with that, his strong arms got back to work.

5

"Thank you for coming. Glad you could make it." Mason mingled with various crew members, shaking hands, moving on until he made it to the edge of the crowd at the graveside. He was satisfied with the good showing from all the teams. Harley had been well-liked and respected in the racing industry.

Too bad not so much in his own family. His ex-wife and children hadn't bothered to show. But there was still time.

His gaze shot to the road where cars lined the curb, stretching as far as he could see in both directions.

Charlie, his current crew chief, stepped up beside him and curled a hand around his shoulder. "I'm sorry about Harley, boss. I know how fond you were of the old man. We all were."

"Thanks, man. I appreciate it."

"Do you think his family will show?"

"It doesn't look that way."

Charlie shook his head, commiserating. "Well, I'm glad you got to his place when you did. That's a tough way to finish out your life, huh?"

"Yeah. But he wasn't alone. He might not have had family or friends surrounding him, but God walked with him through the valley." He should've headed to Harley's house first. Instead, he'd made a stop at the shop and then the fast food joint. Even so, according to the medical team that worked on Harley, arriving earlier that morning wouldn't have changed the outcome.

Charlie nodded. "I hear ya."

Movement along the road caught Mason's attention. Had Harley's family members finally decided to make an appearance?

A tall, slender man and a female walked toward the tent. Suddenly the female turned around abruptly and headed in the opposite direction. The man hurried after her, slid an arm around her shoulders and leaned close to speak to her in low tones, his expression a mixture of worry and concern.

Wait a minute. Was that—

Remi?

She'd come after all!

A grateful sigh lifted his chest. *Thank You, Lord!*

"Excuse me, Charlie." He patted his crew chief's shoulder and hustled toward Remi.

His gaze soaked in the sight of her. She'd pulled her long dark hair into a twist at the nape of her neck. Wearing black dress slacks and a turquoise sweater that clung to her soft curves, her pure and natural beauty made his breath hitch, but the lightly applied makeup couldn't conceal the puffy, dark hollows around her eyes.

Loneliness? Heartache? Or had this guy said something to upset her?

One glance at the man, compassion and tenderness clear in the lines etching his face, told Mason that wasn't the case.

"Remi." He held out his hand. Warmth spread through his limbs at the sensation of satin skin.

Her sweet smile just about did him in. If she hadn't arrived with this fellow, he'd have tugged her into his arms to chase away the loneliness that seemed to plague them both.

"Mason, this is my brother Camdon." She transferred her smile to the tall, suited man standing next to her. "Camdon, this is Mason Mulrennan."

Her brother? Mason tamped down the pleasure that raced through his veins. Of course she'd brought her brother!

He could've kicked himself for not spotting the resemblance between siblings. Dark hair, slender build, striking brown flecks gracing jade colored eyes.

"Glad to meet you, Camdon. You're a lifesaver, man. I appreciate the use of your clothes."

A puzzled look crossed Camdon's face as they shook hands. Pink crept across Remi's cheeks.

"Oh, that didn't come out right." Grimacing, Mason pulled his arm back and scrubbed a hand across his jaw, hoping to hide the silly grin that slid across his face since knowing this was her brother and not a date.

But he'd better set the record straight. Wouldn't want her brother to think badly of him right off. "It's not like…she, I, um—"

"He had a run in with Jumbo, and I let him borrow your shirt," Remi blurted.

Camdon nodded with a wrinkled nose. "We've all suffered similar incidents from that rascal. But the big lug's been through a lot. I think he'll behave better under my sister's loving care."

"I'm sure." That didn't sound right, either. What was wrong with him? Heat burned his neck and made its way up to his face.

He cupped Remi's elbow and leaned close, her spicy scent tickling his nose and igniting even more flames to life. "Thank you for coming."

She smiled, but it was mostly just lip gesture.

"Would you like to sit inside the tent?"

She shook her head and shrunk back. Was that fear flitting across her pretty features? Or just general distaste for memorial services? "No, thanks. I think we'll be good standing out here. Right, Camdon?" She took a step back, glancing to her brother for confirmation.

Camdon nodded and halted her retreat by placing a hand against her back, his black shoes firmly planted in the grass.

The pastor started to speak, and Mason turned his attention to the tent. *Lord, let the pastor's words be Your words. Please don't let Harley's death be in vain. Allow him to bring honor and glory to You in his death, just as he did in his living.*

****

What was she doing here? She shouldn't have come.

Darkness swirled, threatened to overwhelm her.

The coffin. The pastor's message. The finality of death. Never seeing her father again. Whispers. Stares. Pointed fingers.

A tremor started in her legs and worked its way up to her shoulders. She braced her arms across her chest, certain that her teeth would start chattering any second.

Mason angled his head sideways, but she didn't dare look at him or she'd break down. He must be suffering tremendous pain, losing his long-time friend. Her heart ached for him in his loss, but she couldn't stay here much longer.

An arm tugged and tucked her under a shoulder, next to blessed warmth. She looked up and smiled her thanks, her lips quivering.

Mason.

He'd just lost one of his best friends, and he was offering her comfort? Dampness trickled down her cheeks. She sniffled.

A tissue appeared in front of her face, this time from her left. Camdon.

She took it and swiped at her face and nose, grateful for the tenderness and care from both men. She expected it from her brother, but Mason?

Her cheek nestled against the fabric of the man's coat. His clean and spicy scent mingled with the cool outdoors, calming her until the tremors settled. Her body relaxed against his wall of solid muscle. The pastor's words, confident and comforting, flowed through her.

Please, God, I want that peace that the pastor speaks of, and that Mason models with his life, for myself. Please heal my wounded spirit. Help me break free from this bondage of fear that grips me tighter than a vice.

The prayer, along with a sigh, slipped out from the deepest part of her soul. Would God come through? Might He finally loosen the shackles of fear?

Still tucked in the security of Mason's embrace, Remi glanced around the large gathering. Every seat inside the tent was occupied, and a crowd huddled close together outside to hear the eulogy.

If Remi didn't know better, she'd think that Mason's friend was well-liked and respected. But she knew better.

Sure. Some people attended memorials to pay their respects, but others came to gawk. To gossip. Perhaps to snatch a photo of a celebrity like Mason.

Where did she fit in?

She came because Mason cared about this man. But why did that matter? He hadn't been completely honest with her about who he was until she'd confronted him.

She'd do best to remember that he was a celebrity, an icon, worthy of media frenzy.

She stole another glance around the crowd. She didn't recognize any reporters, and she hadn't seen any camera flashes. No hands concealed microphones, just waiting to pop up in front of her face at the earliest opportunity.

Mason's arm tightened around her, as if he could read her thoughts. Again.

Remi snuck a peek at his profile. Freshly shaved jaw. Strong cheekbones. Warm eyes, the color of perfectly roasted coffee beans. A cowlick that always stood up in front, no matter how many times he raked his fingers through it. His usual cheeky grin was noticeably absent today.

Her pulse accelerated, and bumps tingled along her arms, but not from the cool air. Her fingers ached to reach up and touch his rough cheeks, to trail the line of his strong jaw, to glide through his hair to see if it was as soft as she imagined.

Not only was he nice to look at, but the man sure could warm a body.

She blinked, stunned.

Falling for a racecar driver? No! This could not be happening. It couldn't.

No way!

****

"Thank you, Pastor. I appreciate your message more than you can imagine." Mason shook hands with the preacher, but his gaze tracked Remi and her brother as the pair made their way to Camdon's car.

"You're mighty welcome. I was honored to be asked."

He slipped the courtesy envelope into the pastor's hand then practically sprinted to catch up with Remi.

Camdon fumbled for something by his side then pulled out a phone and pressed it to his ear.

Thankfully, a reprieve. Slowing his pace as he neared, Mason made a mental note to thank the man later.

"Sure. I'll be right there." Camdon disconnected and clipped the phone to his belt. "Remi, I need to get you home. That was the City Manager—"

Noting the man's furrowed brow and worried expression, Mason stepped into their personal zone. "I can take her home, Camdon."

Remi's brother arched a brow and glanced at his sister, waiting for her response.

Her gaze jerked to him. She studied him for a few seconds then nodded. "Thank you, Mason. I appreciate the offer."

"You sure?" Camdon asked.

"Yeah. I'm good. Thank you for bringing me. I'll call you later, okay?" She stood on the tips of her shoes to kiss her brother's cheek.

"Sorry to desert you like this." Camdon stared at his sister. As if giving her another chance to change her mind.

"No worries. I'll take good care of her."

Finally, Camdon flicked his head in acknowledgement.

He hustled toward his car, his long stride eating up the distance quickly.

Remi's gaze followed her brother until his vehicle disappeared. She sighed.

"That bad, huh?"

"What?"

"The idea of riding home with me." Disappointment jabbed him in the gut, and fatigue from the long hours spent dividing his time at the ranch and the shop strained his shoulders.

"I'm sorry, Mason. That's not it at all. Really."

Would she ever share what weighed so heavy on her heart? "Ready then?"

"It depends." A dimple flashed unexpectedly. Mischief teased from the slant of her lips.

"On?"

"Which car you're driving."

His eyebrows shot to the top of his head, and his heart lightened. She couldn't be too upset with him if she was giving him a hard time. Could she?

A cool breeze ruffled her hair and carried a sweet and spicy blend of cinnamon and cloves. He leaned in and tucked a loose strand behind her ear. Holding his breath against the intoxicating fragrance and the silkiness of her hair, his gaze trailed the creamy hollows of her neck.

Just as he thought. Touching her could be addictive. His fingers ached to release the clip and run his hand down the entire length of her hair.

She gasped, almost imperceptible, so that he felt her intake of breath more than heard it.

He didn't realize his fingers had slid down to caress her jaw until she eased back, away from his touch, clearing his head of thoughts he had no business entertaining. What was he thinking?

Hit the brakes, Mulrennan! Not so fast.

"It's a good thing I brought the truck, then." He cleared the huskiness from his throat and started walking.

At least his legs functioned properly.

She slanted a sideways glance at him, her lips curving sweetly. "Why?"

"Because if I brought my racecar, you'd have to slide into the seat through the window."

"That wouldn't be a pretty sight."

Oh, he begged to differ. "Are you fishing for compliments? Because if you are—"

"I miss Goliath." She gave him a playful swat on the arm and changed the subject.

"Yeah. Me, too, but I didn't feel right bringing him graveside. He's sleeping in the truck."

She shot him a grin, her face brightening. "Really?"

"Really." Little things sure seemed to please her. How did she handle big things? "It's cool enough that he can stay in the truck with the windows cracked, and I left him some water."

They made it to the parking lot, and Mason pressed the unlock button on the passenger side. The drive to the sanctuary would take forty-five minutes or so. A nice meal might work wonders for damage control with Remi. He glanced at his watch, mentally calculating what he needed to do before he left for the airport. Would he have enough time for them to snag a table in his favorite restaurant? They should be able to swing it.

He opened the door for her. "Want to grab a bite to eat at Kramer's while we're in town?"

Was that fear that flashed across her features? Surely not. What could she be afraid of? Him?

He'd spent days on the farm, just her and him. She couldn't be afraid of him, could she?

"Thank you, but—" Her back stiffened. Her hands clenched at her sides until her knuckles whitened.

Definitely frightened of something, but he didn't have time to press. "Or we could grab something and take it to your house. That might work better anyway, since I have to be at the airport in a few hours."

She nodded, her relief obvious in the way her shoulders relaxed, and her hands flexed. Smiling, she hoisted herself into the truck and slid into the seat. "That sounds nice."

Maybe she just didn't like to go out to eat. Filing that away, Mason walked around the truck and hopped in.

"You're such a sweet boy. I'm so glad you came with Mason." Remi angled sideways in the seat, giving his dog a brisk rub around the ears. She buried her face in his furry neck then planted a kiss on his forehead.

Mason tamped down the envy. Was she as glad to see him as she was his dog? Probably not.

****

"Will you be sorry to see me leave?" Mason. The rascal. Judging by the impish look, he was baiting her.

Remi almost choked on the water sliding down her throat. "No."

He grinned. As if he knew she wasn't being truthful.

Yeah. She'd be sorry to see him go. There. She admitted it, if only to herself.

She stole a sideways glance at him, the last fork of lasagna halfway to her mouth, the tantalizing scents of tomato, cheese and spices drifting up her nose.

As usual, his hair spiked up in the front, but he was missing the customary scruff along his cheeks. His suit jacket and tie draped across the back of the chair. Black curly hair poked out from where he'd unfastened the top few buttons of his burgundy dress shirt. Instead of form fitting jeans for working on the farm, today he wore charcoal gray slacks.

Her eyes wanted to linger, to soak in the sight of him. How did this man always look so good?

He probably even looked fabulous in his racing suit.

She jerked her gaze to Goliath, lazing near the table.

Was she enamored with Mason because he was the only other person besides Jillian or her family who came to the sanctuary regularly? Or because he treated the animals like they were his family, too? Or because he'd wiggled through the cracks surrounding her heart?

Whatever. Remi didn't like it.

There was no future for a racecar driver and a social phobic. She jammed the fork into her mouth and chewed, but the rich cheese and tomato goodness had lost its flavor. She tossed the napkin on the table and shoved her chair back. "Thank you for the ride home. And for dinner."

"My pleasure." His eyes glinted with truth.

Her pulse picked up speed. She hooked her foot against the chair rung and stumbled forward. He reached out a hand to steady her, but his warm grip only made her heart beat more erratically. If only she could turn off her physical response to him!

Just another reason why she shouldn't allow Mason to keep coming back to the sanctuary.

"Thanks." She scooped up the disposable trays and tossed them in the trash.

He followed, carrying the empty cups, but detoured to the sink.

There was that scent again, the one she'd caught a whiff of earlier at the cemetery, when he'd tucked her under his arm. Something spicy with a little citrus mixed in, and definitely too masculine for her peace of mind.

She huffed, confused with the battle going on between her heart and her head. On the one hand, she wanted to tell him never to come back. But if she did, she'd miss—

"Come to the race with me."

She backed into a solid wall of...chest. She turned around to face him. "W-what?"

Some strange emotion glowed from his eyes and curved his lips. "You heard me."

She shook her head. "I'm not. I don't do—"

His expression morphed into firm resolve as he took a step back. "I didn't mean it that way, Remi. You could stay with a friend and his wife in their RV. I have an RV, too, but I don't think it's a good idea for you to stay with me."

That was awfully sweet of him to be concerned with her reputation. But that wasn't what she meant. What would he say if he knew that she didn't do crowds?

Temptation snaked into her heart for a second, but as appealing as the offer of spending time with Mason sounded, she couldn't bring herself to say yes. She gave her head a little wobble. "I can't."

He regarded her. His nostrils flared as a regretful sigh rumbled from his chest. Nodding, he snatched his jacket off the chair and slipped it over his arms. "Next week, maybe."

"Maybe." It was her turn to sigh. She followed him to the door, her footsteps as heavy as her heart. What was going on with her? How had her life suddenly gotten so out of control?

He stopped abruptly and turned. Her palms splayed against his chest to keep from bumping into him.

She dared to look up. Soft brown eyes, the remnants of shock and pain of losing a friend still lingering around the edges, stared back at her. Her limbs felt as if they melted into a puddle on the floor.

What was her mistake? Looking up or walking too close behind him? Or maybe it was inviting him back to her place for dinner. Whatever it was, her lungs refused to work.

His palms cupped her cheeks.

Oh, she was really in trouble here.

Lashes closed over those gorgeous eyes. His head dipped, and his breath puffed against her lips.

She closed her eyes. What would his kiss, *a kiss*, taste like? How should she respond? She'd never been kissed before, never allowed a guy to get close enough. Other than her brothers, that is, but those kisses were just brotherly pecks on her forehead or cheek.

Goliath barked. Enough of a warning to put the skids on her heart and allow her brain to take control once again.

Her eyelids zapped open to find his face dangerously close. Fear ratcheted through her veins. What was she thinking?

She applied some pressure against his chest and stepped back. Not far enough that her heart didn't stop racing and the blood pumping through her body didn't feel as if it zapped her with a thousand volts of electricity.

His palms still cradled her cheeks. When his lashes lifted, surprise flashed across his features. The handsome man was probably accustomed to females fawning all over him. Asking for his autograph. Draping an arm around his back for a picture. Or worse! Kissing him in total fangirl abandon.

Not happening with this girl!

But there was something else in his expression. Respect? Wonder?

"Mason, I, um…" She licked her dry lips but stopped when his gaze lingered there. "I'm sorry."

His lips quirked up on one side. "Yeah. Me, too. But it's okay." He placed a kiss on her forehead. A kiss that felt anything but brotherly.

At least she was back in the safe territory.

"I'll be back on Tuesday."

"You will?" It was her turn to be surprised.

He nodded. "Count on it."

There he was again with that promise. Could she count on him?

He opened the door to the pleasant harmony of frogs and cicadas. Then he stepped into the darkness, his long strides taking him to his truck too fast, Goliath bounding along behind him.

Her fingertips traced a path along her cheeks and forehead as she stood in the doorway, watching the truck wind its way down the driveway.

She'd wanted him to kiss her. More than that quick peck on her forehead.

And that terrified her.

6

Remi closed the gate, careful to make sure the latch caught. She didn't want these newcomers to escape. They were frightened enough without adding to their stress.

"There you go, lady. That takes care of the lot." The animal hauler tugged off his gloves and slid them in his back pocket, doing a little two-step with his boots, one leg slightly longer than the other.

"Thank you."

"You and this animal sanctuary deserve the thanks. It'd be a crying shame for these beauties to be destroyed."

"We'll take good care of them." Four horses, all mangy and skittish, stood stiff and nervous as they surveyed their new home. Briars tangled their manes and scars speckled their flanks. Ribs protruded from gaunt bellies. Poor things. They may not look so beautiful now, but they would after she got them cleaned up and fed.

She sighed. Taking in these four would cost her dearly, though. She couldn't handle any more animals, no matter their horrible circumstances, until she received more funding. She would not jeopardize the animals she was already responsible for.

"Well, you have a good day now, ya hear? God bless and keep up the good work you're doing here." The old man turned and hobbled back to his truck. The engine roared, and dust flumed behind the trailer as it pulled away.

Did you hear that, God? Could you bless me with a way to take care of these precious animals?

She was amazed at how quickly she turned to God

these days.

Mason Mulrennan.

What? The voice sounded as if it came from behind her. She angled her head, looking over a shoulder. Nobody was there.

Mason.

She glanced over her shoulder again, just to be sure. Rattled her head, speared the horses with one last concerned look, and headed for the house.

Her brain was playing tricks on her, that's all. She missed catching a glimpse of the man outside the window, Goliath trotting along beside him as they moved from one chore to the next. She longed for that sudden jolt of energy, that prick of awareness, as she recognized the roar of his truck pulling into the drive.

Okay. So she missed him, the man. But missing him wouldn't pay the bills or feed the animals. Enough already!

If she could help every animal headed to the chopping block, she would. But she'd opened her email inbox earlier to six grant rejections. Six!

It was time to get serious.

Mason Mulrennan wasn't the answer to her prayer for money.

****

"When do you come home?"

Remi's sweet voice broke through Mason's melancholy like sunshine blasting through steel gray clouds on a blustery winter day. She sounded like she sat next to him in the RV rather than the hundreds of miles that separated them by phone.

Mason stretched his legs on the couch and leaned his head back against the pillow he'd tucked against the wall. He'd made himself wait to call until practice was out of the way. It made for a long day. He should have just given in and called her during one of the breaks, but then their conversation might have been interrupted. Hopefully, now they could talk longer.

"Is that your way of saying you miss me?" A smile toyed with his lips while tenderness for this woman settled in his heart.

Remi sputtered. "You're putting words in my mouth."

"Somebody has to do it."

Silence on the other end.

"So maybe *you* didn't miss me, but I'll bet Jumbo did."

Her laughter warmed his belly. "Okay. I'll admit it. Jumbo has been a bit on the sulky side. Nobody to spit at for a few days."

Translation. She missed him.

That was a good thing because he literally ached to see her again. How could that be? He hadn't known her that long to develop such a strong attraction.

"So what's new at the sanctuary?" He changed the subject, fearing he was treading on weak ice.

"We're the proud parents of four horses that would have been destroyed if we hadn't volunteered to take them."

We? He liked the sound of that.

She coughed. "I meant the sanctuary."

He liked the first way better. "That's awesome. What's their story?"

"Abandonment."

"Ouch."

"Yeah. Poor things. They're so skinny."

"They won't be for long. You'll fatten them up in no time."

"I plan to, but if I can't—" Her voice broke off, and after a second's hesitation, she cleared her throat.

"If you can't what, Remi?"

"I didn't mean to bore you with my problems, Mason. How was your day?"

That was an abrupt change of subject. So what didn't she want him to know? He sat up straight. The pillow fell behind his back. He tugged it out and flung it to the other end of the couch. "You could never bore me with your problems, Remi. And besides, the sanctuary isn't a problem. Not with you in charge. You're amazing with those animals."

Guilt pricked him. Why hadn't he written that check, yet? His manpower benefited the sanctuary and his presence offered a chance for them to get to know each other better. But what if she—if the animals—desperately needed the money?

Her silence told him he'd heard the end of that subject.

"Today was practice. We didn't wreck any of our cars, so that was good."

"*Any of your cars?*" she repeated. After a marked pause, she continued. "How many cars do you have?"

He cringed and prayed for the right words. Words that wouldn't put up a roadblock to a budding relationship with this woman he was falling for more every day. "Three of us are racing this weekend."

"Oh."

What did 'oh' mean?

"So that makes three cars you didn't wreck?"

"Yep. Not today." No need to tell her they brought a backup car to every race. Not yet, anyway. She'd learn soon enough. That is, if he could ever convince her to come see him race. "There's always tomorrow."

"What happens tomorrow?"

"Qualifying."

"So more chances to wreck the cars."

"Well, there is that, but the goal is to get the fastest time without wrecking."

"I hope you don't." Her voice came out small, as if on the wings of a prayer.

"Thank you, Remi. Sure I can't talk you into joining me?"

She laughed, but it was more of a nervous sound than from enjoyment.

"I could get you here. If you wanted to come." He'd move heaven and earth—

"Thanks for asking, Mason, but I can't right now. Not after taking in four new sweeties today." Was that relief he heard in her voice?

"I hear ya. Guess I'll see you on Tuesday then." Disappointment swamped him. It wasn't as if he'd expected her to change her mind. But her voice...her voice had watered the tiny seed of hope. Hope that she might want to be with him as much as he wanted her here.

Feeling much like a love-struck teen, he waited for her to disconnect then tapped the phone screen a few times until Angela's picture appeared. He tapped the call icon.

"Hey, Mason. How was practice today?"

"Great. We survived another round. No casualties."

"What's up?"

"I need you to write a check."

7

Remi tossed the last bale onto the ground and stripped off her gloves. Rustling sounded behind her before a llama head plunked over the top of her shoulder. She turned her head, chuckling at the display of lower teeth. "Jumbo, are you being a good boy today?"

She rubbed his neck. "Mason said to tell you hi."

He reared his head, and a hum vibrated from deep in his throat.

"Now don't you go getting upset with me because he's not here. You take it up with him."

Laughing, she exited the enclosure and locked the gate behind her. She stopped at the pen containing Snickers and Reesie. "Reesie, you look like you're feeling much better."

Remi had spent much of the night and today checking on her after Corbin's visit yesterday.

She crossed her arms over the fence rail, enjoying the peaceful sounds of the farm. The swishing of tails and the soft snuffles of the horses. The occasional hum from the llamas.

Hoof beats pounded the ground, punctuating the quiet, then a snort.

"Whoa!" Jillian halted Lightning and dismounted. "Hey, girl."

"Hey to you, my favorite neighbor."

Jillian rolled her eyes. "I'm your only neighbor for miles."

Remi grinned. "Come on inside. I was just fixing to sit down for a bit."

"Great. I was hoping you'd have time to relax and chat."

"Why?"

"No reason. Just needed to get out of the house for a while."

Which meant she was lonely. Remi suspected she knew the reason. Jillian missed Carson. "Want some coffee or hot chocolate?"

"Mmmm. Hot chocolate sounds wonderful. It's so cold today." Jillian rubbed her upper arms, clearly shivering inside her jacket.

Remi led the way inside. She heated a couple mugs of milk laden with chocolate then topped them with whipped cream while Jillian flicked on the television.

"I missed you at church this morning. Thought you said you were coming."

"I'd planned to." Remi sighed, disappointed that she hadn't been able to make the service. She handed Jillian a mug, and they both settled on the sofa. Remi folded her legs under her bottom. "But Reesie came down sick last night. I was up most of the night with her."

"Next week then." No condemnation from Jillian's expression. Only tender concern.

"I'll be there unless I have another sick baby."

"I know. I just wanted to make sure you didn't chicken out on me." Jillian's gentle smile eased the sting.

Remi didn't take offense. Jillian had never chided her about not going to church or about her lack of faith. Her friend faced her own anxiety over the stares and finger pointing at her scars, so Jillian could relate to Remi's paralyzing fear of being out in public. Understood the doubt that plagued.

"I see the horses finally arrived. Looks like they've missed a few meals." Jillian sipped the hot chocolate. She licked the remnants of the white foam off her upper lip.

"You think?" By Remi's estimation, those poor horses had missed many meals.

"You'll fatten 'em up."

"That's exactly what Mason said." Oops. If Remi could've snatched her words back, she would've.

"Mason Mulrennan? I thought you—" Jillian's eyebrows hiked then dipped. Her jaw dangled, leaving her mouth wide open. When she finally spoke again, her voice came out awestruck. "You've been talking to Mason Mulrennan?"

Remi rubbed her forehead, considering the best way to squash this conversation. "Well, not today."

"Not today?" Jillian squealed. She set her mug on the side table and bolted off the couch, snatching the remote and pointing it at the television.

Remi held her breath while the hot liquid swirled around but it never spilled over.

"Why didn't you say something sooner?" Her friend flicked through the channels until landing on the race. She turned around and smiled, arms folded over her chest.

Actually, it was more like a satisfied smirk.

Remi squirmed and shrank back against the couch. "I'm not sure I want to watch him race."

"Well, you may not be sure but I am." Jillian tossed the remote on the coffee table and perched on the edge of the couch.

Remi sipped the hot chocolate, but it did nothing to chase away the chill gripping her insides. What if he wrecked? What if he got hurt? How could she watch that?

She tugged the velvety throw from the back of the couch and held up an end. "Want to share the blanket?"

"No." Jillian tore her gaze away from the television and narrowed her eyebrows at Remi. "You're not warm enough with the fireplace cooking or sipping that hot chocolate?"

Remi shook her head, her teeth close to the chattering point. She snuggled under the toasty blanket, occasionally stealing glances at the TV.

"I can't believe you didn't mention this sooner. We

could have had the race on. We're lucky to see the last few laps."

"Lucky?" This time, Remi's teeth did chatter.

"Mulrennan just might have this one clenched! Can he hold off Salinger for two more laps?" The sports announcer's voice carried anticipation to a new level.

Remi dared a peek at the race just as the camera panned the stands, where thousands of fans stood, cheering and pumping their fists in the air. Did people really get this excited about racing? The camera flashed back to the cars. "He's not ahead by much."

Jillian shook her head. "No. And I surely don't want the guy behind him to win."

"Salinger? What's wrong with that guy winning? He probably wants to win as much as Mason."

"He stole Mason's wife."

"He what?" Remi whipped her head sideways. Sorrow lodged in her belly, anguish for Mason threatening to spill out in tears. And maybe just the tiniest seed of jealousy.

"You didn't know?" Jillian scrunched her cheeks and met Remi's gaze.

Remi shook her head, her voice barely above a whisper. "No. He never mentioned being married."

What else didn't she know about Mason Mulrennan? If Nan hadn't revealed his identity, she wouldn't even know that he was a racecar driver.

"He wasn't married long. Two years maybe? I can't remember exactly. This all happened a few years ago." Jillian sipped her hot chocolate, swinging her glance between the race and Remi. "Mason was going through a slump, and his wife up and dumped him for this other racer, Salinger, who was on a winning streak." Jillian paused for another sip. Again, her gaze tracked between Remi and the television. "It was all over the news. Maybe he just expected that you knew."

Oh, how awful. Poor Mason. Remi shook her head.

"Mulrennan's going to beat him by millimeters! Yes!

Yes! Here it is! Here it is, ladies and gentlemen! The checkered flag!" The announcer practically screamed. The camera panned the crowd, jumping and roaring their applause.

Jillian lunged from the couch, her arms raised in victory. "He did it!"

"Mason won?" Remi bounced up, looking from the television to Jillian for confirmation.

Jillian nodded, her smile taking over her entire face.

"Sweet!" She held up her palm for Jillian to slap.

Her friend complied with a high-five. "Enough to make you want to watch racing, huh?"

Fear caused her tummy to tumble straight to her toes. She jiggled her head. "No. He might get hurt."

"Well, he could." A look of understanding flashed across Jillian's face, as if she'd solved a complicated puzzle. She nodded slowly. "And you might get hurt by one of those horses you just took in."

Her friend's pointed arrow of logic lodged in her brain. Jillian was right.

"Besides the organization has made it much safer for the drivers over the last few years. The cars have rigid standards, and they test—" The house phone rang, interrupting Jillian.

"Sorry, Jillian. Excuse me." Remi left their victory huddle and picked up the phone. "Forever Family Animal Sanctuary. This is Remi."

"Did you see it?"

"Mason?" The race hadn't been over that long. Wasn't he still in his car?

She glanced back at the television. The cars had already disappeared from the track. Wow, that was quick.

"Yeah. It's me. Did you watch the race?"

"Actually, my friend is over—"

"Ouch. I'm sorry. I didn't mean to interrupt. I'll catch you later." He sounded disappointed.

"No. Don't go. Please."

"I'm not interrupting?"

"No. I was just going to say that I caught the last couple of laps. Congratulations on winning. I'm happy for you."

"Thank you. I wish you were here." His tone warmed her, sending tickles of awareness to dance up and down her arms.

So did she. Now. But then, if she had been there, she wouldn't have enjoyed watching him race. Would she?

"Sorry, Remi, but I have to go now. I'll see you on Tuesday."

Right. Tuesday.

As if.

His world consisted of fame and fortune, a direct conflict with her private and secluded domain.

"Sure. Thanks for calling, Mason. Catch you later." Although he had disconnected, the phone clung to her ear, as if it had a mind of its own. She finally slipped it back in the cradle.

"Mason called. Girl, this is serious." Jillian's voice sounded close.

"S-s-serious?" Remi angled over a shoulder and met Jillian's solemn face. "What do you mean?"

Her friend's sandy eyebrows narrowed. She waved her palms in the air then gestured toward the television. "He hasn't even made it to the winner's circle yet, and he stopped to call you. That is so sweet."

"What makes that serious?"

"He cares enough to call." Jillian dipped her head and let out a long-suffering sigh. When she looked up, a giant teardrop trickled down her cheek. "You are important enough for him to want to talk to you, to let you know that he was okay."

Remi reached out and tugged her best friend into a hug. "I'm sorry."

Why didn't her brother come home? Then he'd see how much his family loved him, how much Jillian still loved him, how she'd waited for him, even after all these years.

"Carson will come home, Jillian." Eventually. *Please, God?*

There she was, talking to God again. Would He ever be inclined to answer her prayers with a yes?

Jillian blinked, her long lashes dappled with tears. "Savor this new thing that's developing between you and Mason, Remi. Appreciate the simple gesture of his phone call."

She would if she could, but there wasn't a "new thing" with her and Mason. It wasn't possible. Not with his career and the swarming media that went along with the public spotlight.

No thanks.

Anything between them was just friendship, plain and simple. Nothing more.

Still. She couldn't stop her heart from doing a little victory dance.

****

Mason slithered through the car's slim opening, just in time for the spray of thirty bottles of diet cola, his sponsor and favorite cold drink, to soak him.

Laughing, he wiped his face with a dry towel, thoroughly invigorated from his very abbreviated conversation with Remi, when he'd convinced Charlie to hold the phone to his ear through the car window. What he wouldn't have given for her to be here, to see the checkered flag wave over his car as he crossed the finish line.

Maybe next time.

Hands clapped his shoulders and bodies jostled him to the center of the celebratory circle. Someone jabbed a microphone in front of his face, the reporter attached to it peering at him from the side. Cameras flashed and clicked. His crew laughed and chatted behind him. One of Mason's drivers stopped to shake his hand and offer congratulations.

Mason loved being in victory lane, enjoyed the camaraderie, the spotlight for his team, the adrenaline that pumped through his veins with a win after a hard-fought race.

And winning meant more money for his church and the foundation. More funds to allow him to assist charitable organizations that protected and cared for helpless animals. Organizations like Remi's.

Various news teams hurled what seemed like hundreds of questions at him. He answered the questions, smiling and posing for the team pictures. Finally, he broke free from the celebration and made his way to the RV. Time to change and head for home.

The farther he walked, the calmer the night became. He breathed in the quiet, allowing it to settle over his tense shoulders, to recharge his spirit. *Thank You for the win tonight, Father.*

Footsteps pounded heavy on the pavement behind him. He angled his head around and found Ken, his spotter, jogging. He slowed his pace until Ken caught up with him.

"Great racing tonight, Mason." Ken clapped a hand on his shoulder.

"Thanks, man. Couldn't have done it without you." With the aid of the overhead lamps, Mason made out the heavy smudges above Ken's cheeks, the defeat etching his eyes and mouth. "I have to say, though, for a win, you look pretty dismal."

Ken's huge sigh rattled through the quiet space. "Cindy served me with divorce papers yesterday." His voice broke, a sharp contrast to the celebratory laughter they left behind. No wonder he'd been anxious to get away from the crowd.

"Ouch. I'm sorry." He understood all too well how the pain and guilt from a failing marriage ripped a man apart. Especially a man in this business.

"Yeah. Me, too." Ken's shoulders slumped as if burdened with a heavy weight. The man shuffled along, kicking pebbles with the tip of his steel-toed boot. "It was hard enough to see the kids before. Now I'll never see them."

Yeah. Mason could see how that would be tough. They reached his RV, and Goliath barked a welcome from inside the camper.

Mason turned to face his spotter, but more than that, his friend. "Divorce is painful. No two ways about it."

Ken looked up. His gaze met Mason's. Understanding dawned. "I forgot. I'm sorry."

"Thanks, but I'm in a better place now. God still works miracles. Do you want some time off to see if you can repair the damage before it's too late?"

Respect flowed across Ken's face. "I'm not sure that it's not too late, but I'm willing to try. Thank you."

Mason nodded and plunked a hand on Ken's shoulder. "No problem. We'll get somebody to fill in for you in the meantime. Take as much time as you need."

Ken walked away, his spine a little straighter, a little more bounce in his steps. From the other direction a man and woman drew closer. The woman's voice rose in anger. Her hands slashed through the air as she stomped ahead of the man, disgust in her wrinkled nose, the snarl of her lips, and the furrows in her forehead.

Lisa and Salinger.

A knot pitted in Mason's gut. He swiveled and pushed open the door to the RV.

He hadn't been able to save his own marriage. The very least he could do was give Ken some space to save his. And maybe extend a small amount of grace to Salinger by refusing to witness Lisa's verbal lashing. He closed the door, muffling his ex-wife's hateful words.

Keeping a solid marriage in this business was tough. They were on the road more than they were home. Hanging out with the guys was easier than knowing what to do with a soft, emotional female.

His brain told him that he shouldn't even be thinking about seeing Remi again, should just give up the temptation to visit the sanctuary.

But his heart whispered something totally different.

8

Mason refilled his coffee mug and dumped in a packet of sweetener, hoping the caffeine would fire up his system so he could get caught up with paperwork and go home for the night.

He tossed the plastic stick in the trash and exited the break room, heading down the now dim hall to his office. Footsteps slapped the tile behind him. He glanced over his shoulder.

"Hey, boss." Charlie, his crew chief, sounded weary. The season was starting to take its toll on everybody.

"Charlie."

"Got a second?"

"Sure. Come on in." Mason stepped into his office, the lamp glowing on his desk the only light. Goliath poked his head up from his usual spot on the rug, and then he plopped it back down with a heavy sigh.

Mason could relate.

Charlie sank into the leather chair in front of Mason's desk and rolled his shoulders. "Long day."

"Yeah." It would be an even longer night if he hoped to make it out to the sanctuary tomorrow. No amount of brain scolding could convince his heart not to go.

Remi's sweet spirit and shy manner drew him like a checkered flag. Interacting with all the precious animals was icing on the cake.

"That's a great thing you're doing for Ken."

Mason nodded. So long as it was in his power to help, he would.

"I hope the time off helps and they can get back

together," Charlie drawled.

"Me too."

"I plan to put Shane in his place temporarily. Any objections?"

"No." He shook his head. "Shane will do a good job."

"Well, I wanted to make sure you were good with it." Charlie stood and walked to the door. His fingers curled around the knob.

He should probably give his crew chief advance notice in case Remi ever decided to accept his invitation. "Hey, Charlie."

Charlie angled over a shoulder, his eyebrows arched.

"I'm hoping one of these days you'll have a guest sitting with you on the box."

"Wow! That's news. When were you planning on spilling those beans?" Charlie turned back around and folded his arms, nudging a shoulder against the door jam.

"Nothing to spill, yet. Just wanted to make sure you have an extra seat available on the off chance I can talk her into coming."

Charlie scoffed. "Off chance? What woman would turn down that invitation?"

Mason sighed, scratching the back of his head. "I know of one who has on several occasions already."

Charlie tried to hide his surprise behind a cough, but it didn't work.

Mason frowned. His jaw clenched.

"Not a problem, boss. I'll take care of it." Charlie recovered well. "Is this the same gal you couldn't wait to call yesterday?"

"Yeah. Remi Lambright."

"Remi Lambright?" Charlie's arms unbuckled, and he heaved himself away from the door. "As in the golfer's daughter?"

The golfer's daughter? That was news to him. She hadn't mentioned that anyone in her family golfed.

He shrugged. "I don't know. Can't say I ever keep up

with golf. Are you referring to her mom or dad?"

"Her dad, Connor Lambright. But I'm sure it can't be his daughter." Worry mottled his crew chief's neck and cheeks. Worse than during the race that Mason had been forced to watch from the box, after suffering a mild concussion from a wreck the week before.

"Why couldn't she be his daughter?"

"Sorry, boss." Charlie held up his arm and pointedly glanced at his watch. "Just remembered something the little lady asked me to do on my way home. Gotta go." He practically scrambled through the door, his legs barely keeping up with his torso and arms.

Mason's eyebrows fused together. He tapped out a rhythm on the chair's arm. What just happened there? What hadn't Charlie wanted to tell him?

He scooted forward and typed the golfer's name in the computer's search engine. Scanned the highlights. After several minutes, he stopped reading. Leather rustled in the silent office as he sank back in the folds of the chair.

This was Remi's father? The man who, after a very public divorce, committed suicide? The media had jumped all over that, blaming his wife for the horrendous fall of the golfing legend, the golden boy of the sport.

The golfer's wife? Remi's mother.

No wonder Remi didn't trust him or want him anywhere near the sanctuary. Why would she? He lived in the public arena, in the face of glaring media spotlight, the very people who'd emotionally crucified her mother and caused tremendous pain for her family. On the heels of an already horrifying loss.

Mason blew out a sigh, his thumb tapping out an agitated rhythm on the chair arm. Now that he knew the identity of Remi's father and details of his death, gaining her trust, wooing her respect, might be tougher than he thought.

He took a sip of the coffee, wincing as the nearly cold taste snagged in his throat. How could he get her to trust him? To not despise him or the attention that came along with being connected to a racecar driver?

If he was even to run this race, to have any hopes of seeing the green flag wave over his wooing of Remi, he'd have to come up with a creative strategy. What, though?

Ideas flitted through his brain. He bolted from the chair and opened the side door that led outdoors. "Goliath, you might want to go outside and take care of business. We're going to be here for a while."

9

Remi finished scrubbing and turned off the spigot. She straightened and found herself staring up Jumbo's oversized nostrils. His lips separated, revealing big, lopsided bottom teeth.

"You crazy old softie." Remi stroked the llama's neck. "You get under Mason's skin, you know that? Why can't you stop spitting at him?"

"What would be the fun in that?"

The voice, warm and husky and oh so close, startled her. She whipped around.

Mason! He came. Just like he said he would!

Her heart jigged and jagged. The cantankerous organ refused to settle back to its normal pace.

Mason unlocked the gate and stepped inside. Goliath rushed over to her, his tail whipping back and forth so fast it lifted the back half of his torso. She waited until he sat like a good boy then bent down and rubbed behind his ears. "Hey, sweet thing. How are you this morning?"

"Tired, but as you can see, happy to be back here with all his friends."

Did that mean Mason was happy to be here, too? With her? Remi smiled, joy filling her deep inside, soul-level, at his sweet words.

Remi stretched to her full height, taking in Mason's appearance. Yeah, he had some dark smudges above his cheekbones, and he hadn't shaved in days, but he looked absolutely scrumptious in boots and his well-worn jeans and flannel shirt.

Goliath ambled off to sniff and reacquaint himself with

the llamas, while Mason stepped close. He halted in front of her. His scent, a mixture of spice and woods and the cool outdoors, enveloped her, superseding the familiar animal smells. Except now, his scent was as familiar, as comforting, as the animals.

Fear snaked through her veins.

He carried success and fame well. For now. But that could change. She'd do best to remember that.

"I missed you." His soft words settled over her like a warm blanket on a frigid winter evening. But instead of calming her nerves, they spiked.

She licked her parched lips. How should she respond? She'd missed him like crazy, but she wasn't going to admit that.

A slow smile spread across his face, as if he already knew that. "I hope you don't mind that I—"

Tires crunched in the gravel parking lot. From the sounds of it, a bunch of tires. What was going on?

She angled around him to peer at the long line of trucks snaking the length of her drive. One by one, they squeezed in whatever open space would fit their rigs. When the lot filled, they parked in even rows on the grass. Her jaw dropped.

"—rounded up some volunteers."

"Some volunteers? It looks like the entire population of Harrison, North Carolina, showed up." She blinked. Maybe it was a nightmare. She flicked her eyelids open as still more vehicles piled in.

She hugged arms around her middle as panic set in. What was she going to do with this many people on the property? She'd never be able to get her truck out of the jammed yard and parking area.

A horse! Her eyes darted to the pasture where the four recent newbies grazed. No, they were still too skittish to attempt escape, and she refused to risk injury to them.

She'd have to get to the barn. Saddle Pocono. She could hide out at Jillian's place until all these…*people* disappeared. Picturing the crowd, her heart stuttered, almost stopped, and sweat slicked her palms. She took a step, wobbled.

"Oh, no, you don't." Mason grasped her arm, gently holding her in place.

"Mason, I—" She couldn't seem to catch her breath.

Vehicle doors closed. Laughter and animated chatter. Footsteps on gravel.

Like an ominous cloud, they were all heading her way. There was sure to be a reporter in that swarming mass of humanity.

"Relax, Remi. These are all my friends. They're not here to hurt you. They only want to help." Velvety eyes sought hers, warming the icy chill that had settled deep in her very core.

"Help?" How could they help? Her experience had proven the bigger the crowd, the heavier the emotional punch they walloped. With their stares, hushed whispers and pointed fingers.

"They're going to make some repairs. To the fencing. To the barn. There are some qualified builders in the crowd, and once you give them the go ahead, they'll make those changes you've been dreaming about to your house."

Mason had organized all of this for her? How could he be so nice to her after she'd ordered him off her property and told him not to come back? A huge glob of emotion caught in her throat, but this time it wasn't fear.

Nope. Not fear.

More like resolve. Determination.

She was sliding down the perilous slope toward love, but she needed to put the skids out. There was no way she would allow herself to fall in love with Mason. Not a racecar driver. Not any sports figure for that matter.

But it sure would help if he didn't keep doing things like this.

She shook her head. She must be dreaming. Miracles like this didn't happen in real life. Not hers, anyway. *God, is this Your doing?*

"Mason, I appreciate—"

"Good. Come on. Let me introduce you to some of my friends." His arm slipped around her waist, warming her with a strength and confidence she wouldn't have otherwise.

****

Balancing the ladder over a shoulder, Mason surveyed the results from today's efforts. They'd repaired fencing and replaced dangling wires. They'd made repairs to the barn, freshened up the stalls, and replaced the shutters and some loose boards on Remi's house.

She hadn't agreed to any house construction, yet. Give him time to persuade her. She'd come around.

Smiling, he hung the ladder on the hooks, satisfaction with their efforts swelling his insides, and headed out to check on the animals one last time for the day. Yep. It had been a good day. Remi had talked with his friends, even smiled, but she'd never completely ditched that slightly panicked look since the others showed up.

He stepped outside the barn, Goliath at his heels, and draped his arms over the llama enclosure holding Snickers and Reesie. The late afternoon's light waned into soft evening. He stood there, watching the two animals munch on hay, the sweet smells of the farm drifting over him. He was beginning to love this place as much as the shop.

No need to disturb those two. They had survived all the commotion and appeared settled for the night.

He sauntered over to the male llama pen and slipped inside to check on their water supply. Five giants all lumbered over to see what he was doing. Goliath trotted along the outskirts of the crowd, grinning as if he knew what was coming.

Jumbo stuck his big head over Mason's shoulder. He stroked the llama's neck. "What's this? You playing nice today, big guy?"

"You're a glutton for punishment."

He angled over his other shoulder to see Remi standing a few feet away, his dog now sitting at her feet. How had he not heard her sneak up on him? "You caught me."

He moved away from the fray of animals, closer to Remi. Her spicy scent seeped into his pores and set his heart to wishing for things he was better off not wanting, but he couldn't seem to resist the pull. He inched forward, giving her space, but needing to be near.

She waved a piece of paper in the air, but in the disappearing light, he couldn't make out what it was. "I can't accept this, you know."

Ah. He didn't need to see the writing to know what she held.

The check from the foundation.

"Especially not after all you've done today."

"What? Organize some volunteers for one of my favorite non-profits?"

She angled her head, her lips quirking up on the side. She might've even rolled those gorgeous eyes. "Mason. Really?"

"So I made a few phone calls." He shrugged and edged even closer to her. She didn't back up. That was a good sign.

"I appreciate those phone calls. And everything else."

"I know you do."

Another step. Goliath wandered away, his head to the ground.

"But I can't keep this check."

"Why not?"

"Because it's from you."

"Technically, it's from the Mason Mulrennan Foundation." But even if it was from him, what was wrong with that?

"People would talk."

"Let them." He took another half a step closer.

She shook her head. "You're a public figure."

He understood her aversion to media attention now.

107

Not so much the logic behind that statement. "So is the foundation."

"You're—"

"It's not about me, Remi. The foundation is dedicated to the protection and humane care of animals. I've seen firsthand how important that is to you here at the sanctuary. And, if I was a betting man, I would bet that I wouldn't find another organization that treats their animals better than you."

She sighed, her brows furrowing. "Mason, thank you, but—"

"Why does there have to be a 'but?'"

"Because you're—"

This time he took a giant step closer, until only the piece of paper separated them. That, and her anxiety. He stared down into gorgeous green eyes, wide and afraid. Didn't she know by now that she could trust him? "I'm what?"

"You've done enough already." Her mouth opened as if she wanted to say more, but then her lips clamped together. What had she been about to say?

"I don't think so." Not by a long shot. His fingers slipped around her arms, and he lowered his head until he felt like he was wading through a forest of luscious green foliage. "Remi?"

"Yes?" Her breathing came and went in short spurts, tickling his lips, heightening every nerve in his body.

"You know I would never hurt you, right?"

Her only response was the shuttering of her lashes. What could he do to put her mind at ease?

Her lips tasted sweet, flavored with the sweetened iced tea from earlier. Unsure and hesitant at first, but definitely yielding and soft, she responded to his slight pressure with an intensity he hadn't expected, curling her arms around his neck.

A moan of pleasure escaped his throat. Somewhere in his subconscious, he felt palms brace against his chest, pressing him back. His eyelids flickered open to see fat teardrops trickle down her cheeks.

"You might not *want* to hurt me, Mason Mulrennan, but you will. It's inevitable because of who you are." Remi tore away from his grasp, and then she turned and dashed toward the house.

Stunned, Mason could only watch, his limbs refusing to cooperate. Finally, he forced his voice to work. "Remi, wait! Please!"

A hum sounded from behind him. Then a hiss.

Mason blinked. Oh, no. He'd forgotten about being within Jumbo's firing range. He lunged—

A fresh coat of llama gunk splattered across his back.

He closed his eyes and sighed, exhausted and emotionally drained, scrubbed a hand across his jaw.

Goliath barked at Remi's retreating figure. When she didn't turn around, he whimpered and plopped on the ground, tucking his head between his giant paws, his expression morphing from happy to miserable.

"I hear you, boy." Mason squatted on his heels and stroked the top of the golden's head. "Come on, Goliath. Tomorrow's another day."

He went to rise and spotted a piece of paper in the grass. He picked it up.

The check from the foundation.

His gaze darted to the converted stable, but Remi had already disappeared inside.

She'd rejected his money. The first girl to do that. Ever.

Gratitude and hope bloomed in his gut.

Thank You, God, for leading me to a woman who doesn't want me for the thickness of my wallet.

So she definitely wasn't after him for his money, but it didn't appear she was interested in pursuing a relationship with him at all.

Please, God, soften her heart. She's carrying around a deep wound, one that I can't heal. Only You can. Lord, You know that I won't hurt her, that I wouldn't allow her to be hurt like she was in the past. Help her to see that, and to know that I'm nothing like her father.

****

Remi eased through the front door and locked it behind her. She pressed her spine against the cool wood, freezing clear through her sweater down to her bones. Her breath came in short, quick pants. Her heart pumped fear through her veins at rocket speed.

What just happened outside? Why had she let him kiss her?

Her head wobbled back and forth. He might have initiated the kiss, but she'd definitely kissed him back. She put a hand against her heart, hoping to calm the frantic beating.

The first time she'd allowed a guy to kiss her, and he had to be a popular sports figure? A guy whose face was plastered all over the Internet and television? What was she thinking?

Obviously, she hadn't been thinking, or she never would have let Mason drive onto her ranch in the first place. Or allowed him to keep coming back.

And now he'd raced his way into her heart.

She was in trouble.

She scrubbed a hand across her face and moaned. *Oh, God, if You're listening, I could use some help here. I can't fall for a racecar driver and suffer a repeat of life with my father. Please, please set me free from this fear!*

God hadn't heard her heart's cry about her father. Would He hear her prayer now?

10

Six o'clock on Halloween evening. Like clockwork, tires crunched the gravel driveway outside.

Remi lifted the curtain and peered out the window, avoiding the truck that had been parked out there since this afternoon. And the good-looking man that had stepped out of it.

Good. Camdon was here, toting a large sack. He came bearing dinner, as usual.

Time to face the music, er…the driver.

Remi pulled on a sweater and opened the front door, the chilly breeze penetrating straight through the fleece. She shivered, more from facing the racecar driver than the frosty temperature and the unusually frigid wind.

Her boots pounded the wood slats on the porch. She met her brother at the bottom of the steps. "Hey, Camdon."

"Hey, sweetness." Camdon planted a kiss on her forehead. "How are you today?"

She hadn't given much thought to the significance of the date until Camdon showed up. Why was that?

She gulped. Because a racecar driver had taken over her brain and her heart today, that's why. "Actually, I'm good."

One dark eyebrow hiked high on his forehead. "That's awesome. So you mean I brought all this grub for nothing?" He brandished the white takeout bag in the air. "Two whole baskets of crispy fried chicken with extra sides of slaw and rice. And lots of biscuits."

She smiled. "Enough for one more?"

"Of course. You know I always bring extra for Jillian. Is she here?" His gaze jerked to the spot where Lightning was usually tied up. Confusion crinkled his forehead.

"Not yet." She flicked her head toward the pickup still parked on the other side of the barn. "Mason's here."

His gaze followed hers. Both eyebrows hiked, and his head moved in a slow, thoughtful nod. "Ahh."

She didn't have time to ask what all that meant. She wanted to catch Mason before he disappeared, to apologize for not coming out to greet him earlier.

Who was she kidding?

She just wanted to see…

Goliath. Yep. She hadn't seen the cute Golden all day.

"Go on. I'll start unloading everything." Camdon's brown eyes encouraged. His head bobbed toward the barn.

"Thanks." She didn't need any more coaxing. She practically sprinted, her heart tripping out an anxious rhythm.

At the barn door, a deep voice belted out the tunes to a song, what sounded like a praise song.

Remi halted outside. With eyelids pressed tight, she listened to the words. Worship. Soul. Holy. The message in the song, and the heart of the messenger, floated in the air like a leaf, whispering words of love directly to her heart. The song ended, and Mason's voice faded to a hum.

She took a slow step into the barn, her heart hammering against her chest. "Hey."

The brush resting along Pocono's back stilled. Goliath, who'd been slumbering against the wall behind Mason, stretched and meandered her way, his tail curling high above him. She leaned down to scratch behind his ears, avoiding Mason's eyes as he slid an appreciative gaze over her.

"Hey yourself. I was wondering if I was going to have to go inside and drag you out."

Her lips curving at that prospect, she rose and mashed her hands in her pockets. "I'm sorry I didn't come out earlier."

"Scared?" His brown eyes dared her to say otherwise.

"Yeah."

"Scared *and* honest." He tilted his head back, his laughter loosening the anxiety that had coiled all afternoon.

How could he have this effect on her? One minute she dreaded seeing him, the next, her entire body tingled with anticipation.

"I wish the other drivers were as scared to see me coming as you are." His cheeks, still scrunched with humor, relaxed. "But you know there's no reason to be frightened of me, Remi. I would never do anything to hurt you."

He kept saying that, but he didn't know anything about her or why she was so nervous around him. Was it time to tell him the sordid details of her past?

But, if she did, he'd hightail it to that fancy truck of his and race right out of her life.

Isn't that what she wanted? Remi didn't know anymore.

She took a deep breath and mustered her courage. "My brother is here. Camdon. You met him at the funeral for your friend."

Mason nodded, and the brush continued sliding along Pocono's back. "I saw his car drive in."

"He brought some fried chicken. Would you like to join us for dinner?"

The brush stopped abruptly. Mason stepped away from the horse and brown eyes bored into her. As if he ripped her chest wall away and revealed the nightmarish fear that kept her captive all these years.

Gripping the brush in one hand, a curious expression flitted across his face. "Dinner with you and your brother? Are you sure?"

She cocked her head, considering his question. It was just dinner. And Camdon and Jillian would be around, so there wouldn't be a repeat of yesterday's kiss. Why did she find that slightly disappointing? She shook it off. "Yeah. I'm sure."

He stared at her for all of thirty seconds, his eyes warming, his lips curving into a delicious smile.

She struggled to keep her breathing even. "My friend is also coming."

His smile turned into a laugh. "Reinforcements, huh? That's probably a good thing."

Remi turned to leave but couldn't resist another glance over her shoulder at the attractive man. The way his muscles rippled underneath his long-sleeved shirt. The powerful slant of his jaw. The caring, tender expression on his face whenever he looked at her. Which he was doing now.

She gulped and scrounged up the remnants of her courage before she backed down. "Come on in when you're done. And bring Goliath."

"Give me a minute to clean up, and we'll be there."

****

Mason leaned back in the chair and sipped the sweet tea, enjoying every minute of being included in Remi's tight circle of family and friends. Sharing dinner and fellowship with her brother and best friend gave him a better glimpse into her life.

"Well, sis, I've got an early morning meeting tomorrow with the City Manager, so I need to hit the road back to town." Camdon pushed his chair back and rose to his full six-foot plus height.

"Yeah, me, too." Jillian scooted out of her chair.

"You've got a meeting with the City Manager?" Shock resounded through Remi's voice.

He narrowed his eyes at the alarm blaring from her face. Or was that dread or fear of being left alone with him?

Chuckling, Jillian slipped her arms into a sweater, allowing Camdon to help her with the sleeves. "Hope not. But I do have a shift tomorrow, so I need to get going."

Mason rose, too, although he had no intention of leaving just yet.

Camdon stepped away from the girls' goodbye scene. "Mason, I'm glad you decided to join us tonight."

"Yeah. Me, too." His gaze darted to Remi. She glanced back at him, smiling, that cute little dimple showing off.

Camdon caught the exchange. His forehead scrunched, and he lowered his voice. "I appreciate your help around the sanctuary."

"No problem." Mason couldn't tear his gaze from Remi.

"I don't know how you manage your shop and volunteering here."

Volunteering? He no longer considered his work here as volunteering. Hmmm…why was that? He swung his gaze back to Camdon. "I guess a person does what's important to them, right?"

Camdon stared at him. Questioning his motives? Finally, Remi's brother shrugged. "Well, thank you. And I know my sister appreciates it as well."

"I'm happy to do what I can, but it's not nearly enough. Remi needs more volunteers during the week."

"You've done a lot, especially rounding up all your friends yesterday, but I'm not sure Remi would feel comfortable with that many volunteers around the place very often."

"Yeah. I get that," Mason agreed.

"Take care." Camdon extended his hand, and although his expression was kind, Mason heard the hint of stern warning in his voice.

Message received. Loud and clear. Take care of his sister.

"I intend to." Mason acknowledged the warning with a nod. "I'm sure I'll be seeing you around."

Camdon's eyebrows narrowed, his concern for his sister obvious. "Yeah? You plan to stick—"

"Yeah, what?" Remi slid in next to her brother and

snaked an arm around his slender waist, her face tipped adoringly up toward Camdon.

Mason tamped down the envy. *Come on, man. This is her brother.*

Camdon slipped his arm around Remi's shoulders and planted a kiss on the top of her head. "Yeah. I'm just leaving. I'll walk Jillian to her car, er, horse. Will you be all right tonight?"

Remi's face darkened briefly, but she mustered a sweet smile with watery eyes and nodded.

Camdon pulled her into a hug and whispered something in her ear. Her dark head bobbed again.

Sudden waterworks and a secret message. What was up with that?

Mason wandered into the kitchen and busied himself with making coffee while Remi followed Camdon and Jillian to the door.

He twisted over a shoulder. Remi stood, staring out into the darkness for a few minutes before closing the door and pressing her forehead against the wood. Something was definitely up tonight. What was it?

"Thanks for inviting me to dinner. Hope you don't mind if I stay for coffee."

She startled. As if she'd forgotten he was there. "No. That's fine. Coffee sounds great."

He handed her a cup.

"Thanks, Mason. Come. Sit down." She parked herself on one end of the couch.

He debated for about ten seconds on whether he should take the armchair. Maybe she wouldn't be so nervous if he wasn't sitting right next to her. And that might be the only way he could keep from pulling her into his arms. From attempting a repeat of yesterday's kiss.

Nah. He couldn't resist the opportunity to be close, so he sank down next to her, allowing a couple feet of clearance between them.

Goliath was sacked out in the corner of the family

room. A fire glowed from the hearth, casting a soft light across Remi's smooth face. The only sound in the big room was the dog's snore and a clock ticking from the kitchen.

Mason sighed and sipped the warm liquid, contentment rippling through his chest. What a perfect way to end the evening.

Remi hadn't touched her coffee. Her head dipped.

He put the cup down and angled toward her. Reaching out, he nudged her chin up with his thumb. "Remi? Would you rather I leave?"

A sheen glazed her emerald irises, showing off those amber specks. She shook her head. "No!"

"What's wrong, then?" He toyed with the tips of her silky hair before hooking it back behind her ear.

A huge sigh erupted from her chest. "You're so sweet, Mason. Even after I've been so…unwelcoming."

"Sweetheart, you don't need—"

She stilled his hand by bringing it to her cheek and cupping it with her own. "Yes, please. I need to explain."

He nodded and waited for her to go on. When she released his hand, he draped his arm along the back of the couch.

"When I was ten, my father—" Her voice broke. She cleared her throat.

He stroked her hair. Everything in him prodded to tell her that it was all right. She didn't need to explain. But the only way she'd heal was to talk about it.

"My father committed suicide. On Halloween night."

Ouch! Today. How could he have forgotten the significance of the date from all the articles he'd scoured? No wonder her brother was so concerned tonight.

Mason blinked, but other than that, didn't show any reaction or offer useless words. He just kept stroking her hair, letting her get out of her system words and emotions that hadn't been resolved for more than a couple of decades.

"You might have heard of him?" Her gaze darted to his, tiny autumn specks of worry shimmering from her eyes now. "Connor Lambright? He was a pro golfer."

How should he respond? He hadn't heard of him until Charlie mentioned—

She didn't wait for his response. "My mom had just filed for divorce. He was the golden boy of golf at the time, and it was unexpected. The newspaper reporters, the tv sportscasters, they all blasted my mother, citing the surprise divorce papers for his suicide. Well, the divorce might have been a surprise to them, but it wasn't to our family."

It was his turn to sigh. "I'm so sorry, Remi."

She nodded. "Yeah. Me, too. Because I really like you."

Hope blossomed, overflowed in his chest. He scooted closer.

"But it can't go anywhere."

Then withered just as quickly. "Remi—"

"Don't you see, Mason?" She lifted her face, pleading with him to understand.

Wasn't happening.

"You live, no, you thrive, in the media spotlight every day. As much as I might like the chance to get to know you better," her eyes, although glittering with uncertainty, narrowed with determination, "to pursue what might be happening between us, there's no way I could subject myself to that horrendous ordeal all over again." Her head wobbled back and forth, her face growing more agitated with every warble.

"Oh, Remi." He curled his arm around her shoulders and tugged her to his side. He held her, his chin resting on her head, until the tremors stopped racking her body and her breathing became even again. His lips whispered a kiss against her silky crown. "Sweetheart, I'm sorry. About your dad. About the media attack. I'm sorry for the pain you still feel."

He tugged her back so she could see the promise in his

eyes. "I would never allow the media to hurt you like they did your mother."

"But that's just it, Mason." Pain seeped into her voice, stiffened her spine. "It might have started with the media, but it didn't stop there. We'd go into town and find people huddled together, whispering and pointing their fingers at my mom and us kids. The kids at school picked fights with my brothers..." Her lips clamped together, and her head and shoulders slumped. "Things got so bad that my mom finally moved us to the country."

His anger escalated. So much pain directed at her family. He couldn't do anything about the past, but he could certainly do damage control from here on out.

"If something happened to you…" Her voice tapered off, and her lips quivered.

All that she'd been through, and she was worried about him?

He cupped her cheeks and leaned toward her until only an inch separated their lips, the soft glow of the fire and the warm spicy tones of her perfume a tantalizing combination. "Remi…"

This time her face stretched to meet his, her lips red and full, begging to be kissed.

He took his time obliging, lingering, teasing, tasting the sweetness.

He pulled back and pressed his forehead against hers. "Remi, God decides when I go home to heaven. Whether that's in a racecar or just sitting in my office chair, it's up to Him."

He heard her soft intake of breath, but he had to go on. "You don't need to face this alone. God will walk this path with you, just like He does with me. He can take that fear and replace it with peace. This is your time to heal."

****

"I have prayed for healing, for a relief from this dreadful fear. Not just of the media but going out in public. But God doesn't seem to hear my prayers." Her voice came out louder than she'd intended, but his words made her downright mad.

She'd prayed for healing to overcome her social anxiety. Many times. But it hadn't gotten her anywhere. No. God had chosen to respond to her cries by sending Mason Mulrennan into her life.

A racecar driver. Not exactly the perfect recipe for healing. How could being under the media microscope be the answer to her prayer?

Mason must have noticed her throbbing vein. He caressed the stiffness around her neck. "He heard your prayers, sweetheart. I'm here."

"So you're saying you're God's answer to my prayers? How can a racecar driver possibly be the answer to heal a social phobic?"

"That's not what I meant. I'm here with you. When was the last time you made a new friend?"

Ouch.

"Or allowed someone besides Jillian and your family to help you out here at the sanctuary?"

Double ouch. His words pinned her against the couch with laser precision.

"And you survived an invasion of about fifty people yesterday."

She had, hadn't she? A tiny seed of triumph sprouted in her belly. "Well, I hid most of the day."

"But you didn't bolt."

"I thought about it, but there wasn't a clear getaway. God would have had to part the Red Sea for me. Apparently, He didn't see fit to make that happen."

He threw his head back and laughed. "You are so refreshingly honest."

She liked the hearty sound of his laughter, the little crinkle lines that shot out from his eyes, his relaxed posture. Mason Mulrennan was totally okay with his own skin, whether he was here at the sanctuary or standing in the winner's circle with a microphone sticking in front of his face.

Maybe God had put him in her life so she could learn from him.

He rose onto those incredibly long legs of his and held out a hand. She took it, and he tugged her off the couch. And right into his chest.

"Come to the race, Remi." Simple words that meant so much more coming from his husky voice.

"Mason, didn't I just—"

He sheltered her in his embrace, tugging her so close that her words were muffled against his shirt. She breathed deep of citrus and spice, of fresh outdoors and fried chicken. He made saying *no* so hard.

"Mason, I can't."

"Maybe not yet. But I know you will." His words rumbled against her head where his cheek rested.

Did he? Because she sure couldn't see it happening.

Not in her lifetime.

11

"Come on. No arguing. It's time for you to relax." Mason tugged Remi's hand until she stood up. She'd been holed up in the house all afternoon, and now she sat hunched over the keyboard of her laptop. Invoices, checks and paperwork scattered across the kitchen table.

Since he'd arrived at the ranch this afternoon, she hadn't made it outdoors one time. Too busy or was she avoiding him?

His lips quirked up on one side. That wasn't happening. Not if he could help it. Especially since he'd rearranged his schedule so that he could fly out in the morning rather than tonight.

"Relax?" she muttered, sliding her warm hand from his grasp to stretch her arms above her head and then roll her shoulders. "Who has time to relax? I've got a ranch to run. Animals to feed and take care of."

"Not tonight. You have the night off. The animals are all fed and tucked in for the evening." He dangled the bursting-at-the-seams picnic hamper in front of her. "And you have to eat."

Her eyes brightened, and she perked up. Now he knew what motivated her. Food.

"You did all that?"

He waggled his eyebrows. "The animals part. Not the picnic. I thought we could spend a quiet evening together. Just you and me."

Goliath let out a single bark, loud and echoing through the tiny house.

Mason's gaze shot to the Golden sitting on his

haunches next to them. He rubbed the soft fur on Goliath's head, trying to glare at him but not succeeding all that well. The dog couldn't take a hint, and he surely wouldn't stay behind. "Correction. You, me, and Goliath."

Remi tossed that mane of silky dark hair back and laughed. She crouched and rubbed the canine's ears. "That's a good boy. You've trained your master well."

She rose and lifted her pretty nose in the air. "Thank you, Mason. Actually, something to eat sounds awesome and it smells divine. What's in there?"

"Dinner."

She gave him a playful swat on his upper arm, and he felt the magnetism that constantly drew him to her all the way through his denim jacket. He grabbed her hand and took his time bringing her palm to his lips, his eyes never leaving hers.

Amber specks burned like melted gold against the backdrop of her green eyes. She drew in a sharp breath. Her body stilled in anticipation.

He kissed the soft flesh on her palm and then guided her hand gently back to her side. This woman made his heart flap like crazy, but he didn't want to do anything to jeopardize the tenuous thread that held them together.

"Ready?" Willing his primary organ back to a normal rate, he swept the air with his arm, inviting her to the front door.

She might have smelled crusty bread from the roast beef sandwiches, strong cheese, and oatmeal cookies with chocolate chips from the basket, but all he breathed in was her jasmine and spicy cinnamon scent as she passed by. That, and a slight whiff of chocolate and peanut butter from her latest candy binge.

In two long-legged steps, he beat her to the door and opened it with a flourish. "After you, milady."

Smiling, she complied, and they stepped onto the porch. Brilliant white stars glittered across a not quite dark sky, the giant moon already hanging high and bright on the horizon.

Dinner under a star-studded sky with Remi. Was he sure he could handle this? No. Not at all. But he was going to give it his best shot.

****

The wonderful fragrance of a surprise dinner enticed Remi off the porch. She followed Mason's boots closely, just like Goliath.

He was so sweet to feed and take care of the animals, but he hadn't stopped there. Somehow he'd managed to scrounge up dinner for them, too.

When had he done that?

She ran a hand through her hair, flipping it away from her face. So absorbed in paying bills, she really wasn't sure what time he had arrived at the ranch. Or even what time it was now.

Judging by the darkening sky, it had to be late. And it was…wasn't it Thursday? He should be gone already!

She gasped and touched his forearm, feeling her pulse rocket at the muscles that bunched underneath her fingertips. "Mason, why are you still here?"

He grabbed her hand with his free one. "Worried about me?"

"Of course not." Well, maybe just a little.

Llama heads popped up as they trekked across the yard and toward a grassy knoll. A couple hums sounded, but they were too far away that Mason didn't even flinch.

"My flight isn't until tomorrow."

"So does that mean the race is later?"

"No. That means I rearranged my schedule so that I could spend more time with you." He angled his gaze in her direction. In the waning light, she made out his boyish, hopeful expression.

He'd already given her the gift of time on so many occasions, and again tonight. Her heart soared with this tiny glimpse of his vulnerability.

But, what was she supposed to do with that?

12

"I told him no." Heat blasted Remi's face as she opened the oven door and slid the cake pans out. She placed the round pans on the counter and turned around, planting fists on her hips, the hot pads dangling from her fingers. She shot her best glare at her mother. "Whose side are you on anyway?"

"I'm not taking any sides, honey." Lessa looked up from tossing the salad.

Jillian's blonde eyebrows arched, but she kept silent. She poured iced tea into a glass then moved on to the next. Was that a smirk she was trying to hide?

Everyone was ganging up on her. Well, not quite everyone. Not yet, anyway. But Remi was sure that once Camdon and her stepfather Ryan came inside from checking and feeding the animals, they'd join in the fray.

"Well, it sure seems like you're taking his side. You, too, Missy." Remi narrowed her eyes at her friend.

"Wait a minute. I didn't say a word." Jillian held up her palms in surrender and blew her wispy bangs up with a puff.

"You didn't have to. I saw that smile trying to creep out." Remi folded her arms.

The front door opened, and Camdon and Ryan walked in. Both men glanced around the room.

"What's got you all worked up, Remi?" Camdon's hands connected with her waist to guide her away from the sink. He pumped soap into his hands then scrubbed them under the faucet while Ryan headed to the bathroom to wash up.

"Mom thinks I should have gone to the race this weekend with Mason. And Jillian's siding with her."

"From what I've seen and read about him, Mason seems like an honorable fellow." Camdon reached around her for the towel and dried his hands. "I don't think he would expect you to sleep with him if that's what you're worried about."

She scoffed. "That's the last thing I'm worried about. He's been a perfect gentleman." Too perfect. He was bound to have a dark side. Wasn't he?

"Then why say no?" Lessa opened the fridge and pulled out bottles of salad dressing.

Remi took a giant gulp of precious air then let it out slowly. Focused her attention on stirring the stew simmering in the crock pot. "Because I couldn't say yes."

"What are we talking about?" Ryan joined them in the kitchen and planted a kiss on the top of Lessa's head.

Lessa gazed up at Ryan, adoration softening her face. Years after the divorce, her mother had found peace and contentment with her high school sweetheart. Ryan had left right after graduation to pursue his dream of flying planes for the military. How different their lives might have been if Ryan had stayed.

Maybe then Remi wouldn't fear people so much that she couldn't even eat in a restaurant or break out in a cold sweat when someone walked toward her. Or panic when a kind and generous man set his heart on getting to know her. She set the wooden spoon down, closed her eyes and rubbed her face.

"Not what. Who. Mason Mulrennan. The racecar driver." Camdon rehung the towel.

At the mention of Mason's name, Remi's hand dropped away, and her eyelids bolted open.

"Ah." Ryan nodded, but he still looked confused. "Why?"

"He invited Remi to the race. Actually, he's invited her a few times now." Jillian retrieved bowls and salad plates from the cabinet.

"Way to throw me under the bus, *girlfriend*." Would sarcasm work with this crowd? Remi didn't think so.

"Well, we can at least watch it on TV." On the way to track down the remote, Ryan stopped to cradle Remi's cheeks in his thick palms. He gave her a peck on the forehead. "If he's the man for you, honey, eventually saying yes will become easier than saying no."

Remi couldn't stifle the sigh that leaked out. Was that why it had been so difficult? Why she felt so torn up inside about not going? Because saying no was becoming harder every day?

"He's right, you know."

Remi stared at her mother, saw the love and understanding on her face. The hope that Remi might finally conquer this battle.

The television flickered on, and Ryan flipped through the channels until he found the race. "Here it is. They haven't started, yet."

The camera panned the colorful cars lined up behind the pace car. Remi spotted Mason's number. Her heart stuttered. Her jaw slacked.

The green flag waved, and the car engines roared as they accelerated. Jillian and Camdon stepped closer to the screen.

Not Remi. Her legs threatened to give out. She planted her hip against the kitchen island, covered her mouth with her hand. If she closed her eyes, she could still feel the tingling, the playful teasing of his lips. Could still picture the tenderness of his smile, the tiny crinkles around those warm brown orbs.

She let out a long sigh and looked up, catching her mother's concerned gaze.

Her mother curled an arm around Remi's back. "Don't give up on the power of love, honey."

"Love?" Remi stuttered. Her palm flattened against her heart.

Was this what love felt like? Thinking about him all day long, and then again after she'd crawled under the covers at night, when he managed to wriggle into her dreams.

Lessa smiled. "Just like the pastor talked about today. There's no room for fear in our lives when we experience God's perfect love."

Remi remained silent. She'd felt the pastor's gaze drilling through to her very core. As if he'd preached that message directly to her. But how could he have known before today that she would brave going to church?

"Honey, you can trust God with your fears. And your man." Lessa flicked her head toward the race. "He'll take care of both."

"How can you say that?" God hadn't kept Remi's father from destroying his life and those around him. "What about Dad?"

Lessa sighed, but her expression was one of peace and finality. "Honey, your father chose death over life because it was less painful. For the same reason, you're willing to give up on love. Because it terrifies you. But is that really how you want to live?"

The truth of her mother's words rammed the breath back into Remi's lungs. She slumped back against the counter and stole another glance at the race.

Cars whizzed around the track faster than she could keep up. The numbers and their positions scrolled across the top of the screen. Mason appeared to be running in fourth position.

He was a man of faith, confident and committed. He'd shown her his character over the last few weeks. But was he a man she could count on for a lifetime? Not to be so full of himself because of the constant media attention and the groupies who followed him from track to track? Would he stick with her when times got tough?

What if, like her father, he went through a losing streak and couldn't regain his momentum? What then? Would he still be the same man?

****

Ten laps to go.

Mason steered through turn two, gripping the wheel until he was sure his knuckles were white underneath the protective gloves. Sweat dripped down his back. His neck ached from four hours of constant stress.

Closing in on the end of the season, drivers were scrambling for points. Some of the wildcards ran all over the field, making stupid mistakes like cutting too close when they passed, and the tires weren't holding up like they should. Two of his drivers had been knocked out of the race since the midway point.

Mason didn't like racing under these conditions. Somebody was bound to get hurt. And he sure wasn't looking forward to being that somebody.

He pressed the gas then backed off slightly to go around turn three. The car behind him hit the gas and nudged Mason's rear bumper. Mason fought the natural turn of the car. Saved it. He punched the accelerator, and his car shot forward.

Nine laps to go. He was still in good shape for a win. If he could only keep these yahoos from acting crazy.

Another lap down.

Eight more, and he was closing in on the back of the pack. Ahead of him, a car turned sideways and rammed into the rail then slid down the track. Cars hit the brakes and jammed together. Smoke covered the track.

"High or low? Which way?" he muttered, concentrating on finding a way through the carnage of steel.

"Slow it down. Cars all over the track." Shane, the replacement spotter, practically yelled into the radio.

Mason mashed the brakes, sailing straight into the cloud of smoke, totally dependent on the spotter's instructions.

A mangled car drifted up the track in front of him. He jerked the wheel hard to the left.

A car slammed into the back of Mason's, sending him

into the fray of spinning cars.

****

"Oh, no!" Remi buried her face in her hands. An arm closed around her shoulders, but she didn't dare open her eyes to see whose it was. She didn't care.

Someone had crashed into Mason's car, careening it into a huge pileup.

Remi trembled. What if he was hurt? Worse! What if he was killed?

She bolted from the couch and fled to the kitchen. She couldn't just stay here and do nothing. But what could she do? How could she find out if he was all right?

Her gaze drifted to her phone.

No. She couldn't call him. He'd just been in an accident, and she didn't have any emergency contact numbers.

"He dropped the window net, Remi." Jillian's words should have soothed her nerves, but they didn't.

"They do that to let everyone know they're okay." Camdon glanced over his shoulder.

Chilled to the bone, she paced the kitchen floor, rubbing her arms. Why hadn't she just gone to the race like he'd asked? She could have been there, could have seen with her own eyes that he was all right.

Because she'd allowed fear to rule her life. As usual. And she was getting might sick of it.

Soft footsteps padded the ceramic tile behind her. An arm slipped around her shoulders.

She didn't need to lift her head to know that it was her mother. She recognized the comfort of her mother's warm hug and the vanilla scent. Fingers squeezed her shoulder. "Honey, he'll be all right. He's out of the car and headed to the infield hospital."

"The hospital?" Did her heart just stop? She couldn't breathe.

Camdon walked into the kitchen and poured another glass of iced tea. "Remi, it's protocol. When drivers are involved in an accident, they are required to be checked out in the hospital. But he doesn't appear to be hurt too badly. He walked to the ambulance."

"Well, he was limping a little, but he'll probably be all right." Jillian rested her forearms on the counter, a sly look on her face.

Remi's jaw dropped.

Mason was limping? She closed her eyes, and her chin dipped to her chest. *Oh, dear God, please let Mason be all right! Please hear my prayer this time!*

Her phone vibrated in her jeans pocket. She dug it out with shaky fingers and fumbled it on the floor. She bent to scoop it up, her heart stuttering and stopping at Mason's smiling image on the screen. Relief made her legs go weak, and she fell back against the counter. "Hi."

"Hi, yourself. I wanted to let you know I'm okay. Just on the off chance you were watching." His deep drawl reached across the miles, his tender concern settling the tremors and warming her from the inside out.

The man just plowed into a dozen cars, but he cared enough to call and let her know he was all right? A sigh came from the deepest part of her soul.

"I was watching." She looked up to see four necks craned in her direction, curiosity all over their faces.

Mercy! Couldn't a girl hold a private conversation in her own house?

"Yeah?" Pleasure mingled with the disbelief in his voice.

"Yeah. Everyone's here. Jillian. My brother. My folks." She glared at the lot of them before twisting around to face the sink.

"Wow. Sounds like a crowd. I won't keep you then."

"Mason?" She held on to the phone as if it was a lifeline. She needed to hear his deep voice, yearned to see those crinkles that fanned out from his eyes, to smile at his contagious rumble of laughter.

Craved his touch. And those oh-so-sweet kisses.

But she had to settle for a staticky connection and a few hundred miles of space between them.

"Yeah?"

"I'm sorry you wrecked your car."

"It's just a car." His voice held the tiniest note of frustration.

It might have been just a car, but he'd been in it.

"We lost three cars today. Not a good day for our team, but each of us walked away from the devastation. Remember what I said, Remi? God can take your fear and replace it with His perfect peace. He can heal you if you'll let Him."

"Is that what you do, Mason? Otherwise, I don't see how you can buckle yourself into a car and drive so fast." Or handle the hundreds of television cameras and microphones jammed in his face afterward.

"It's the only way, Remi."

"If you were here, I'd give you a hug." And maybe a kiss, but she kept that to herself.

An awkward silence widened the gap between them. Maybe she'd said too much. She blew out a breath. "I—"

"Sorry, sweetheart. My crew chief was talking in my other ear. I'll collect on that hug when I see you. Soon. Very soon."

The call disconnected, and she realized she was smiling. She slid the phone back in her pocket and turned around to find four anxious faces peering at her, the house eerily quiet. "What?"

"So, he's okay?" Lessa asked first.

"Yeah. He's fine." Remi sighed, and probably didn't mask the dreamy expression quickly enough.

"More than fine if the gleam in your eyes means anything." Jillian gloated.

Remi glared at her. "You're not helping matters."

One blonde eyebrow hiked in challenge. "It depends on which matter you're referring to."

Lessa hugged her. "I'm so glad, honey. But if he asks

you to go to one of his races again, you should probably go. You might feel better about what he does, and you'd see for yourself that he was all right."

Remi nodded. *If* Mason asked her again, she had every intention of saying yes.

****

Remi punched the pillow a couple times then rolled over on her other side with a huff. She'd been in bed for over an hour now, but sleep? Forget about it.

One thing kept her awake. Rather, one *man*.

A certain good-looking charmer who was wooing her with his sweet phone calls and generous help on the farm.

Was he for real? She'd been lonely for so long, maybe she'd just cooked up a companion. Like children playing with their imaginary friends.

A helicopter's chuff-chuff sounded far off, growing louder as it neared. Strange. She'd never heard a helicopter flying around the countryside of Harrison at midnight. But then, she was usually asleep by now.

Remi pushed the comforter off and slid out of bed. She padded to the window in bare feet and lifted the curtain.

The helicopter sounded as if it hovered directly over her property now. She angled her neck, looking out the window in both directions. Then it zoomed over the house, and a spotlight aimed straight down. In her yard.

What?

She hurried to the front door and braced herself for a blast of cold air. When she flung the door wide, the chopper's rotors slowed, and the engine finally stopped its straining.

What she didn't brace herself for was the man who hopped down from the enclosed cab. Or the dog that followed.

"Mason." The name came out on a whisper, from the very core of her damaged spirit.

She stepped out on the porch, hugging her chest, and moisture leaked from one eye. She brushed it away with her sleeve. Was it stupid to cry because a man visited a gal at midnight, by helicopter?

Mason reached the end of the chopper's blades and stretched to his full height, slanting his cap-covered head to the house. With the help of the bright moon, she made out the droop of his shoulders, the heavy trudge of his steps. Even Goliath moved a little slow.

Not her. She took the steps two at a time then her bare feet glided through the wet grass to greet him. A couple feet away, she slowed to a stop.

Now that she was closer, she could see the smudges of fatigue lining his eyes. But, as tired as he must be, he still managed a warm smile and opened his arms wide. "I came to collect on that hug."

She didn't hesitate. She flew into his arms, resting her cheek against the coolness of his leather jacket. She closed her eyes and breathed in his essence, rejoicing in the fact that he was here, safe and no worse for the wear.

Was this a gift from you, God? Did you hear my prayer?

****

Mason's arms closed around Remi and she snuggled against his chest, all warm and cuddly in her fleece pajamas.

He sighed, exhausted, bruised and banged up, but content. He'd made the right choice asking his pilot to swing by here.

With his cheek resting against the silky smoothness of her hair, he closed his eyes and savored the rapid rhythm of her heart. So fast, it rivaled his own.

Oh yeah. He wouldn't mind coming back every Sunday night from four days of tracks and life on the road, from male egos and flinging testosterone, to Remi's sweet embrace, to seeing the relief and welcome slide across her face. But then, he'd rather have her with him.

Hmmm…tough choice.

When she pulled back, he lifted his head to see what was in her eyes. He liked it.

The upcoming winter might be slinging its icy darts at them, but Remi reminded him of springtime. Of tiny buds popping out from dormant trees into an explosion of vibrant color. Like witnessing a new day dawning on the horizon. A new beginning.

Her fingers grazed his jaw, his rough whiskers making a scratching sound against her soft hand. He stilled her hand with his own then pulled it to his lips and caressed the inside of her palm. "I missed you."

She angled her head, that cute little dimple flashing and long brown wisps of hair sticking up in all directions. "Did you?"

He leaned down and kissed her until she couldn't possibly doubt his words. When he finally pulled back, he traced her bottom lip with his thumb. "Yeah."

"I missed you, too." Tremors shook through her. From the cold?

He couldn't let her get sick, could he? He tugged her back against his chest. Her breath tickled his neck, and her arms wound around his shoulders like they were made to fit. Cinnamon, jasmine and berries mingled with the scents of the animals, grass and hay. All scents he'd come to love as much as rubber and steel.

Reluctantly, he stepped back, away from the fire she sparked in his veins. If he didn't leave soon, he wouldn't be able to. She was too innocent, his faith too precious, to go down that road.

But tonight, his need was overwhelming and his loneliness intense. He wasn't looking forward to going home to the big, empty castle.

"I need to go, sweetheart." He planted a soft kiss on the top of her head and nodded in the direction of the chopper, his prearranged signal with the pilot. The engine whined, breaking the stillness of the night.

"Do you mind if I come back tomorrow?" There was no way he could wait until Tuesday to see her.

A shaft of moonlight spotlighted her dimple and the

glimmer of a sweet smile. "I'd love that." Her glance pinged to the chopper and back to him. "But maybe leave the escort behind?"

"A chaperone isn't such a bad idea." Maybe she didn't need one, but standing here in the yard under a star-studded sky, holding her so close he knew she wore nothing under the fleece pajamas, staring into those sleepy amber-flecked eyes, he was barely hanging on to his last thread of self-control.

God, help me be the man Remi needs. Use me to help her crush those fears and take back her life so that we can walk Your path together. I love her, Lord.

13

Mason locked the gate to the llama enclosure and headed to the barn. Time to head out for the weekend.

Again.

How could the week have disappeared so quickly?

He sure didn't like leaving Remi every Thursday, knowing that he wouldn't see her again until Tuesday. Four whole days of not seeing her beautiful face, not hearing that soft tinkle of laughter, not stealing a few minutes to share coffee and a chat. And occasionally, a kiss.

His sigh came out loud enough that Jillian could probably hear it down the road. Trotting alongside, Goliath looked up at him with big, mournful eyes. Mason patted him on the head as they continued their trek. "Sorry, buddy. Didn't mean to scare you. It's getting tougher to leave every week, isn't it?"

He made sure all the tools were picked up and put away and grabbed the handful of dirty shirts. Jumbo was a little more sociable these days. Only three crud-blasted shirts in the stack. He grinned. Crazy, lovable llama.

What if Angela hadn't asked him to check out this place? He might never have met Remi or these precious animals, who'd quickly become his friends too.

Doubt pricked him. Maybe that wasn't quite accurate according to a recent sermon at one of the tracks. The way he understood the pastor's message, so long as Mason stayed in close fellowship with the Lord and stepped out in faith, the Lord would shape his path.

And that path had led to Remi. So, even if Angela

hadn't sent him, the Lord still would've found a way to connect their paths.

"Come on, Goliath. Let's go say good-bye to our girl." The dog bounded alongside as they made their way to the renovated stable.

It was growing on him. Remi's soft touches made it homey and comfortable, giving it a much more lived in feeling than his house, which felt colder and more sterile every time he walked in the door. Maybe he should invite her over to come up with ideas on what he could do to make The Castle feel more like a home.

Or maybe he just felt more comfortable here because this is where Remi was.

He pressed the doorbell three quick times before going in, their code.

She sat at the table, hunched over a laptop, one palm holding her chin, the other hand fluttering over the mouse.

More grant research probably. Stubborn little thing kept refusing his check.

"You know I could save you a lot of time," he growled. Goliath sauntered over to the area rug in the family room and plunked down.

She tore her gaze away from the monitor, appreciation glowing from her face. "I know, but I can't let you."

The same argument every time he brought it up, and he hadn't won, yet. "One of these days you will."

"You think so?" Her tone full of challenge, she hiked that cute little chin.

In two steps, he was at her side. He reached out, tugged her off the chair, and swallowed her in his arms. He kissed her, slow and teasing, loving the way her lips and heart responded to his touch.

"Yeah. I think so." Confidence oozed from his voice.

A soft gurgle came from her throat, and those gorgeous lashes finally fluttered open. "Is it time to go already?"

He could get lost in those flecks. They changed from brown to amber, depending on the lighting and her mood.

Right now, she looked like she was in the middle of a wonderful dream. Dare he push the issue?

He nodded and pressed his forehead to hers. "Go with me."

That woke her up. Her shoulders reared back, and fear darkened her face. She turned her back to him. "I…"

He waited, unwilling to let her off the hook this time. He wanted her there, and he knew she longed to be there, too. Could she do it? Would she say yes?

He rubbed her shoulders, loosening the panic that tightened her muscles.

After what seemed like an entire thirty seconds, she swiveled, forcing his hands to drop to his sides. "All right. I'll go. But I can't leave today. Can I come on Saturday?"

Joy exploded in his chest and spilled over to his face. He pumped a fist along his side. "You bet! I'll send Sam for you. Do you mind riding in a small plane?"

Her head dipped as if shamed. "I'm not afraid of heights. Only people."

"Hey." He hooked her chin with his thumb and nudged it up. "You don't need to be frightened of Sam. He's worked for me going on ten years now. He wouldn't say or do anything to hurt you. You have my word." A fierce, protective urged welled up inside. He didn't think he needed to warn Sam, but he would if it meant shielding Remi from any more pain.

She nibbled her upper lip. He longed to tease the worry from her lips, but he was running out of time. Now that she was coming, he'd have to work tonight to clear some time for her this weekend.

"I trust you, Mason."

"That means a lot coming from you." He would move heaven and earth not to damage that fragile thread of trust. Which brought up another issue. There was no way she could stay in his RV. He wouldn't risk shredding her reputation, giving the media something new to gnaw on.

"Uh, Remi…" He scraped fingers across his whiskered

jaw.

"Yeah?"

"As far as sleeping arrangements—" His boot tapped a nervous rhythm on the floor.

"I can't stay with you." Was she asking? Or telling?

"I was just getting to that." He nodded his agreement. "You can stay with some of my friends in their RV at the track or I can get you a hotel room nearby."

Her lips pressed together in a thin line as indecision flitted across her face. Would she change her mind about coming?

"I'll stay with your friends." She squared her shoulders, determination straightening her spine.

"Thatta girl. You'll like Michelle and Geoff." He allowed himself one last lingering kiss, something to hold him until Saturday. Reluctantly, he pulled away, his fingers sliding around the cold door handle.

"Goliath, come." Mason needed to get going. He had a ton of work to do now that she was coming. Plus he figured it would be a good idea to leave before she changed her mind.

****

She should change her mind. Could she really do this?

Remi glanced at the time on her phone. Five thirty on a Friday night.

Should she try calling Camdon at the office? He definitely wouldn't be at home, yet. With all the city functions he attended, the man never kept normal hours. She tapped the screen to connect. It only rang a couple times before he picked up.

"Hey, Remi. What's up?" Papers rustled in the background. As she'd expected. Still at work.

"I've decided to go."

"Yeah?"

She'd surprised him. His office chair squeaked, and she pictured him leaning all the way back, giving her his full attention now. His dark eyebrows would be well up on his forehead, and right about now he was probably rubbing his temple. She smiled at the image.

"I'm impressed. When are you leaving?"

"Tomorrow." A tiny snake of fear slithered in, casting doubt on her decision. Had she experienced a temporary moment of insanity when she'd said yes to Mason? What had she been thinking?

It all came back to her. The loss she felt every weekend at not seeing him. The dread that he might be involved in another accident, and how long before she knew that he was safe.

Or it could have been from that kiss. He'd set her limbs on fire, sparking tingles from her toes to her heart.

"What time?"

"Huh?" Her mind snapped back to now. She rubbed her arms, warming the shivers that spiked.

"What time are you leaving tomorrow?"

"Oh. About nine. Mason's sending his pilot to get me."

"I'll be there."

She smiled. She knew he'd say that. It was just like her brother to make sure she'd be all right. And to celebrate a milestone.

But, did she really have the courage to go through with this?

****

"You can do it, Remi." Jillian glanced over at her from atop Lightning's back, her tone soft and encouraging. They'd ridden Lightning and Pocono hard, and now were taking their time heading back to Remi's barn.

"I hope so." Remi sighed, enjoying Pocono's peaceful, easy gait after their gallop session and the quietness of the countryside as the sun began its ascent, bringing the day to life. Awakening the panic that she'd done her best to bury since agreeing to go to the race.

She tugged some chocolates from her pocket and held out her palm to Jillian. "Want one?"

"No, thanks. Did you say Camdon was coming?"

"Yeah." Remi glanced at her watch, squinting through the glare to make out the time. "He should be here soon." She unfolded the wrapper and tossed the chocolate piece in her mouth, stuffed the soiled wrapper in her pocket.

"Between the two of us, we'll make sure you get on that helicopter." Jillian nodded once.

Fear crashed into her tummy like a boulder avalanche. Could she really do this? Leave the refuge of the sanctuary and surround herself with...people? People she didn't know? People that might—

She took a deep breath, corralling the fear. *God, if You're there, please help me get on that chopper.*

They reached the barn and swung down from the horses. Remi removed the saddle and brushed Pocono's back.

"I'll be right back." Remi led Pocono to his stall while Jillian finished grooming Lightning. Her best friend had agreed to stay at the sanctuary and attend to the animals. Camdon would assume animal duty for Jillian's shift at the fire department on Sunday.

As she latched the door, hooves clomped through the barn behind her as Jillian escorted Lightning to a stall.

"Be a good boy for Jillian and Camdon while I'm gone." She buried her face in Pocono's neck, taking small comfort in the horse's strength.

Jillian came beside her and gave her a one-armed hug. They laced arms around each other's waists as they exited the barn.

The tires of her brother's silver car scrunched through the gravel and grinded to a stop. One long jean-clad leg appeared then his entire body popped out of the car.

Remi couldn't contain the chuckle, a familiar reaction upon seeing her brother get out of his car. He was just too tall a guy to drive such a compact sedan.

"Looks like reinforcements have arrived." Jillian smiled at Remi's brother.

"Good morning, sweet brother of mine." Remi planted

a kiss on his cheek, inhaling the familiar notes of cedar and basil from Camdon's cologne.

"Morning." Her brother's early morning voice rumbled close to her ear.

"Work late last night?" With so many evening functions to attend for the job, Camdon wasn't usually an early riser.

"Not too late."

"I see you didn't come dressed to work today." Jillian teased, running her gaze down to Camdon's white tee, covered by a suit jacket.

Frowning, Camdon glanced down at his attire. "What do you mean? I'm wearing jeans and boots."

"This is as close as he comes to casual wear, Jillian. You should know that by now." Remi giggled. When the twins were younger and tried to pull their occasional prank, she could always tell them apart by how they dressed. Even casual, Camdon pressed his jeans and wore a dressy shirt. Carson, on the other hand, didn't mind looking scruffy, even down to the shirttail that hung out. In high school, Carson wore his hair longer and rarely shaved.

"Funny girls." Camdon scowled and linked arms between them. "So how are my two favorite gals this morning?"

Fear reared its ugly head again. Remi swallowed and licked her dry lips.

"Someone has a bad case of nerves." Jillian cocked her head at Remi.

"Figured as much." Camdon smiled, sweet and encouraging. "Is your bag packed?"

She nodded, still not trusting herself to speak. Would she be able to spit some words out by the time the pilot arrived? Or should she just call this whole thing off right now?

Her hand slid into her pocket and gripped her phone.

An unusual noise disrupted the normal sanctuary sounds of animals munching and the occasional swishing of horses' tails. She tilted her head, listening.

A chopper's rotors. And judging by the sound of it, almost here.

"It's time." Camdon said quietly, halting the trio's walk to the house. He chucked her chin up with his thumb. "You sure you're okay with this?"

Her lips quivered. Was she?

An image of Mason popped up. The contagiousness of his grin, the confidence in his shoulders, the encouragement in his voice. His promise that he wouldn't let anyone hurt her.

So far, he'd kept that promise, including getting rid of that pesky reporter.

She sucked in a breath, expanding her lungs and puffing up her chest. Determination lifted her chin and straightened her shoulders. "Yes. I'm going to do this."

"Aww! I'm so proud of you." Jillian squealed and tugged her into a hug, twirling them around in circles. When she finally let go, Camdon deposited Remi's bag on the ground.

The chopper approached the landing zone, kicking up dust and making it impossible to hear what Camdon was saying.

Remi held up her hand, motioning for him to wait, that she couldn't hear. The rotors finally stopped spinning, and the engine cut off. She turned back to her brother. "What did you say?"

"I said, 'I knew you could do this.'" Camdon kissed the top of her head. "Don't worry, Remi. Mason's a man of faith. He'll take great care of you."

She nodded, squashing back the fear and swiping at the moisture collecting on her cheek.

"And if he doesn't, he'll have to answer to me." Camdon's lips thinned, eyebrows narrowed.

"And me!" Jillian added.

A loud bark snagged Remi's attention back to the helicopter. What?

Goliath hopped out and bounded her way. A man wearing an olive green jumpsuit followed, but at a much slower pace.

Remi waited until Goliath sat, and then squatted to scrub the dog's ears and neck. When his big tongue lapped her cheek, she giggled. "Goliath, you crazy dog. What are you doing here?"

Remi's stomach knotted into tight coils as the pilot's boots crunched through the gravel. She hugged Goliath then stood as the man caught up to them.

"Sam Wilson." He held out a hand.

Remi studied his leathered, worn-looking face, looking for malice and curiosity, but saw only kindness. She shook his hand. "Remi Lambright. This is my brother, Camdon, and my friend, Jillian."

Sam nodded, shaking hands all around before returning his attention to her. He flicked his head toward the dog. "Mason asked me to bring the pup, so you'd feel more comfortable."

Her lips formed a silent 'oh.' "That was so sweet. How thoughtful of him."

Sam scratched the back of his head, trying to keep the grin from sliding across his face, but failed. "I agree, but you might not want to say that to him in front of the guys, ma'am."

Camdon laughed. "He's got a point, Remi. You might want to save that just for him."

She smiled, but nerves made her head wobble and her knees buckle. "Would you excuse me for a minute?"

"Sure. Take all the time you need. We'll be a few minutes getting back to the airport, and then about another hour in the air."

"Thanks."

Remi bolted for the house, knots bunching in her stomach. Footsteps crunched behind her, but she ignored them. She needed a minute to think. Was she doing the right thing? Could she go through with this?

She reached the bathroom and closed the door, her fingers gripping the cool enamel of the tub as she sank onto the edge.

Oh, God, sending Goliath along so I wouldn't be so frightened was such a thoughtful thing for Mason to do. Help me go through with this, to show him that I trust him. I can't do this on my own. I need Your help.

There. She said it. Finally admitted the truth, that she needed God, what she suspected she'd known all along.

A small knock sounded on the bathroom door. "Remi?"

Jillian.

"I'm all right, Jillian. Give me a minute, and I'll be out."

She could do this. She would do this. Not just for Mason, but for herself. She stood and splashed cool water against her hot cheeks. Tucked her hair back in a ponytail.

She took in a deep, calming breath. Exhaled. Better. She opened the door to Jillian's concerned look.

"You gonna be okay?"

She took another breath. "Yeah. I am."

****

Beef scented smoke drifted into Mason's face as he stabbed the potatoes with a fork and lifted them off the grill and onto a platter to join the steaks. He swiped a sleeve across his eyes then lowered the lid to the grill and turned back to the cluster of chairs situated around a small table outside his RV.

Some of his closest friends were here. One of his drivers, Geoff, and his wife, Michelle. His pilot, Sam. His car hauler, Mike, and his wife, Kristin.

And Remi. Someone special. Someone he hoped would become more than a good friend.

Next to him, Goliath panted in anticipation of scooping up any juicy tidbits that might fall his way. Mason set the platter on the table, and Goliath plopped down on the ground with a disappointed huff.

"Looks like we're good to go." With a wink at Remi, he

sank into the lawn chair next to her and downed a long swig of water. He set the bottle on the ground and reached for Remi's hand, twining their fingers. Hers, so soft and feminine against his calloused ones. How was that possible when she worked so hard outside every day?

He looked up and caught the knowing smile between his longtime friends, Geoff and Michelle. They'd been married a good ten years, but no kids yet, so Michelle travelled with her husband during the race season.

"Pray with me?" Mason bowed his head and said a blessing over the food, his fellowship with God drowning out the sounds of motors revving around the track as the drivers prepared for the Saturday night race.

Was Remi having a good time? Or was she still nervous? When Sam had finally arrived at the track, Remi had stepped out of the rented van, as frightened as a skittish cat, her face as pale as a sheet of paper. He'd worried about leaving her alone when it was his turn on the track. But, Michelle had curled her arm through Remi's, taking the newbie under her wing and giving a rundown and tour of the track. He made a mental note to thank Michelle later.

Reluctantly, he released Remi's hand to pass the platter of steaks.

"Mmm, this smells wonderful, Mason." Michelle carved off a piece.

"And tastes better than Louis's," Geoff said, around a bite.

"Ouch. Don't let Louis hear you say that." Mason cut into his steak and slid a sideways glance at Remi as he speared the piece and aimed at his mouth.

She swallowed, concentration furrowing her smooth forehead. "Who's Louis?"

"Mason's chef," Michelle answered.

Remi's jaw dropped. Those sweet green eyes shot to his. "Your *chef*?"

He narrowed his gaze at Michelle. Maybe he wouldn't

thank her after all. The chunk of beef clawed all the way down his throat. He took another swig of water and rubbed the back of his neck. "It's not how it sounds."

"No?"

He shook his head, debating his next words.

Mike saved the evening. "Louis cooks for the entire team. Most of us don't have the time or the proper facilities to cook so he does it for us. It's more efficient that bringing food in or everyone having to leave the track."

"Oh."

Remi's shoulders seemed to loosen up a little more with every bite. By the time they finished the meal, she reclined in her seat and pressed a hand against her middle. "That was delicious, Mason. Thank you."

He took hold of her hand again and smiled. "You're welcome. Glad you enjoyed it." And he hoped there would be plenty more meals like this together.

Geoff stood and stretched his arms above his head. "It was mighty good, Mason. Thanks for inviting us."

Michelle stood, too, along with Kristen and Mike. Sam started clearing the table, tossing paper plates and crumpled napkins in the trash can behind the RV. Goliath trotted after Sam, his fluffy tail waving. Before they made it around the trailer, Sam tossed a chunk of beef to his canine buddy, who snatched it out of the air.

"Hey, I saw that!" Mason chuckled as he stood to wish his friends a good night.

"Remi, we'll leave the door unlocked for you. It won't be hard to find your bed." Michelle laughed, her arm snaked around Geoff's waist.

****

Alone. Finally. With a man who was quickly becoming a necessity in her life. Someone she needed to see and be near every day.

What was she thinking coming here this weekend?

Mason turned to face her and his palms cupped her

cheeks. In the soft light of the moon and the glow from the track's floodlights, his brown eyes blazed warmth and appreciation. Her heart pounded so loud that it almost drowned out the growl of the racecars in the background.

His lips feathered a touch against hers for a second, sweet, but oh, much too short. When he grabbed her hand, her lashes fluttered open. Had she just dreamt his kiss?

"Come on. Let's sit for a bit before I take you back to Geoff and Michelle's." His grip was strong, but gentle, as he led her to a chair. Goliath lifted his head from his spot in the grass then plopped it back down with a moan.

Mason scooted his chair closer and dipped his head back to gaze at the star-studded sky.

A powerful desire to reach over and run her fingers over the stubble along his jaw, to touch him, came over her. What would it hurt? Instead of stifling the urge, she gave into it.

He pressed his lips against the tender skin of her palm, burning a trail to her wrist—

He stopped abruptly and settled their twined hands on top of her leg. "I made a few mistakes with a past relationship, Remi. I don't want to make the same with you. I want to do this right."

"You're talking about your ex-wife."

Surprise flitted across his face, and then acceptance. He nodded. "Yeah."

"Are you referring to marrying her in general?"

"That and so many other things. Like not putting God front and center in our relationship. If I had done that and not rushed things, I would have saved myself a lot of heartache."

"Why didn't you?"

"Patience isn't one of my strong traits, I'm sorry to confess."

"That doesn't sound like you."

"That's because I learned my lesson. The hard way."

"I'm sorry she hurt you." And she was. She dug her free hand into her pocket, tugged out some candy. "Want one?"

He smiled and accepted the chocolate-peanut butter treat. "Is this the equivalent of kissing a boo-boo?"

She'd prefer kissing him, but she wasn't about to tell him that. Instead, she unwrapped the candy and popped it into her mouth while he did the same.

His deep, melodic voice drew her back to his profile again as he stared off into the darkness, regret lining the hard ridges of his face. "For so long, I prayed this one prayer. For a wife. For someone to come home to. A soul mate to share my life. When Lisa came along, I thought she was the answer to my prayers. But I should have known better." Remi felt, more than heard, his sigh.

"How could you have known that she wasn't an answer to your prayer?"

"She didn't share my faith." His gaze connected with hers and lingered, as if beseeching her to understand. "That much was obvious from the beginning, but I ignored it. Thought she would change once we were married."

"And she didn't?"

He shook his head. "No. She gave up all pretense after we were married."

Remi certainly understood that. The camera brought out the best in her father. He'd reserved the worst for home.

"I want what my parents and my friends have."

"What's that?" She angled her head to study him, curious. This was the first time he'd mentioned his parents.

"The love of a lifetime. A solid relationship centered around their faith and their love. I won't settle for less the next time."

A fierce longing for the same ignited within her, zapping all the way from her toes to her head. She pushed it down. Absolutely not. She couldn't.

He was an athlete, a public persona, and extremely handsome. He probably had women hanging all over him most of the time. "You'll find it. I'm sure you get a ton of female attention. There's bound to be somebody for you in that crowd."

He scoffed, more like a loud bark, and shook his head. "No. Definitely not."

"Why not? Are you trying to tell me that you don't have a huge female fan base?" Here it was. The moment of truth. Would he be a man of honor or lies?

He dropped his head before spearing her with his dark gaze. "Actually, I get more female attention than a man has any business with."

There. She knew it. But now she was confused. How could a man of honor and faith have women hanging all over him? The two didn't seem to go together.

"But I'm not interested in any of those women, and my friends will confirm that I don't allow groupies to get anywhere near me." Serious brown eyes, dazzling with the warm color of roasting coffee beans, drilled into hers.

"No?" She gulped. Could he hear the frantic beat of her heart?

What happened to that barrier of protection, that giant wall of privacy, she'd erected around herself to keep from getting hurt?

Mason Mulrennan had crashed right through it, that's what.

He shook his head, a slow back and forth motion, while he raised her hand, caressing the sensitive spot of her wrist with his lips again. "They only care about the size of my wallet. Not in getting to know the real me." He thumped his chest. "That's why I didn't correct your original assumption about me being a vet, Remi. I hoped, I prayed, that finally I had a fighting chance to meet someone who didn't know my name."

He looked down for a few seconds before wounded eyes lifted to meet hers. "Someone who might eventually be interested in me for just me."

She swiped at a tear trickling down her cheek. She knew all about people trying to get at her for what she could give them but in her case it wasn't her wallet. It was news reports, magazine interviews, any scoop on her father. And then the general public assuming the worst about her family based on what they read or saw online.

They didn't know squat. They certainly didn't know the pain, the deep emotional wounds that their words inflicted. The consequences, like Carson's absence and the hole his leaving meant for their family. And for Jillian.

Or Remi's social disorder. How a simple dinner like tonight's caused such fear and anxiety that she'd considered catching a flight back home this afternoon. If it hadn't been for Michelle's kindness and Mason's continual popping in and out to check on her during his times on the track, she wouldn't be here now.

"Come on. I'll walk you back." Mason tugged her up from the chair, and Goliath bolted off the ground, his tail waving.

They walked in a companionable silence. The whine of the motors, the soft padding of their rubber soles on the grass, Goliath's pants, and the occasional RV door closing was comforting. Not as peaceful as hearing the animals munching or their tails swooshing at the sanctuary, but…comfortable.

Or was it just because she was with Mason?

"Hey, Mason!" A male voice yelled, and a metal fence rattled. "Mason Mulrennan! How about an interview before the race tomorrow?"

Goliath assumed a defensive stance and ripped off a few ferocious barks.

Remi startled. The air whooshed from her lungs, and she almost tripped.

Mason waved a hand in the air in acknowledgement, but his other arm tucked around her waist, bringing her snug against his side. He leaned in close. "It's all right, sweetheart. The gate's locked and secured. He can't get in."

He veered away from the main walkway and led her along a hidden, private path, tucked in the middle of RV's, Goliath trotting beside them.

She stole a sideways glance at Mason. His determination to protect her was obvious in the tight line of his lips, the clenched jaw, the rigid set to his spine. Even so, his grip was gentle.

"Here we are." He stopped walking and tugged her against his chest. Citrus and spicy berries, lavender and wood mingled with the cool outdoors to send her pulse to skittering and her heart to racing. In a good way, not from the fear the reporter invoked a few minutes ago.

Yes, indeed. Mercy! The man in front of her was totally responsible for this spike in her pulse.

Her arms somehow managed to find their way around his neck. Had he put them there?

His head dipped agonizingly close, and his lips finally met hers. The perfect balance of sweet from the chocolate and spicy from the steak sauce. Mmmm…

He pulled back too soon and pressed his forehead to hers. "Good night, sweetheart."

"Night."

He opened the door for her, and she slipped inside the RV, lit only with a night light in the kitchen area. She locked the door, and then rolled back the shade.

Mason headed toward his place, his wide shoulders powerful and confident, his back straight. Until he bent over to pat the top of Goliath's head.

The racecar driver wasn't ashamed or embarrassed to show his vulnerability, and so far, he'd been a man of his word, a man of honor and faith, and the night hadn't been that scary. She'd actually enjoyed spending time with Mason's friends. And being with Mason was so much sweeter than spending the weekend alone. Maybe this is what healing looked like.

Thank You, God.

14

"He's gonna get the checkered flag!" Charlie bolted off his seat on top of the pit box, hands clenched around the rail. "Go, buddy! You've got it!"

"What?" Remi squealed and rose to lean against the rail next to the crew chief. Mason was still a few cars back from the front. How could Charlie predict that? "Mason's going to win?"

"Sure looks like it." He tore his gaze from the race to glance at her briefly. "He's had a few close races lately but no wins. You must be the lucky charm."

"Ha! Not hardly. This is awesome teamwork, pure and simple, and Mason's excellent driving skills." She would hardly consider herself anyone's lucky charm, let alone Mason's. She turned her attention back to the car speeding toward the finish line.

"Go, Mason, go!" She chanted, not bothering to scream. Mason wouldn't hear her, and she'd only blast poor Charlie's eardrums.

"There's a certain pretty lady cheering you on, buddy. Go get 'em." Charlie's voice sounded clear over her headset.

She gaped at the crew chief, but Charlie only chuckled. Her attention returned to the race, and Mason's severely dented car. Did the car have enough oomph to make it to the flag first?

She held her breath. Finally, Mason zoomed past the last driver that stood between him and the win, staying well to the inside. The cars raced underneath the checkered flag, waving above them.

Laughing, she threw her arms in the air.

"Woo-hoo! Yeah! Thanks, everybody. Great job today!" Mason hollered through the headset, clearly exhilarated. Across the track, Remi made out Mason's fist pumping through his open window.

"Backatcha, Mason. That was some spectacular racing. Way to steer clear of Salinger." Charlie tugged off his headset and faced her. "Let's go."

"Go?" Fear churned in Remi's belly as she pulled off her headphones.

Charlie moved to the stairs and turned to extend a hand.

Remi's legs refused to cooperate. "Go where?"

"To see Mason."

"Oh. Okay." She was good with that. More than good, she confessed to herself.

She followed Charlie, slogging through the masses of racing teams, keeping her gaze glued to the crew chief's back, ignoring the swarm of bodies as they scurried to prep the cars to leave the track.

A bead of sweat trailed down the hollow of her spine. These men and women were just trying to do their job. No cause for alarm. If she kept telling herself that, she might be all right.

There was a break in the crowd, and she angled around Charlie to peer ahead. Caught a glimpse of the throng hustling in the same direction as them. Men and women toting cameras and microphones. Her heart plummeted, and her brain zapped an instant message to her legs.

No!

She wasn't going in there. No way.

She slowed her pace, allowing Charlie to widen the gap between them. He must have noticed that she wasn't directly behind him because he glanced over a shoulder, eyebrows raised in question.

"I'll catch up with Mason later." She couldn't stop the trembling that rattled her shoulders and limbs then her teeth started chattering. Would Charlie notice?

He turned around to face her, his head slanted, his expression uncertain. "Are you sure? Mason will want you to be there."

He wanted to please his boss, but she couldn't help him. This was just asking too much.

She nodded and waved him on. "Yeah. I'm sure. You go. I'll be all right." And she would be. Once she reached the sanctuary of her home and was surrounded by her beloved animals instead of this horde of reporters. How she would manage that, she wasn't sure yet, but she'd find a way even if it meant renting a car and driving all the way back to Harrison.

She turned around, scanning for the entry to the RV parking. So many people rushed by, jostling her from all directions. She closed her eyes, blotting them out of her vision, her pulse hammering with every bump and elbow to the back. She pressed a hand to her forehead, nausea welling up her throat. She had to get out of here.

God, thank You for letting Mason win and allowing me to see it. But I can't take this crowd anymore. Please help me find a way home.

A light touch landed on her shoulder. "Remi?"

She swung around. Somehow managed to lift her eyelids, heavy with fear and tension.

"Oh, Sam. Hi." Her voice came out husky. She sniffled and swiped her face with the back of her hand.

"Why aren't you celebrating?" He flicked his head toward the mass of people thronging around Mason and the prized car.

She didn't dare follow his gaze. "I—"

Wait a minute. Sam had been headed in the opposite direction. Was the pilot her ticket out of here? Maybe he could get her to the airport. She could take it from there. "Sam, are you on your way somewhere?"

"I'm fixing to shuttle a few guys to the airport. Why? You need something?" His look was curious and friendly.

He could help her.

Thank You, God! You sure do work fast. "Do you think I could catch a ride?"

"Sure. Can you be ready in," he glanced at his watch, "say, ten minutes?"

She nodded. She would be happy to leave right now if he gave the word.

"Good. Meet me at the same spot where I dropped you off." He started to walk away then swiveled, as if he forgot something. "But, fair warning that it'll be a while before we leave for home. I have to make a couple trips back and forth before everyone's at the airport and ready to go, and Mason has to stay for the interviews." His eyebrows sloped together, and a frown marred his face. "Mason may want you to wait—"

She shook her head, cutting him off. "No. That's all right, Sam. Something's come up, and I need to get home. I'll take care of the return flight, but thanks. I'll be ready and waiting for you."

You'll take care of that, too, right, God? You've gotten me this far. I trust You to get me all the way home.

Now that the immediate area had thinned out, she looked around for the RV entrance. There it was. She hustled to Michelle and Geoff's RV to collect her bag and write Mason a note.

A good-bye note.

She was a coward. But if God loved everyone like she'd heard in chapel that morning, then He loved cowards, too.

****

Where was she?

Mason ignored the woman in front of him, clutching a microphone, waiting for the camera guy's signal. She could wait.

He scanned the crowd, searching for any sign of a certain dark-haired beauty, the only female he really wanted standing next to him.

He spotted Charlie, but he walked into the circle alone.

Remi should have been with him. Disappointment slinked into his gut.

Charlie clapped him on the shoulder. "Great race, buddy."

"Thanks. You, too. Where's Remi?"

Charlie took off his cap and scratched the top of his balding head. "Funny thing, boss. We were headed this way, and then she said she'd meet up with you later. She looked pale, like she didn't feel so good. I figured she might've needed to use the restroom."

Not good. He opened his mouth to respond—

"In three. Two. One. We're live." The reporter turned her full attention on him.

He fielded her questions, forcing a smile to his face, but that was next to impossible.

What was going on with Remi? Was she sick? Had she stayed with Charlie the entire race? He should have warned Charlie about her condition and given him a code to relay over the radio.

As the interview tapered off, he scrubbed a hand across his whisker-heavy jaw. Impatience made his answers terse and brief. He longed to get back to the RV and check on Remi.

"So would you like to tell us about your latest love interest?"

Mason's head snapped back to the reporter, and although he smiled, his tone turned frosty and firm. "My personal life is off limits. I hope you all enjoyed spectacular racing today. Thank you."

He turned away from the microphone, signaling the end of the interview. Now to get the pictures out of the way, so he could check on Remi.

****

"Thanks for coming to get me, Camdon."

Parked in the arrival lane at the airport, her brother stood next to the open passenger door. A couple cars waited further up the lane, but mostly the airport was deserted and quiet.

Camdon held out his arms, and Remi stepped into them, drawing comfort from his strength. Finally, she pulled away and slid into the car's leather seat, the warm air coming from the heater and the comfort of her brother's kindness putting an end to her trembling. She stowed her bag on the floor. "Sorry to drag you out of bed."

"I wasn't in bed yet, so it's all good. But even if I was, you know I'd still come for you." He shut her door with a quiet click and walked around the back of the car, his long jean-clad legs sliding in the driver's seat with ease.

How did her brother do it? How did he manage to stay strong while she and Carson fell apart at the seams? She sighed and hugged her arms. Her voice came out hoarse. "What were you doing still up? It's after midnight."

His shrug was his only response as he put the car in gear and concentrated on the road.

Ahhh. Light bulb moment. She slapped a palm against her forehead. "You were expecting me to call, weren't you?"

His head flicked toward her briefly before angling back to the road. "Actually, you lasted a lot longer than I thought you would." Pride and— was that amazement? — tinged his voice.

He turned onto the entrance ramp to the interstate. Just a few more minutes and she'd be home. Far away from the fast cars and the swarming media with their giant cameras.

Far away from Mason.

Her brother might be proud of her, but she wasn't. And she was pretty sure Mason wouldn't be, either.

She closed her eyes and leaned back against the seat, weary from the constant battle between fear and longing, the need to be whole and healed.

She wanted to believe in love. Desperately wanted to believe. But a happily-ever-after ending just wasn't a reality for her and Mason.

****

The crowd had finally dissipated and most of the teams had pulled out. Mason hustled to the trailer, his racing shoes pounding the grass in the quiet night.

In the darkness, Mason made out the white piece of paper attached to the door. He clenched his fists, his heart plummeting to his toes. He snatched it from the door and scrambled inside to read it.

Mason, I'm so happy for you! You won! I had so much fun watching you race. Thank you for inviting me.

You probably suspect by now that I wasn't feeling well, so I caught an early flight back home. I'm sorry that I couldn't hang out with you after the race, but just seeing all the cameras and reporters swarming around you made me realize just how impossible a relationship between us would be. I can't tell you how sad that makes me.

Hoping and praying all the best for you, Mason. You deserve it.
All my love, Remi

He crumbled the flimsy paper in his hand, a giant glob of emotion crawling down his throat and settling in his gut.

What could he do?

He could guard her privacy, could shield her from reporters and their nosey questions, but he couldn't protect her from her own fear. That, she had to fight for herself.

And, for them.

Would she consider him worth fighting for?

15

"So other than when you saw the crowd of reporters huddled around Mason after he won, you had a good time?" Jillian hiked a boot against the rustic wood of the barn's exterior.

Remi tossed the hay, scattering some extra clumps for Reesie and Snickers. "Yeah." She'd had a great time. As much as it hurt to admit.

"Would you go again?"

"He'll never ask." With a heavy sigh, she turned the spigot on and draped the hose over the trough. No. He'd never ask.

"Why do you say that?"

"Because I left him a note."

"Oh." Jillian's blonde eyebrows furrowed in the middle.

Remi quickly averted her gaze back to the hose, turned off the faucet and draped the hose around the hook.

"And?" Jillian's tone was quiet.

Or maybe she was just too tired. She straightened, her muscles screaming and her eyelids heavy. When Camdon had finally dropped her off at one o'clock this morning, she hadn't bothered to go to bed, knowing she'd never be able to sleep. "I told him I didn't see how a relationship between us could ever work."

The day's light didn't make that decision any wiser or better. But there it was.

She stomped inside the barn, plucked a couple pitchforks from the hooks, and handed them to Jillian. Then she tossed a bucket into the wheelbarrow and steered the unwieldy thing toward the first stall.

Jillian's boots clomped behind her. "You know he'll be back."

Remi unlatched the door to the empty stall and shoved the wheelbarrow in. It clunked on the ground. "No, he won't."

Would he? She wasn't so sure. Her brain had been so addled last night, her emotions so tangled, that she couldn't even remember what she wrote in the note. The urgency to leave still made her tummy ache and her shoulders tense.

Mason deserved someone who could share in his success, someone who didn't mind being in front of the camera. She wasn't that person, as much as she wanted to be with him.

They set to work mucking out the stall and fluffing it with fresh bedding then moved on to the next one. Usually this chore brought her peace, satisfaction. Today, not so much. Discouragement as heavy as bricks weighted her shoulders. Even the grant award she'd found in her email inbox earlier hadn't soothed her heart or cleared the tension.

"I can't do it, Jillian." She didn't blink. If she did, the tears would surely fall. She'd cried enough tears in her lifetime. She speared the waste and flicked it in the bucket, caught tears swelling in Jillian's brown eyes as she leaned against the pitchfork.

"You can, Remi. You're stronger than you give yourself credit for. Remember graduation?"

She stopped digging and straightened. A sigh lifted her chest. "Yeah."

"You were determined to make your mom proud. To show her honor and respect after all the years of people saying those hurtful things. It took months of practice, but you did it."

Remi nodded. Her best friend had gone with her to the auditorium every day after school for months to watch her practice walking the stage.

"Think of this relationship with Mason in the same way, Remi. It'll take practice, and it won't be easy, but you can do it. If Mason is worth the effort." Jillian tilted her head to study Remi. "Is he? Worth the effort?"

Just thinking about the man made her pulse rocket. Her heart ached with longing. She missed him already.

It didn't take long for her to decide. She nodded. "Yes. Definitely."

Determination firmed Jillian's jaw, and her normally full lips flattened. "Then we need to get busy."

****

"So what do you see in Mason Mulrennan's future?" Nan Greenway, the reporter for *Athletes in the News* magazine, leaned forward in her chair, her pen poised above the paper, even though she was also taping their conversation. A slim leg crossed a knee, and her four-inch spike of a heel jiggled.

The leather of Mason's office chair creaked as he fidgeted. He scrubbed a hand across his whiskered jaws, weary to the bone. He'd gotten home at two this morning, but he hadn't slept.

He probably should have cancelled this interview, but at least it wasn't televised. The world wouldn't see his droopy shoulders or the frustrated look he flashed the reporter.

He chuckled, but it was more from a desire to bring this interview to a close than mirth. "Another car for the team. Hopefully, a championship."

Judging by Nan's frown, that wasn't the answer she was looking for. Well, too bad. This interview was over. He stood and rose to his full height, towering over the lady still sitting in the chair as if she had nowhere to go, nowhere else she'd rather be.

Well, that wasn't his case.

He held out a hand, forcing the reporter to get up. "Thanks for the interview, Nan. I'll look forward to reading the feature next month."

"I'm not quite done with my questions—"

"I'm sorry." He glanced pointedly at the clock in his office. "I have another appointment."

And he did. With the Lord. He needed time to shut the door to all the interruptions, time to get up close and personal with his Father. A few moments to allow raindrops from heaven to pour down and soothe his battered heart.

He walked over to the open door and swung it wide, waiting for Nan to take the hint. With a huff, she leaned over to pick up her oversized bag, displaying a huge gap in the front of her silk blouse.

He averted his gaze with a sigh. Why did women do that? Did they think he would be even remotely interested? Or that he'd give them more of a newsworthy scoop? Thanks to his mom's advice, he'd always maintained an "open door" policy when it came to women in his office.

Nan took her time collecting her belongings then wobbled over to him in those high heels, stopping directly in front of him, her strong perfume reeking of some floral scent that would have been best left in the ground. So strong, his eyes watered.

She looked up at him, a coy expression on her face. "How's it going with the golfer's daughter?"

If she thought that would rile him enough to give her an answer, she was mistaken. Even so, his jaw clenched at her rudeness.

"Have a good day, Nan." With a firm hand against her back, he guided her out the door. Once she passed, he closed it and pressed his back against the cool metal.

Was this type of rudeness what Remi and her family had endured all these years? How could he possibly understand how to deal with the hurt and pain that she carried around on those tiny shoulders? And how could he, a racecar driver whose livelihood depended on media popularity, keep her and their relationship out of the public eye? Questions like this were bound to surface repeatedly.

Was it fair to expect her to change, to overcome her adversity to the media? His heart sank. Not if Nan was any indication. He certainly wouldn't throw Remi to the wolves.

God, how can this be? I finally meet a woman who doesn't care about my money, but she can't handle my career. Did You allow me the joy of getting to know Remi, of loving Remi, only to leave us like this?

He didn't think so, but a little time on his knees wouldn't hurt.

16

Remi tugged a piece of candy from her pocket and took her time unwrapping it. She plunked it in her mouth and rested her forearms on the pasture rail.

Mason hadn't come today.

So that was it. He'd finally admitted to himself that there couldn't be a "them."

She sucked on the chocolate until she tasted the creamy peanut butter, watching the llamas grazing about the field. A cool breeze lifted strands of her hair, wrapping it around her eyes. She brushed it away. Her fingers came away moist.

She'd missed him today. Missed the roar of his truck as he pulled in the driveway. Missed seeing his broad shoulders as he slipped in and out of the pastures to feed the llamas and the horses. Missed lingering over lunch with him, talking, and catching a whiff of his distinctly masculine mixture of woods and fresh outdoors.

And yeah, she missed his kisses. The feel of his strong hands wrapping around her waist and his lips connecting with hers. Missed hearing him whisper that all things were possible. That "they" were possible.

Was a relationship with Mason a dead end? Did it have to be? Would she be better off without him in her life?

No. She bounced out of bed on the mornings that she knew he was coming. He made the days so much sweeter, so much brighter with his presence.

She couldn't bear the thought that he wouldn't be dropping by anymore.

Her stepfather was right. Saying yes to Mason was so

much sweeter than saying no.

God, I'm so sick of being afraid to live my life. I love Mason. I don't want this to be the end but rather the beginning. Help me to overcome this fear that's literally strangling me. Help me be the woman You created me to be.

She lifted her face to the sky, draped with streaks of pink and purple, and allowed the gentle breeze to cool her skin and for God's whisper to sink deep into her spirit.

You can do it.

How?

With My strength.

She closed her eyes and bowed her head. In the quiet part of her soul, she knew what she had to do.

****

Mason signed the paper with more of a flourish than usual, and then flicked the pen out of his hand. It landed on the wood desktop with a ping. Leaning back in the chair, he sighed and rammed a hand through his hair.

"Tough day, boss?" Charlie lounged in the doorway with his shoulder propped against the frame. How long had he been standing there?

Frustration and indecision churned in his gut. "Not so much tough as long."

"Maybe you're not where you should be."

He scowled at his crew chief.

Charlie only shrugged and ignored his glare. "You haven't been in the office on a Tuesday or Wednesday for weeks now."

He huffed. "Don't remind me. My inbox is overflowing."

"So maybe your head says you should be here, but your heart's telling you otherwise."

Mason picked up the pen and fiddled with it, tossing it in the air and catching it, letting Charlie's comment slide.

"So what are you doing here today? Why aren't you at the sanctuary?"

"Giving Remi some time."

Charlie scoffed. "Some time? For what? To forget about you? To rethink getting involved with this whole—" Charlie swept an arm around the office "—racing business?"

Mason shook his head, sorrow filling the hollow chasm in his heart. He scrubbed a hand across his whiskered cheeks. "I can't do this to her."

Charlie closed the door and shuffled into the office, sinking deep into the chair in front of Mason's desk. "Does this have something to do with her father?"

Mason pinched the bridge of his nose. Nodded.

"I thought it might."

"She has a tough time dealing with reporters. After my interview with Nan Greenway yesterday, I can see why."

"Didn't go well?"

"Nah. That's not it. Nan's just doing her job. But that's just it. Reporters tend to get a little nosey. The less scrupulous ones dig and poke around until they get the dirt they're looking for. If they hurt someone in the process, that's just a casualty of the job. A cost of doing business."

"You don't want Remi to get hurt."

"That's the last thing I want. But a relationship with me is bound to bring the reporters crawling out of the woodwork."

"Want my advice?"

Mason swallowed, hesitated. "She made it clear—"

"Well, you're getting it anyway. Remi's a special lady to have survived what she did and not be bitter or resentful. I remember when her daddy died. The media tormented her momma, blamed her for his death, and the whole family took the heat. Remi's made of tough stuff. More than you give her credit."

"That's not true. I give her lots—"

"I'm not finished. If God means for you to be together, He'll work it out."

Charlie had a point there.

"But that's not going to happen with you sitting here in

this office."

Ouch. That's exactly what he'd been telling himself every day this week.

"She came to the race, didn't she?"

Mason nodded.

Charlie's head bobbed as he continued his tirade. "The little lady stayed to the very end. That says a lot right there. She cares about you enough to face those demons."

A smile tugged at Mason's lips. The first all week.

"She might've gotten a little queasy thinking about the crowd there at the end, but that doesn't mean she didn't give it her best shot."

Remorse slammed through Mason. Yeah. She did. She had lasted all day Saturday and then until the race was over on Sunday. He'd introduced her to his friends, left her alone with them, and she hadn't complained once about being out of her comfort zone. She was a real trooper.

"So why aren't you there giving her your best shot?" Charlie glared at him.

"What do you mean?" It was a good thing his crew chief had worked for him a long time, and Mason trusted his opinion and respected his advice. Otherwise, he might have kicked the man out of his office.

"With her background, my guess is it took a lot for her to be there for you. I'm sure she feels bad about leaving, probably even hurting in here." Charlie thumped his chest. "But that just means she could use your support and encouragement more than ever right now. More than she's ever gotten from anyone before." Charlie's jaw tightened, and he growled. "But that means you have to be there for her. Not this 'give her some time' business."

Mason rubbed the back of his neck. Was Charlie right? Was he hurting Remi more by not being there for her?

17

"I trust you, Lord." Remi whispered at her reflection in the mirror. She swiped the brush against her cheeks until a rosy blush appeared.

"I will not be afraid." She dabbed some lipstick on her lips. When was the last time she'd worn makeup?

"What can man possibly do to hurt me anymore?" She paraphrased the verse she'd memorized over the last couple of days. *Thank You, God, for those sweet words of encouragement. I needed them.*

She shoved the makeup bag back in the drawer and, taking a deep breath, opened the bathroom door.

Four heads turned in her direction, all with anxious faces.

"I'm fine," she reassured. And she was.

A sigh welled up from her chest. She'd be a whole lot better if Mason was here, but she'd burned that bridge. He hadn't shown up at the ranch all week, and she couldn't blame him. Not after the note she'd left him.

But, she had to do this for herself. To face and slay the dragon of fear. The demon that paralyzed her, the one that kept her from living a normal life and prevented her from a lasting relationship with a man who had proven he could be counted on.

Camdon appeared next to her. His dark eyebrows hiked, and tiny furrows buried into his forehead. "Everything's set up outside. Are you ready?"

She nodded. "Yeah. I'm all set. Let's go."

Her fingers gripped the doorknob, but she hesitated as emotion crawled down her throat. She turned around to face her mom and stepfather, Camdon, and Jillian. "Thanks you, guys, for coming. I love you."

They took turns hugging her, bolstering her with their encouraging words. Finally, she pressed her shoulders back, sucked in a deep breath, and opened the door.

Lights flashed. Voices mumbled, speaking into microphones. Television cameras pointed in her direction.

She froze. Gulped. *I trust You, God. Render them powerless to hurt me with their words anymore.*

Her mother and Ryan stepped to one side, Jillian and Camdon appeared at her other side, their arms circled around her back. She could do this. God was with her, protecting and uplifting her with her family and friends.

She stepped to the microphone that Camdon had placed at the top of the stairs. With weak and unsteady legs, she glanced out at the crowd. Except for Nan Greenway's smirk, the rest of the reporters appeared friendly and interested.

Remi cleared her throat.

****

Mason mashed his foot harder against the truck's gas pedal, an urgency to get to Remi eating a hole in his heart.

"Why did we wait all week to come see her, boy?" Mason muttered, glancing back at Goliath. The mournful glaze in Goliath's eyes condemned him even more.

Because he'd let his stubborn pride get in the way, when he should have been loving and supportive, that's why.

He could kick himself, but then, Jumbo would probably take care of any necessary humbling measures.

Slowing, he flipped the blinker to turn into the sanctuary's parking lot but was forced to stop in the road. Cars were parked haphazardly, tightly squeezed together, lining the drive from the barn to the road.

Mason rubbed a hand across his face. The excitement over seeing Remi curdled in his gut. What was going on?

He slammed the truck in PARK, barely allowing the

vehicle to stop before he took off jogging for the house, Goliath scampering beside him. Whatever was going on, he should have been here for Remi. He sprinted around the barn and stopped cold in his tracks.

"Whoa, boy!" he commanded, and Goliath obeyed, sitting on the grass, panting with his tongue hanging.

Remi stood on the front porch, surrounded by Camdon and Jillian, and two others, and a mass of people— media? —huddled at the foot of the steps.

His heart plummeted to his toes. What happened? Why hadn't she called him? He could have interceded, taken the pressure off her. He would have handled this for her. Gladly.

"So, although we're currently filled to capacity, last week we were awarded grant funding and we anticipate additional grant monies to be awarded soon. That means we can accept more endangered animals to protect and love, more animals that can call Forever Family Animal Sanctuary their permanent home." Remi spoke into a microphone, her arm encompassing the pastures.

Her gaze landed on him, and her jaw dropped. She locked her lips, swallowed, and continued. "You can see we already have many animals to take care of, and volunteers are always appreciated."

Her gaze stayed locked on his, as if she spoke directly to him. He refused to release her eyes, drawn like a honeybee to a beautiful, fragrant flower.

And she was. An inner beauty glowed, not only from her face but in her confident poise, surrounded by her loved ones.

He should have been up there with her. He fit in that category. But then, if he had, he would have tried to shield her, and she wouldn't experience the freedom of unshackling the chains of terror that had confined her for so long.

His heart soared, proud of her for taking the first step to conquer her fears. And it was a giant one.

Did this mean she was giving them a chance? That she'd changed her mind about him? About them?

A smile lifted the corners of his mouth, and he felt better, lighter, than he had all week. He winked at her.

She smiled and finally dragged her eyes away. "I'll accept a few questions now."

Reporters fired questions at her, and she responded with grace, her enthusiasm for the animals contagious. All around, men and women smiled as she talked about the llamas.

"One more question," Remi announced, flicking a long strand of dark hair behind an ear.

Mason longed to touch it, to run his fingers through the silky mass.

"How did your father's suicide influence your decision to run this sanctuary?" Malice edged Nan Greenway's tone.

Remi's chest heaved as if she struggled to breathe. The smile slipped, and her lips moved but no words came out. Her brother and the other man huddled closer to her, circling their arms around her back.

Mason pushed through the throng of reporters, skirting to the outside, bypassing the cameras, Goliath right on his heels. He should be up there, fielding their questions, protecting his girl—

Remi's sweet voice broke through the anxious murmuring of the crowd.

Mason halted next to the bottom of the steps and glanced up at her.

She lifted her chin and pressed her lips together, her expression solemn. When she spoke, her voice came out steady and firm. "Twenty years ago, my father took his life. I'm not proud of that, but I won't apologize for it, either. Taking his life was his choice. His decision doesn't reflect me, or the value I place on life. It's part of my past and a key factor in who I am today."

Her gaze locked on Nan then skittered to him. She

didn't need his protection. This spectacular performance was all her. Pride puffed his chest, and joy exploded across his face.

"But, *my future*, *my today*," she thumped her chest, "is my life, and what I make of it and how I respond is my choice." Her shoulders dipped slightly, as if all her energy and courage had been depleted. "Thank you for coming."

It took him two strides to reach the top of the stairs. He squeezed in beside her and gathered her in his arms, delighting in the feel of her, the scent that was all Remi. Farm and family, roses and cinnamon.

"Great job, sweetheart," he whispered.

How he'd missed her! Why had he thought giving her time and space was a good idea? Nothing came to him, definitely not with her hair tickling his cheek.

Thousands of cameras clicked. White lights flashed.

He released Remi only to cup her elbow. "Come on. Let's get you inside."

He kept his body in front of Remi, shielding her, but angled back to Camdon. "Can you take care of these people?"

Camdon nodded, respect in his eyes. "Sure. If you take care of my sister."

"You got it." Happily. He'd take on that responsibility for the rest of his life. But Remi probably wouldn't be interested in that proposition just yet. Especially since he hadn't kept his promise to protect her, to be here when she needed him.

He ushered her inside the house, along with Jillian and another lady. Judging by her body build and dark hair, he'd guess this was Remi's mom and the other man outside with Camdon, her stepfather. After Goliath trotted inside, Mason closed the door behind them, leaving the two men to manage the crowd. The dog sauntered over to the fireplace and plopped down on the hardwood to scratch his neck.

"Mason Mulrennan." Smiling, Mason extended a hand

to Remi's mom.

"I'm Lessa Worth. Remi's mom." Ignoring his hand, she wrapped him in a warm hug instead.

Over Lessa's shoulder, he saw a tear slip down Remi's smooth cheek. She swiped at it with her arm.

He caught her gaze and held it. When Lessa backed away, he held out his arms for Remi.

She didn't hesitate. Just stepped right into his embrace. A peace, a sense of rightness, nothing like he'd ever experienced, filled him from his toes to his head.

"You came." Her cheek and both palms pressed against his cotton shirt, muffling her whisper.

"I should have been here sooner." He settled his temple on the top of her head, relishing the silkiness of her hair.

She shook her head. "No. Your timing was perfect. Just when I needed you."

Thank You, God.

He held her in his arms until her limbs relaxed. Because he really didn't want to let go.

"You did great, honey." Lessa's voice sounded as if it came from far away.

Possibly because he'd drifted into a vision of the future. Sharing successes like this with Remi and her family, her friends, and those wacky animals she considered family. Sharing hugs and kisses and...life.

Remi pulled away, her hair mussed from his whiskers. She looked adorable. "Thanks, Mom."

"I knew you could do it." Jillian bobbed her blonde head, sporting a confident smile.

Remi took turns hugging her mom and best friend. "Thank you."

The door opened and the men walked in. Remi introduced her stepfather.

"They're all gone. Every last one of them. Great job, Remi." Camdon gave his sister a one-armed hug.

"Yeah. Especially with that last reporter's question."

Ryan shook his head. "There was absolutely no need for her to attack. You handled it exceptionally well."

Mason agreed. He wouldn't have done as well if he'd been the one up there answering the questions. He might have hopped off that makeshift stage and—

Lessa glanced at her watch and nodded at Ryan, flashing an unspoken message. "Well, we need to be going. We promised Judy we'd stop by and relieve her for a couple hours. Call us if you need anything, honey."

"Yep. Me, too. Got a full day ahead still at the office. See ya, sis."

"Wait for me." Jillian trailed after the family.

The door closed behind them, a blend of shoes and boots clomping down the front steps. Then, silence descended on the room. Except for Goliath's soft snore.

"I was waiting for Jillian's excuse, but she didn't offer one," Mason said, smiling. "I think they just wanted to give us some time alone."

Remi's chin dipped, shyness prevailing over spunk this time. "Probably."

He nudged her chin up. Staring into those beautiful green eyes, he lost himself in the specks of amber twinkling back at him.

A sigh lifted his chest, and a moan erupted from his throat as his lips sought hers. He kissed her, deep and long, a kiss that parted the skies and gave him a glimpse of what heaven on earth would be like. A kiss that made him long for more than what he had now, more than just the huge empty shell he came home to half the week, more than just a career that was meaningless if he couldn't share it with her. So much more than just a kiss. It was a powerful meeting of their hearts.

When he finally pulled back, her lashes draped those stunning amber flints. He rested his forehead against hers, waiting for her to open her eyes, knowing she felt the connection as deeply as him.

Finally, her eyelids fluttered open.

"I'm glad they did."

"Did what?" Her eyelids shuttered again, and her breathing was ragged.

He smiled at her breathless tone. "Left us alone."

"Oh." She blinked and flashed a dimple. "What? No chaperones today?"

He held her hand and tugged her to the couch. "Come here."

She sat, and he sank down next to her, leaving no space between their hips. He curled his arm around her shoulders, and she settled her palm and head against his heart.

That was better.

His entire week righted itself. Went from downright lonely and miserable, to warm and comfy just from being in her presence.

He wished he didn't have to leave tonight. He'd wasted a whole week without her.

"What was that big old sigh for?" Her words came out husky.

"I would pay an exorbitant amount of money to redo this week."

Her head lifted from his chest. She flashed him a hazy, dreamy-eyed look, as if she'd almost drifted off to sleep. "Why?"

"Because I spent all week alone when I could have been here with you."

"You honored my wishes." Was that regret in her tone, too?

"Yeah." He angled his head to study her. "But did you mean it?"

"Which part?"

"That a relationship between us would be impossible. Because from where I'm sitting it's a done deal." He grinned, feeling suddenly playful, not wanting to waste another minute of regret.

"At the time."

"What changed?"

"I did."

He hiked his brows, waiting for her to elaborate.

"I discovered that saying yes is so much sweeter than saying no."

"You'll have to explain that one."

Smiling, she tilted her head up to look at him. "I missed you. Plain and simple."

He couldn't resist another kiss. "I like plain and simple."

She chuckled. "I bet you do."

"I missed you, too. What do you want to do about it?"

A puzzled expression crossed her cute face.

"Come with me tonight," he urged.

Her brows furrowed. Was she going to say no?

"Remember what you just said about saying yes."

"Camdon's getting ready to go out of town, and Jillian has a shift tomorrow. The animals—"

Ah. How could he forget her family? "Sunday then. It's the last race of the season, and I'd like for you to be there."

He wanted her to be there for every race, not just the last, but he'd settle for this one.

18

A tap bumped the back of his car. Fighting the natural instinct of the tires to spin, Mason wrangled the car into submission.

If another driver wanted to take him out, it would be here, curling around the final turn. He couldn't spare a glance in the mirror. "Who is it?"

"Salinger. Don't worry about him. Just give it all you got." The spotter's voice came through the radio with only a hint of worry.

Another tap, this time much harder, and Mason wrestled the steering wheel to keep from wrecking. Salinger's car zoomed alongside. Mason glanced sideways to catch the man's wicked grin as he rocketed by.

He should have known Salinger would try to take him out. The guy couldn't win by hard racing alone. No. He had to resort to pushing and shoving to be the first one under the checkered flag.

Well, Mason wasn't playing that game and not just because Remi watched him from the pit box. He was known for racing hard, but fair, and he wouldn't tarnish that image just to get a win.

He tamped down the urge to turn the steering wheel into the back of Salinger's car and mashed the gas pedal to the floorboard. This was it. Just ahead, the flagger leaned over the track, poised to wave the coveted flag.

His car gained some traction, but he wasn't going to make it. The tires were shot.

The checkered flag waved over Salinger's car.

"Great job, guys! You worked your tails off this week.

Sorry I couldn't get the win for you, but it was a great season." Easing his foot off the accelerator, Mason removed his gloves and unhooked the window shield. He whacked a glove against the steering wheel and turned onto pit road.

With Remi watching, he'd hoped for a win. But she might not be so frightened on pit road like she had been about winner's circle. The media didn't swarm like an angry beehive here, and it cleared out fast. Actually, now that he thought about it, second place was a blessing this week.

He tossed the gloves aside and killed the engine. He pulled himself through the open window, stretched and turned—

A body slammed into his chest.

A warm female body.

He didn't have to look to know who it was. Her signature scent, cinnamon and citrus with just the slightest hint of jasmine and roses, only minus the scents of the farm, drifted up, smelling so much better than oil and rubber. Her face settled against his chest, and he could feel her heartbeat even through his layers of fireproof clothing. Silky strands of long dark hair blew in his face and tickled his cheek.

Remi.

"I was so worried about you at the end when that guy was trying to make you crash, but you did great." Arms wound around his neck, and he pulled back far enough to gaze into the most beautiful face he'd ever seen. Joy and excitement mingled with worry.

If he lived to be a hundred, he would remember this moment forever. He sighed, contentment and joy filling his soul.

A win on the track didn't matter tonight. This was the true victory.

She tugged his head down and her lips connected with his. Her kiss was just like her, sweet and undemanding, gentle and unassuming. He deepened it, and she didn't seem to mind.

Cameras clicked and lights flashed through his subconscious.

He pulled back, his lips a whisper away. "You good with the cameras? An interview or two?"

She nodded, and he didn't see the least bit of hesitation in her expression.

"That's my girl." Pulling back, he slung an arm over her shoulder, holding her close. He didn't want her to pull the disappearing act. If she'd let him, he would help her through this.

A reporter stepped up to them and jabbed a microphone in Mason's face. Remi shifted under his arm, trying to detach herself.

"Stay with me?" He slid a strand of hair away from her eye.

"Stay with you?" Fear flashed across her face.

"This interview won't take long, and I'd like to see you home this time."

She pressed her shoulders back and nodded, clamping her lips together.

He smiled and tightened his grip, holding her snug to his side.

Finally, he'd met a woman who so obviously didn't care about fame or fortune. Remi cared about him, for who he was inside. *Thank You, Lord.*

****

Remi bit her bottom lip. What had she just agreed to? Had she just opened herself up to another round of pain and humiliation from the media?

Mason tugged her close to his side and she closed her eyes, praying for the strength and peace that she now understood only came from God.

She inhaled deep of gasoline and burnt rubber, but she also caught of whiff of pure Mason, some blend of wood and soap that mingled with the cool air. Her arm tightened around his waist for support, bolstering her courage.

Mason answered all the reporter's questions with his customary confidence and humor, earning a few smiles from the reporter. Just like he'd won her heart.

"And I take it this lady is someone special?" the reporter asked, hinting around for a scoop.

She caught her breath and looked up.

Crinkle lines fanned out from Mason's warm brown eyes, and his gaze never wavered from hers. His lips curled up, soft and cute, as if keeping a secret. "Oh yeah. She's special all right, but we'll save that for another day."

Could he feel the frantic rhythm of her heartbeat underneath all the layers of his racing uniform? Her legs threatened to give out on her. His grip tightened.

When the interview finally concluded, Mason tugged her to a secluded area near the pit box and hugged her. "Thank you for sticking with me, sweetheart."

Special? Sweetheart? A longing started in her toes and raced all the way up to her heart. Was sticking with him a real possibility?

"Ready to go home?"

"That sounds wonderful."

He slung an arm around her, and they ambled toward his RV, their pace slow and easy.

All around them, the track bustled with activity. The same noises as last week, the same frenzy of movement as race teams packed up and got ready to leave, but tonight she felt different. Not so incapacitated or frozen with fear. With Mason's arm around her, she could almost ignore the sounds and the commotion.

Mason stopped at the door to the RV, sliding his hands to her hips and tugging her against his rock-hard chest. His dark eyes pleaded. "I have a couple more interviews to do, but they won't take long. Will you stay here, or will I come back to a note?"

Funny thing was, she didn't have any desire to go back without him. She liked the idea of sticking around to wait for him. "I'll be here."

Relief broke out on his face, and his shoulders relaxed. "Good."

He leaned down, his palms framing her cheeks, and kissed her. Teasing and playful, yet gentle and soft, when his lips pulled away, she wanted more. So much more.

"Now that the season is over, we can really spend some time together." His husky voice sent her heart into overdrive.

"Oh yeah?" She flashed him her flirtiest look. Not that she'd ever practiced that much, but she gave it her best shot.

He chuckled. "You'll have to do a lot better than that if you want to get rid of me."

"Who said I wanted to get rid of you?"

"Changed your mind, did you?" His eyebrows dared her to challenge him. That, and his smug expression, so different from the vulnerable little boy look a minute ago.

"Maybe." Definitely.

"Give me a few minutes. I'll be back as quickly as I can, and then we can go home." He planted a swift peck on her head and opened the door for her. He turned and his long legs gobbled the distance back to the track at a rapid pace.

Home. Yeah. That sounded nice, but not as comforting as it used to be.

Standing on the step in the doorway, she admired his powerful shoulders until he disappeared in the darkness.

She knew he'd be back soon, just like he promised. Because he was a man of his word.

A man she could count on.

19

"I'll be back later tonight. You guys behave." Remi stroked Jumbo's neck, the fiber silky against her palm.

The rascal split his lips to reveal his bottom teeth.

Laughing eased the nerves threatening to swallow Remi whole. "You're a silly guy, you know that? I love you."

She turned and secured the gate then made her way toward the house, tugging her sweater tight against her chest, fighting off the chilly breeze that swept across the yard.

Mason would be here soon to pick her up and take her to his house for Thanksgiving dinner with his family.

She jerked the front door open with more force than she intended. Was she ready for this?

Meeting Mason's parents, his sister and her husband? Becoming more entrenched, more firmly rooted in his life?

Little late for that, wasn't it? She scoffed as she pulled a mug from the cabinet and filled it with lukewarm coffee.

What was she doing? With a tummy churning with nerves, the last thing she needed right now was coffee. She dumped the black liquid in the sink and rinsed out the cup.

She couldn't imagine Mason not being a part of her day, not showing up at the sanctuary every afternoon with his quirky smile and whiskered jaw. Couldn't forget how lonely and isolated she was until Mason roared into her driveway that first time and helped deliver Reesie.

She pulled out a piece of candy, unwrapped it and popped it in her mouth, her lips curving as she chewed. How could she have ever mistaken him for a vet? Ha!

Truck tires ground into the gravel outside, and a door

opened and closed. Paws bounced across the front porch and skidded into the wood frame of the house. She met Mason and Goliath at the front door.

"Hey, beautiful." Mason took his time kissing her, the woody fragrance of his cologne drifting in with the cool breeze from the open door.

She wasn't complaining. His kiss heated her insides and raised goose bumps along her arms.

When he pulled away, he pressed his forehead to hers, his arms still draped around her back.

"I might need another one of those. Just to calm my nerves."

He chuckled. "I'm not sure if that's a good thing or bad."

"Good." Definitely. Positively. Divine.

"We keep that up and we won't make it back. I'd much rather stay here with you, cuddling in front of the fireplace and keeping each other warm." His labored breath whispered against her heavy eyelids.

A sigh lifted her chest, and she opened her eyes, pulling back a little, feeling her stomach tense at meeting his family, at leaving the sanctuary of her comfort zone. "Do we have to go?"

Mason cocked his head, his brow bunching. "No. I suppose we don't have to."

Really? That was great—

He grabbed her fingers and brought them to his lips, planting a slow caress on the top of her hand. "But I would love for you to meet my parents and my sister and her husband. You'll like them, Remi. They won't hurt you. Can you trust me on that?"

How could she not trust him when he looked at her like that? Confidence in her— and was that really love? — all wrapped up in one seriously rich and luscious cocoa-eyed gaze.

She nodded, shivering.

He rubbed her upper arms, and the warmth of his

touch seared through her sweater. "Besides, I've got a ham in the oven with a boatload of scalloped potatoes to go with it. Not to mention a giant chocolate chip cheesecake for dessert."

"A gal's gotta eat." She pulled away and stepped through the open door then waited for him at the top of the stairs.

Chuckling, he pulled the front door closed and stood beside her. His knuckles grazed her cheek, sending shivers racing down to her toes. "You're sure about this, sweetheart? I don't want to pressure you into something that you're not ready for."

That was so Mason. Kind. Considerate. Loving.

How could she not be ready and willing to meet his family?

She refused to let the nerves win. She nodded, lifting her chin and pressing her shoulders back. "Yeah. I'm ready."

****

Mason parked the truck in front of The Castle and killed the motor. The engine ticked a few times then silence, except for Goliath's panting in the cab.

He glanced over at Remi.

She was staring out the passenger window, her fingers pressed against the glass. She turned to him, her eyes unreadable, her voice hesitant. "This is where you live?"

"Yeah." He cleared his throat.

"It's so...big."

He let out his breath on a sigh. "Yep. That it is. And incredibly lonely."

"I could see how that would happen. Do you ever get lost in there?"

He chuckled. "Truthfully, most of the time I only use a couple of the rooms, my bedroom and the living room. Occasionally, the kitchen. I'm really not home that much to wander around the other rooms."

Her fingers reached out to touch the glass again.

"You ready?"

"To meet your family, yes. To step into this gigantic house, I'm not so sure."

His heart plummeted to his boots. He grabbed a hold of her free hand. "Why?"

She turned to face him but stayed tucked in the shadows. "I guess because it reminds me of how far apart we really are."

"I'd say only a couple feet separated us right now, but we can change that pretty quick. Come here, beautiful." He tugged her as close as he could, instantly regretting that he'd brought the truck with a center console rather than the car. "Then again, maybe not."

She threw her head back and laughed.

He ran his fingers through her silky mane. "If it makes you feel better about going inside, I'll confess I'd much rather be with you in your house."

"Oh? Why's that?" She angled her cute little head to the side, her eyes like emerald orbs.

"It reflects you. Your character."

She scoffed. "Do you mean socially unacceptable or unfinished?"

He shook his head and nudged her chin with his thumb. "No. I mean intimate. Just the right size. Perfect."

"Nobody's perfect, Mason." She tucked his hand in hers. "Especially not me."

"People can be perfect for each other. God designed it that way."

"How did you end up marrying Lisa, then?"

"Had I listened and waited for Him that never would have happened." There was a whole lot more he'd like to say on this subject but not now.

No. When he finally told Remi how he felt about her, he wanted it to be special. Not while they sat in the truck parked outside his house with his family waiting on them to arrive. And he definitely didn't want to rush her.

"Sweetheart, your home is your sanctuary, and it's filled

with everything you love. That's the way it should be. That's what a home is. Not this," he cocked his head toward The Castle, "giant shell of a house. Yeah, I know it's colossal, but it's cold and empty, hollow, too. A home shouldn't be that way. It should be filled with love and laughter, with family and friends. But that's the way it will be tonight. Because you're here with me."

Her eyes swelled, and her lips curved. She swiped at her cheek with the arm of her sweater.

Soft leather creaked as he leaned in, taking his time kissing her, cherishing the feel of her arms wrapped around his neck. When he pulled back, he was satisfied that he had helped her relax and alleviated some of her fear, but she'd warmed him from the inside out. He needed to escape the tight confines of the truck. "You ready?"

"Now I am." Her words came out husky.

He opened the door and allowed the frigid air to cool the hotness racing through his veins. Goliath bounded down after him, and he walked around the truck to open Remi's door.

Would she be as ready when he admitted how he felt about her? Or would she run to the sanctuary of her home, afraid of everything he stood for?

20

"You've got a big job today, Reesie. Think you can handle it?" Mason attached the custom designed collar around the llama's neck and stood back to admire it. Goliath sat at Mason's feet, solemnly staring at the collar.

Mason pulled a treat from his pocket and tossed it to the dog. "Here you go, boy. Sorry, Reesie's gonna cover this one, but you'll have a much bigger job here soon. I hope." And prayed.

He turned his attention back to the llama. "You look great. Now don't get dirty in the next few minutes, okay? Remi will be out soon, and we'll take this thing off your neck."

Mason patted the llama's rump and made his way out of the enclosure, the sun casting its first glorious rays of the morning across the grass. Dew shimmered like the diamond he'd just attached to Reesie's neck. Not a spot of clouds speckled the brilliant blue sky. A perfect morning for proposing.

Mason paused, resting his forearms on the top of the gate, smiling as Goliath rolled around in the moist grass. Jumbo's head bobbed up from grazing in the adjoining enclosure. He sauntered over to the fence, still munching.

Mason narrowed his eyes, steering clear of the big fellow. Although it was still a love-hate relationship with that one, he'd gone from never seeing a llama before his visit to Forever Family to them totally winning him over. How quickly they'd grown on him. Friendly and inquisitive, they were such fun to be around, and he didn't think he'd ever grow tired of caring for them.

If Remi gave them a chance.

Would she?

God, You brought me to this place, to Remi. Help her see that we belong together. That with You, all things are possible.

He turned and headed to the barn, determination and anticipation making his steps light. With a long to-do list before their big dinner tomorrow, he'd feed and care for the animals so Remi wouldn't have to worry about them.

All the animals except Reesie. He'd have to concoct a reason for her to feed Reesie. That was the only way she'd find her surprise.

Better get to it. He had a lot to do.

****

Remi stepped out of the shower and quickly dried off, pulling on jeans and a sweater.

Today was Christmas Eve, and she had a lot to do before Mason came over to help her get ready for the big get-together with their families tomorrow.

She smiled, thinking of how sweet he'd been over the last month. He'd shown up to help at the sanctuary every day since racing season ended.

He'd lived up to his word. And then some.

She lifted the curtain by the front door and glanced out. Joy jolted through her veins. Mason's big black truck was parked outside already.

She filled two coffee mugs and headed to the barn, her steps light and her heart soaring to see him.

Goliath bounded over to greet her. She set the mugs down and scratched his belly for a bit. "I have to find your daddy, darling boy. Sorry."

With a moan, he curled up in the straw, resting his head on a giant paw. Chuckling, Remi picked up the mugs and went in search of Mason.

As usual, the man was humming. Remi tiptoed toward the sound and leaned a shoulder against the frame of the open stall, waiting for him to realize she was there.

When he looked up, a wide grin brightened his face.

She loved it when those crinkles fanned out from his warm brown eyes.

"Hey." His greeting was soft and welcoming. In two steps, he took the mugs from her hands and placed them on top of the stall gate then tugged her hips toward him.

She wrapped her arms around his neck, smiling up at him. He smelled wonderful. Of hay and woods, of outdoors and manly soap. "Hey back."

Standing on the tips of her boots, she pressed her lips to his and deepened the kiss when he tugged her even closer, holding her tight against his chest. Being in his arms felt so right, so comforting. She felt protected, loved, even though he'd never uttered those three special words to her.

He might not have said he loved her, but he'd shown it. He'd juggled the demands of his career and shop to help her at the sanctuary. He'd rallied his friends to remodel and renovate the house and barn. He'd even offered her money, but she'd refused every time. She wouldn't take his money. His presence in her life meant more than his money.

She pulled back with a smile. "You're here awfully early this morning."

He reached for the coffee and handed her a mug. "Didn't want you to worry about things."

"When do you ever let me worry about things?"

"That's good. I want you to feel that way."

"Protected and shielded from life's worries?"

"If I could do that, I would, but that's not up to me. That's up to God, but I promised Him I'd do my best to help Him out."

She chuckled.

His knuckles grazed her cheek and slid down her jaw, his deep voice husky, his coffee-colored eyes intent, serious. "Seriously, sweetheart, I want you to feel, no, more than that, I want you to know, that I'm here for you. That you can count on me."

Had he read her mind? How could he have known

what she'd wanted, what her soul longed for, all these years? Her eyes watered, and a huge lump refused to slide down her throat. "Thank you, Mason. You don't know how much that means to me." How many times she'd prayed for that very thing.

He sipped his coffee, keeping his gaze on her over the top of the mug, but a mischievous sparkle glinted from his eyes, replacing the seriousness from the moment before.

"So what do you want to tackle first?" They walked into the main part of the barn. Goliath's head lifted, but the dog didn't get up.

"Reesie still needs to be fed, and then we can move on to the dinner setup."

"Sounds like a plan." She filled a bucket with grain, but before she could pick it up, Mason grabbed the handle and scooped the bucket off the floor.

"I can carry that," she protested.

"Not while I'm around." He took off for the pasture, Goliath trotting along beside him, fluffy tail waving from side to side.

She had to admit that she didn't mind letting Mason carry the load if she could see that view all the time. A denim jacket strained against broad, powerful shoulders, narrowing to tapered hips and long legs. And a devoted animal journeying with him through life.

His boots stopped clomping at the barn opening. He angled over a shoulder, caught her ogling, and grinned. "You coming?"

Goliath barked, as if to say, "Yeah. Come on. Let's go."

They walked out into the sunshine together. If someone had asked her last year if she'd ever feel comfortable with a man around her farm, she'd have vehemently denied it. Amazing the difference God, time, and a certain man, made.

She glanced sideways at him, noting his clean shirt. "Did Jumbo get you again?"

Scoffing, he unlatched the gate and slid it open,

gesturing for her to go in first. "Nah. I think I finally have the big guy figured out."

She slid past him, grinning. "You mean you calculated the correct distance necessary to stay out of his firing range."

Goliath bounded through and took off running through the field. Mason closed the gate. His boots clomped against the wet grass as he caught up with her. "That works."

His smile could melt her in a puddle right here on the ground. A contented sigh rippled through her chest. If only this day, this moment in time, could last forever.

Snickers's head popped up from grazing, and she lumbered their way. Reesie followed, practically skipping behind her mama.

"What's that on her neck?" Remi squinted, trying to focus in on Reesie, but Snickers kept cutting in front of the little one, blocking Remi's view.

Mason knelt and held the bucket out, enticing the animals closer.

Remi stroked the cria's neck, her fingers coming in contact with…a collar?

She unbuckled the black collar and took it off. A tiny box dangled from the middle like a charm. What? Who could have put a collar on Reesie?

Mason?

She glanced at the man who had brought so much sunshine, so much warmth and laughter, into her lonely days.

The man, who was now kneeling, one denim knee soaking in the dewy grass, the grain bucket discarded to the side. Snickers was going to town.

"Remi." Mason took the buckle from her trembling fingers and held her hands. "Have you forgiven me for not letting on about who I was when I met you?" His brown eyes bored right through flesh and into her soul.

She nodded. That seemed so long ago. And how could

she possibly stay mad at him?

"I would never deceive you intentionally, but I'm grateful for that chance for us to get to know each other. Because in that brief window, without either of us really knowing the identity of the other, God gave me the most wonderful gift. Time with you. I never meant to hurt you, sweetheart. You know that, right?"

"I—" She sniffled, nodded again when words wouldn't come.

"Good. Because I meant it when I said, I don't want you to worry. I'll do my best to protect you from the outside world, if that's what you want."

She grazed his cheek with her fingertips. "Over the last few months, I've realized that I can't live that way anymore. I don't *want* to live in fear, and I refuse to let it rule my life."

"That's my girl." His face glowed with pride as he took her palm and caressed it with his lips. "When I'm with you, I never want the time to end, and when I'm not, I count the hours until we can be together again."

"I do the same."

"What do you say we change that?" He opened the tiny box and held up a ring, silver and sparkly.

Her jaw dropped, and her mouth formed an "oh," but all ability to speak coherently left her.

"Remi Lambright, I loved you from the moment you walked out that barn door. I love you when you're sweet and sassy, and I love you when you're shy and timid. I promise you'll hold my heart forever. Will you marry me?"

"Yes!" She threw her arms around Mason's neck, and he settled her on his thigh, still kneeling on the damp ground, and kissed her, taking his sweet time. She didn't mind a bit.

Goliath must have. He barked, loud and insistent, then stood and walked over to them, waving his tail, sniffing at the leather collar.

"He's reminding me that I forgot something

195

important." Mason took her hand and slid the ring on her finger. "I'm looking forward to the day you become my wife, Remi Lambright."

"Me, too." A deep longing rippled through her body, and she trembled.

As one they stood, and he hugged her tight, his jaw resting on the top of her head. She could stay in this position all day.

"Want to fill that house with as many kids as we have animals?"

She reared back, laughter filling her heart and joy overflowing. She angled her head up at him, challenging him with her expression. "That's a mighty big proposition, mister. Think you're up to it?"

He narrowed those dark eyebrows, love and devotion shining from his face. "You better set that date pretty soon. You know I'm always up for a challenge."

21

"Why do you have to be so secretive? I'm going to see it when I open my eyes anyway." Remi stepped carefully into the barn, her vision covered by a cloth while Mason's large hands guided her shoulders.

When his lips connected with her neck, she squealed, then laughed. "Hey, no fair. I can't see."

"Sorry, couldn't resist. I promise to behave now if you promise not to grumble about surprises."

Her heart melted at his thoughtfulness, and citrus and sandalwood mingled with the smells of horses and hay, leather and mustiness. Pine and cinnamon, ham and Christmas scents drifted through the barn. An intoxicating combination made especially more vivid with the blindfold. She angled her head toward Mason, his hands moving with her. "It smells wonderful, Mason."

"Different, huh? But I kinda like the hay and horse smell better."

"I was referring to you."

He rewarded her with another kiss, but this time to the top of her head. His breath tickled her ear. "Are you ready?"

"More than ready." He'd shooed her out of the barn yesterday and called a few friends to help him decorate for the family get-together today. He hadn't allowed her back in until now.

"Okay. Here goes." His voice sounded almost child-like in its excitement, and his fingers fumbled with the tie. The fabric dropped away from her eyes.

Her lids opened to a Christmas fairy tale. Her jaw

dropped. "Wow!"

"Do you like it?"

"How could I not like it?" She spun around, taking in the entire space.

White lights draped from the rafters, adding a festive sparkle to the interior. A giant fir towered in the corner, gorging with twinkling lights, pinecones and cranberries. Colorful gifts mounded under the tree and spilled over onto the bales of hay next to it. Tables, covered with spotless white cloths, displayed fine china and cranberry colored candle centerpieces, greenery and more pinecones. Outdoor gas heaters, situated throughout the barn, warmed the wide-open space to a comfortable temperature.

He'd even decorated a couple long tables with those stainless steel serving trays for the food her family brought. A man with a tall white chef's hat stood behind one of the tables, his arms tucked behind his back. She smiled a greeting then turned back to Mason.

"It's absolutely stunning, Mason! Thank you." Covering his cheeks with her palms, she gave him a kiss he wouldn't forget over the course of the evening.

Mason cupped her elbow. "Come on. Before everybody gets here, I want you to meet Louis."

Mason made the introductions, his arm draped around her back, encouraging her with his tenderness.

"So you're the famous Louis. Your ham is scrumptious." Mason had brought her a sample earlier.

"Thank you. It's a pleasure to finally meet you, ma'am. Mason speaks very highly of you."

"And you as well." Her gaze took in the chef's cap and carving knife. "Call me Remi, please. It looks like you planned to serve, but I hope you'll join us for dinner."

An uncomfortable look crossed his face, and he glanced at Mason. Mason spoke up. "We'd love for you to join us, Louis. It's Christmas, and this isn't the racetrack where you have to feed a bunch of people in a hurry. It's just a few family and friends coming tonight."

Appreciation and respect glowed from the chef's face, and he bobbed his head once. "Thank you. I'll be happy to join you as soon as everyone goes through the line."

"Good. Please excuse us. I have something to show Remi." Mason's hand moved to her elbow, and he guided her outside.

Stars twinkled from the now dark sky, and after leaving the warmth of the barn, Remi shivered and rubbed hands along her sleeves. Mason tucked her under his arm, generating a different kind of warmth. "We won't be out here long. I have another surprise for you."

"Another surprise?" She sighed, content and secure. This man was so good to her that even the thought of the first large get together at her place didn't upset her tonight.

He tugged her to a stop when they reached the enclosure containing Snickers and Reesie. With his arm still wrapped around her shoulder, he hiked a boot up on the wood rail.

Remi took her cue from him, letting her head settle against his solid chest. It was a beautiful night for stargazing. And she couldn't think of a better Christmas present than being here with Mason.

Usually, when they came to the fence, Snickers and Reesie were quick to make an appearance. Where were they?

A head popped around the corner of the barn, followed by another.

She squinted, trying to focus. Those heads definitely didn't belong to Snickers and Reesie. What was going on?

In the dim light cast by the florescent bulbs over the pasture, she made out two silkies timidly stepping into view, curiosity winning over their initial shyness. Ungroomed fiber hung limply, almost to their padded feet, but worse than that, she could tell that the llamas were terribly emaciated.

"Oh!" With trembling fingers, she unlatched the gate

and crept inside the enclosure. Mason's boots thudded the ground behind her.

She stepped closer, not wanting to scare them but needing to get a better look to see what she was dealing with. Knots and snarls coated the fiber on the one with the white head and black and camel-colored streaks. Open sores spotted the legs of the caramel colored llama.

"What's going on? Where did these two sweeties come from? And where are Snickers and Reesie?" She glanced sideways at Mason, caught the crinkles around his eyes.

So he had something to do with this. What, though?

"Snickers and Reesie are fine. I moved them into the back pen for tonight. I wanted to make it easy for you to see these two. Remi, meet your Christmas gift."

"My Christmas gift?"

He nodded.

Her gaze landed on the two gaunt llamas again. His Christmas gift?

"Not impressed, huh?" He must have seen her confusion. He brushed a wisp of hair behind her ear, amusement in his tone.

She leaned into him. "You might have to do a little sweet talking."

His eyebrows arched, and his mouth curved up on one end, mischief and delight warring across his face. "I can do that."

He smelled so good and looked even more scrumptious in his pressed cotton shirt and denim jeans. Talking was the last thing on her mind. Kissing? Now that sounded more like it. Her gaze speared his lips. Her fingertips trailed his jaw.

Apparently, he had talking on his mind, not kissing, because he took hold of her hand, stilling it. "We'll get to that in a minute, sweetheart, but let me explain. I don't want you to be disappointed in my gift."

"I'd never be disappointed in you."

"Don't say that. You haven't watched me race too

many times. I'm sure one of these times you'll be disappointed."

She shook her head. "Not going to happen. That's not in my DNA."

"You're doing a great job of trying to sidetrack me." He smacked his forehead. "Focus, Mulrennan."

She chuckled, and both llama heads popped up. Loud hums sliced through the air, breaking the quiet of the evening.

"Uh oh." Mason took her hand and pulled her back quickly.

She glanced back at their scared faces. "Maybe they've never heard laughter before? Poor things. We'll have to see about changing that."

They stopped at the fence, and he settled his back on the wood rail, tugging her against his solid chest, linking his hands around her waist. "That's exactly what I'm trying to tell you."

She must have missed his point. She shook her head. "I don't understand."

"These two represent my commitment for what you do, for your life's calling." The expression on his face was intent and serious as he cradled her hands in his big ones. "But what you do is also important to me. I want it to be *our* life calling. I spotted a news article about this pair. They were about to be destroyed."

She nodded, her gaze traveling back to the two animals. "I can see why. They're going to need a lot of help. Not many people or organizations would be willing to invest the time and effort."

He chucked her chin back in his direction with a thumb. She would never tire of looking into the depths of those eyes.

"They've lived through suffering and pain, but with our help and God's providence, they'll make it. And even if they don't, we will."

Her mouth formed an "oh." Would she wake up one

day to find that Mason was a figment of her imagination? Or that she'd gone to bed after one too many nights watching romance movies to find that this was all a dream?

"We've both lived through pain and suffering and survived by the grace of God. We survived, Remi, but that doesn't mean we don't carry our scars forever."

Didn't she know that?

"You've been hurt by the media. I was burned by a woman who I thought loved me but was only after my money."

"I'm sorry, Mason. You know that's not how I—"

He squeezed her hands. "I know it's not, honey. That's the reason for my gift. My hope. My commitment. My love. I'd like Forever Family to mean *our* Forever Family."

She wanted that, too, but she was still confused. "What are you saying, Mason?"

"Two things. First, that I love you, Remi Lambright. More than I ever thought possible."

"Mmmm…I like the sound of that." She leaned against his chest and wrapped her arms around his neck. Loving the way she was free to run her fingers through his hair, to nibble on his neck, to breathe in his essence, sandalwood and lavender and some kind of citrus.

He moaned, sliding his arms around her lower back. "When we get married, I want it to be 'we', not 'I.' Do you agree?"

She nodded. She didn't have much, but he could have anything he wanted.

"When you hurt, we both hurt. When you rejoice, I'll be rejoicing with you."

She got it so far.

He tugged something from his back pocket and handed it to her.

"What's this for?" She eyed the black leather wallet.

"It's all yours."

She shook her head, pushing it away, alarm chasing away the contentment that had settled in her belly. She squeezed the words past parched lips. "I don't want it."

"I know you don't want it, sweetheart, but I want to give it to you. From my heart. It's ours, not just mine anymore. God's gifted me with this to help you, to help this sanctuary."

"I'd rather sign a prenup agreement, Mason. That way you'd know—"

"There's no need for a piece of paper to be confident of what I already know in my heart to be true."

"But—"

"Please, Remi. Allow me the joy, the pleasure, the privilege of sharing this with you. All of it. The joys, the triumphs, the work, the finances…" He swept an arm through the air, encompassing the pastures and her beloved animals. "That's the true meaning of my gift."

What a treasure! How could she refuse when he was so sweet?

****

"The last one's for Mason." Remi leaned down, scooped up the last package from under the tree, and handed it to him.

He took the small package, wrapped in red paper with a white bow, and stared at it while ooohs and ahhhs came from all around. His gaze took in the scene.

After eating, they'd gathered around the giant tree, sitting on hay bales, unwrapping presents, soft Christmas music playing in the background. His parents, Patsy and Larry, had finally made it back from their two-week tour of the Caribbean islands, just in time for the Christmas celebration. Against the doctor's orders, his sister and brother-in-law had decided to join them for a couple of hours.

Mason narrowed his eyes at Angela. She looked uncomfortable. She kept blowing out through her mouth, and her hand curled around her mound of a belly. She'd surely need some help getting off that hay bale.

Jillian and Remi's mom had been here most of the day,

cooking and helping in the kitchen. Ryan had spent the day helping Mason set up in the barn. Remi hadn't batted an eye when Camdon brought a friend, Sierra, and her teenage daughter, Violet. Although Mason had talked Louis into joining them for dinner, he'd disappeared shortly after that, leaving just family and close friends for the unwrapping of gifts.

This was the first time he'd ever experienced Christmas in a barn. They would definitely do this again. There was something so homey and comfortable, so humbling and almost ethereal about celebrating the birth of Jesus in a barn. With the makeshift manger scene by the tree, the lingering animal odor and even the straw, the actual birth of Jesus in a stable became much more vivid and real.

"You've already given me a present." He tugged Remi down on his lap and pressed his lips against her silky hair.

"Ack! Enough of this mushy stuff." Camdon groaned, but he was smiling, especially when Sierra gave him a playful swat on the arm.

"Get used to it." Mason warned, and Remi's cheeks turned a beautiful shade of pink.

"Open it." She nudged.

He complied. With his arms still wrapped around her, he managed to tear off the paper. He lifted the lid to the box and pulled out a framed picture of the two of them, taken at the last race, with "May 18th" written with a sharpie across the top.

"May 18th," he read aloud.

Could it be what he thought it was? His head snapped to her, eyebrows arched, pulse racing in wild anticipation. "May 18th?"

She nodded, smiling.

He bolted from the bale, lifting her petite frame off with him. He twirled her around, shouting. "We're getting married on May 18th!"

He stopped, long enough to kiss her, just to make sure this moment was real. Pulled back when hands slapped his back and congratulations were offered.

A crowd had gathered around them. Love and happiness glimmered from Remi's face. He cupped her cheeks with his palms.

"Remi Lambright, you have made me the happiest man alive tonight. On May 18th you'll become my bride. You're the woman God made just for me, and I love you beyond my comprehension."

His gaze traveled over the faces that were so dear to her, men and women that would become his family soon, and then moved on to his family before turning back to gaze into the depths of her emerald eyes. "I can't keep life from hurting you or causing you pain, but I can promise you this, sweetheart. To the best of my ability, I will protect you, and I will love and cherish you always and forever."

He kissed her, to the tune of sniffles, lots of them, and pleas for tissues.

"Oh!"

That was a different kind of cry. A groan. His eyelids bolted open. Angela, with both hands splayed against her belly, panting in quick, short bursts.

"Oh!" Even louder this time.

Mike's jaw dropped, and he stood, frozen in place, eyes wide.

"Looks like the baby's coming." Remi stepped away from him, taking her warmth with her. In two steps, she was next to Angela, draping an arm around his sister's shoulders. "Let's get you inside the house until the ambulance gets here."

Remi glanced at Mike then speared him with her confident gaze. "Mason, can you call 9-1-1 and then show Mike into the house?"

Nodding, he pulled out his phone.

Remi led Angela from the barn, her dark head angled toward his sister's, whispering words of encouragement. Together with his mother, they led her indoors, Lessa scurrying ahead to open the door.

Mason gave the dispatcher the requested information and disconnected. He turned to his brother-in-law. "Come on, buddy. Looks like it's going to be a long night."

Epilogue

"You look beautiful." Jillian's fingers trailed along the gauzy veil then down the back of Remi's wedding gown.

Remi studied her reflection in the full-length mirror leaning against her bedroom wall. Caught the longing on her friend's face, the tears streaming down her cheeks.

The silky material rustled as Remi turned and grasped both of Jillian's hands in hers. "Thank you, Jillian." She hugged her best friend then stepped back, smiling. "Soon I'll be dressing for your big day."

Jillian scoffed and swiped at the moisture gathering on her cheeks, smearing her mascara. She shook her head. "Not anytime soon, but I appreciate the sentiment."

Remi snatched a couple tissues from the nightstand and handed it to her friend.

"Thanks. But I'll need more than this to fix my face. I'll be right back." Jillian pulled the door open and sidestepped Lessa.

Her mother came up behind her and adjusted her veil. She wore a smile like Jillian's, minus the longing. "You look as beautiful as I knew you would, honey."

"Thanks, Mom. Can you help me with my necklace? My fingers are shaking too much to work that clasp." Remi handed her mother the strand of pearls.

"You think mine will be better?" Lessa chuckled but took them with trembling fingers.

Remi turned back around at the cool touch of her mother's fingers on the back of her neck. "There you go, honey. Turn around. Let's see."

Remi pirouetted, stopping to face her mother.

Her mother nodded, her chest lifting with a deep breath. Her fingers trailed a wisp of Remi's hair until it disappeared under the veil. "You've come a long ways over the last few months, honey. Mason is good for you."

"Who'd have ever thought that I'd marry a racecar driver?"

"God knew what He was doing when He brought Mason into your life."

Remi smiled, remembering that first meeting.

A knock sounded on the bedroom door. Lessa cracked the door open, whispering to whoever was outside, then swung it wide.

"I'm heading outside, Remi. Love you." Her mother blew a kiss at Remi and kissed her husband's cheek as they passed.

Her stepfather stepped into the room. "Whoa! I'm not used to seeing you all gussied up. You look beautiful."

"Meaning I don't look beautiful in jeans?" Remi teased.

Ryan scratched the back of his head, his forehead furrowing. "Uh, that's not quite…you look beautiful in whatever—"

Remi decided to let him off the hook. Chuckling, she rubbed the back of his suit jacket. "It's all right, Ryan. I know what you meant."

It wasn't often he saw her wearing a dress. Or makeup. Or with a silly grin plastered on her face.

Relief swept across his features, and his eyebrows lifted. "It's time, Remi."

A heavy lump crawled down her throat. It's not that she wasn't ready to marry Mason. After more than five months of seeing him every day, of falling deeper in love with him, she was more than ready to dive into the next chapter of their lives.

They'd only invited a few guests, mostly family and a smattering of friends. But the media had their ways of sniffing out events like this. She wanted this day to be special, without worries about media hounds and paparazzi barging in to spoil this precious occasion with their endless questions and clicking cameras.

Mason had taken every precaution to keep the news from spreading, and the ceremony private, including hiring a security firm out of Charlotte.

Ryan patted her arm. "It's all right, honey. You don't need to worry. Everyone that showed up was on the guest list. Mason made sure of it. Every time I turn around, I'm bumping into one of those security folks. They're scattered all over the animal sanctuary."

Relief flowed through her like a cool glass of sweet iced tea on a scorching summer day. She nodded. "Okay, then. I'm ready. Let's do it."

She circled her arm through the crook in his and allowed him to lead her out of the bedroom. The house was quiet. The only sound she heard was the faint music filtering in from the reception tent set up on the grounds.

They reached the front door. Ryan stopped and leaned down to kiss the top of her head. "I'm proud to call myself your father, Remi."

A tear leaked from her eye, and she sniffled. "Let's go before I chicken out."

He shook his head. "Not likely. You've overcome so much to get to this point. You're brave and courageous, and Mason knows what a fine woman he's marrying."

"You made sure of it, eh?" Smiling, she gazed up into the eyes of the man who'd brought the sunshine and laughter back into her mother's life.

His tone was serious, along with his expression. "I would have a problem with you marrying the fellow," he flicked his head toward the door, "if he didn't love and honor you like you deserve. I might not have birthed you, Remi, but I love you as if you were my daughter."

"I love you, too, Dad." There she said it. The first time she'd ever called him by that title.

He sucked in a breath, and she ignored the moisture leaking around his eyes. He patted her hand then tugged the door handle. "Come on. There's a great guy out there waiting for you."

Mason was more than a great guy. He was *the* guy for today, tomorrow, and the next day after that. "Yeah. He is."

Jillian stood on the front porch, waiting, two simple bunches of roses in her hand. Her sandy eyebrows arched. "Ready?"

Five o'clock, and the sun dazzled against a bright blue sky, not a cloud in sight. A perfect afternoon for a wedding.

"What are we waiting for?" She grinned. Now that she knew there weren't any photographers or media hounds hanging around, her tummy felt lighter than it had in days.

"You, but now that you're here, we can get this show on the road." Jillian handed her the bridal bouquet.

"Thank you, sister of my heart." Remi gave her bestie a quick hug, the scent of roses mingling with the sweet smell of cake and punch that drifted from the reception table. "See you at the front."

Jillian's jade gown swirled around her bare ankles as she pivoted, starting the short procession. She reached the bottom of the steps and waited for the signal, poised in front of the carpet runner leading to the area where the wedding ceremony was to be performed.

Ryan kept pressure on Remi's arm tucked through the crook in his. Was he afraid she might bolt?

Not a chance. She wanted the handsome prize at the end of the runway.

Mason Mulrennan. A racecar driver. Who'd have guessed?

A smile teased the corners of her lips. God had used a racecar driver to work a miracle in her life, healing her from the bondage of fear and shame.

The first strains of music sounded, and Jillian stepped onto the carpet.

At least a hundred chairs packed with guests lined both

sides of the path, but Remi only had eyes for the man standing tall and proud, his powerful shoulders stretched wide over long legs, hands folded behind his back, a handsome, enticing smile on his lips. His warm eyes beckoned her forward like a sandy beach drew an ocean's wave.

Camdon stood next to her groom with the same pose, just taller and thinner. Goliath sat on his haunches next to Mason, a black bow tie draped around his furry neck.

Just ahead of them, Jillian stumbled, almost fell forward, but recovered by extending her arm. Her blonde head swiveled from left to front, and her movements became awkward and gangly, uncoordinated, unlike her usual graceful, athletic style. What was wrong?

Ryan tightened his grip on her arm, frowning, and turned his head sideways.

Remi leaned around him, following his gaze.

A man strode toward them, his long-legged gait eerily similar. Her jaw dropped then she let out a tiny squeal. "Carson!" She tore away from Ryan's grasp and, lifting the bottom of her gown, took the couple steps to reach him with lightning speed.

Her brother swallowed her in his arms, his grizzly face resting on the top of her head.

"You came." Joy filled and expanded her heart to overflowing.

"Did you think I would miss my little sister's wedding?" His jaw rumbled against her head, tugging on her veil, and she knew from the sound of his gruff voice that he was trying to compose himself. Her arms reached all the way around his back, with length to spare. He was so thin.

She gave him a moment then pulled back to look at him. A scruffy black beard covered his face, and his jeans were worn, his shirt ragged and too thin for the cooler spring temperatures. A book bag hung from one boney shoulder.

"Did you just get here?" she whispered.

"Yeah. Took me two weeks, but I made it. Just in time, by the looks of things." Brown flakes speckled his green eyes. He looked more weary than adventurous after more than ten years of wandering, as his gaze looked longingly at the converted stable. "I suppose I don't have time to shower or change."

She loved her brother, but she wasn't willing to wait one minute longer to become Mrs. Mason Mulrennan. "Not on your life, Carson Lambright. It might have taken you two weeks to get home, but you had more than ten years, and I've made this sweet guy—" Remi flicked her head in Mason's direction then back to Carson "—wait far too long already. You're fine just as you are." And he was. She was so happy to see him. She didn't care how he was dressed. "Go on up to the front row and sit with Mom."

Ryan clapped a hand on Carson's shoulder. "Your mom will be thrilled to see you, Carson. I'm glad you came home."

"Ryan?"

"Yeah."

Tears leaked from Remi's eyes as the two embraced. She swiped at them with the tip of her finger. When Carson pulled away, his cheeks were moist, too.

The music changed to the wedding march, and guests from both sides of the aisle stood, their faces angled to the back.

Carson slipped off to the side, behind the last row of guests. Far enough that he wasn't visible from the smiling faces pointed in her direction.

Remi swallowed. Time to go. Did she call attention to her brother by asking Ryan to escort Carson to the front row to sit next to Mom?

She wouldn't appreciate if someone did that to her, and she didn't think Carson would, either.

"Would you like me to walk with you to the front?" Ryan offered her brother.

Remi held her breath, her fingers almost crushing the long rose stems she clutched in her hand.

Carson tugged a chair from the last row. "Thanks, Ryan, but I think I'll just take a seat in the back for now."

Remi hesitated. Would he slip away again before she had a chance to talk to him?

"Go on, Remi. I'm here to stay. We can catch up later," Carson whispered, his expression solemn and weary as he nodded toward Mason.

She let out the breath she'd been holding, releasing Carson back to God. How easy it was to give a problem to God, but then try to take it back.

She didn't need a second invitation to marry the man she'd found stuck close through tough times. A man who showed her that he wouldn't give up or wave the white flag of surrender. A man who, through his patient love, had encouraged her to stretch her boundaries and freed her from the chains that had taken over her life. She'd become stronger, braver, than she ever dreamed possible.

Yeah. He was a man she could depend on. But he was so much more.

A soft breeze ruffled Remi's dress and she shivered, but it was more from peace and contentment rippling through her body than the cool air. If she could wake up every morning for the rest of her life tucked in Mason's arms and gaze into his sweet, adoring face, it wouldn't be long enough.

They shuffled up the aisle. Faces of friends and family watched quietly, their mouths forming silent "ohs."

She practically floated to the front, but she could reach Mason faster if she weren't shackled to Ryan. Could this man walk any slower?

"In a hurry?" Ryan grinned down at her, laugh lines fanning out from the corners of his eyes.

"Whatever gave you that idea? Do you think you could step it up a bit?" She cracked with a smile.

Ryan complied, stopping in front of the preacher and

kissing the top of her head. Then he took a seat next to Lessa, who was dabbing her cheeks with a tissue. He wrapped an arm around his wife's shoulders and drew her tight against his side.

Remi turned to face her beloved. His brown eyes simmered with love and tenderness, warm and velvety as roasting coffee. His rough palms cupped her cheeks, and he leaned down, taking his time kissing her.

When he pulled back, she could barely breathe, so much raw emotion filled her lungs.

"I love you, sweetheart, forever and always," he whispered.

Her free hand reached up to graze his jaw, and she smiled into his adoring face. "I love you, too."

Loving Mason meant prying loose the iron hold that fear held over her heart for too long. While Mason had shown her that love was worth the risk, God had showered her with an everlasting love and promises that if she trusted Him, she had no reason to be afraid. Nothing the media printed or that people whispered about her could ever hurt her. The only way for that to happen is if she allowed it. Loving Mason, loving God, gave her time to heal.

Life was all about choices. Some people, like her father, chose death over life. Chose a release from the pain and temporary suffering over living through it and becoming better and stronger for it.

She couldn't change her father's decision, any more than she could change what people thought about it or what they said, but she refused to live under that murky shadow another day.

This day, she chose love and life. Joy and peace. Sunshine and laughter. Healing and freedom from the chains of fear.

She chose God and Mason.

"Dearly beloved. We are gathered here today…"

Thank you for reading *A Time to Heal*! I'm so honored that you chose to read one of my stories. If you enjoyed it— and I hope you did!—please consider sharing your thoughts on Amazon. Positive reviews, even just a couple of sentences, help other readers discover new-to-them authors. Happy reading!

Would you like a peek at *A Time to Build?* Of course, you would. How can you not want to read about the prodigal Lambright and the woman who's pined for him all these years? Will they finally get their happily-ever-after?

1

The prodigal son was back.

Carson Lambright slid the book bag off his shoulder and slipped into the back row, ignoring the heads slanting in his direction, the whispers behind cupped lips, and the pointed fingers.

Didn't they know gossip wasn't polite?

Some things never changed. Like rumors and how they raged through the small town faster and with more ferocity than a wildfire.

"Excuse me." He scooted past a middle-aged couple he didn't recognize. The woman, with blonde hair piled high on top of her head in a stringent bun, gasped and jerked her partner's arm before digging a phone from the bowels of an enormous bag.

Her fingers blazed across the screen. Probably tapping out a status update to all her friends.

By now, the entire population of Harrison, North Carolina, knew Camdon's twin was back.

He groaned. A wedding was supposed to be about the bride and groom, not the wayward son finally returning home.

Scowling, he settled into a thinly cushioned seat, relief flowing all the way through to his aching limbs. After two weeks of hiking, dealing with bleeding blisters and hitching rides when he could get them, he wasn't turning around just for the sake of a few gossips.

Not after he'd made it home and hugged his little sister. He might have sorely misjudged the timing but leaving now would break Remi's heart.

It wouldn't be too healthy for his, either.

He could hardly wait to wrap his arms around his mama and meet the man who'd won over sweet, painfully shy Remi. He wanted to slap his twin on the back, and then slither into an oversized sudsy bathtub to erase the grime and dust he'd accumulated over the last thirteen years.

If only a bath could erase his mistakes, his failures, as easily.

A late spring breeze drifted over him, ruffling the flimsy material of his cotton shirt and wafting through the holes in his last pair of jeans. Scratching his scruffy beard, he slumped low in the seat, finally forcing his shoulders to relax and allowing his eyelids to droop, the long years of wandering sinking into a weariness that went bone deep. He could probably sleep straight through until Monday without moving a muscle.

But he wouldn't.

He sat up straight, determination to stay awake lifting his shoulders and resolve stiffening his spine. He hadn't traveled all this way just to reconnect with his family. No, he planned to track down Jillian Sutthill. He owed her an apology. One that was over a decade late.

Why did it always take something catastrophic to make a person long for what could have been? To make a person take stock of their blessings and realize what they'd given up or taken for granted?

He shook his head. What made him think Jillian was still in Harrison? Likely, she'd moved on. Probably living in a house with a white picket fence, three kids, and a perfect husband who doted on her. That's what she deserved, anyway.

Him? He'd never deserved her love. Not then and definitely not now. But, at least, he'd feel better after he apologized. Then, maybe he could move on with his life. Tuck the pent-up dreams and the "what if's" behind him, where they should have stayed all along.

He scraped a hand across the stubble smattered across his cheeks. Besides, what he deserved and what he wanted were two different things, and right now, neither mattered. And with no immediate job opportunity on the horizon, he'd have plenty of time to sleep.

Sighing, he blinked back the weariness and rolled his gaze along the handful of people lined up in front with the pastor.

His brother, Camdon.

Man, how he'd missed his twin. He'd even missed his brother's controlling nature, but that wasn't something he'd admit to Camdon.

The groom, famous racecar driver Mason Mulrennan. All fancied up in a black tux and pinning Remi with a love-struck gaze. If it weren't for all the pictures plastered over the news, Carson would never have guessed that the guy was a celebrity athlete. With his sister's extreme social phobia, how did she ever hook up with him?

He'd have to ask Camdon. His gaze shifted to the next person in line.

The bride. His baby sister, dressed in a silky white gown, her long hair pulled back in some type of fancy knot under that veil.

When he'd left, hadn't she been just a kid? The last thing lodged in his brain was her giddy excitement over finally getting her driver's license. Camdon had gotten on to him for teasing her unmercifully about being an old lady before she could actually drive, but she hadn't seemed to care. She'd just smiled sweetly and swatted at his arm. Now here she was, all grown up and glowing with a peaceful radiance.

Carson swiped a sleeve across his face, blotting out the moisture burning his eyes. He'd stayed away too long. He refocused on the next person in line.

Sunlight dazzled from the late afternoon sky, glinting like diamonds from a halo-like crown of the blonde-haired beauty standing next to his sister.

Jillian?

He straightened in the chair, sucking in a long breath, holding it until his lungs practically burst with the effort. It couldn't be her, could it?

Camdon had never mentioned Jillian.

Granted, he'd only called Camdon occasionally, just to let him know that he was still alive and to pass the news along to his mom. Not that his less-than-sporadic calls would stop his mother from worrying. But, talking to his twin was his way of holding on to that tenuous strand linking him to his family without the guilt. And Camdon wouldn't break down like his mother or sister would.

No. His brother was always a solid rock on the phone, just like he'd always been for their family after their dad's death.

Unlike him.

But Camdon hadn't bothered to let on that Jillian had matured into this stunning creature or even that she still lived in the area. Not that he'd ventured to ask about her.

What had he expected? That when he left, she wouldn't stick around either? *Get real, man.*

"Mason, you may now kiss your bride." The kindness in the pastor's voice snagged his attention back to the couple, now locked in a lingering man and wife kiss.

But the beautiful woman's silhouette drew his gaze. Was it really her? She'd always been beautiful, but now...

Now she was a stunner. A jade gown dropped midway to her slender ankles. Delicate lacy sleeves highlighted well-defined muscles. The silky material hugged her form and accentuated her curves.

He didn't like the direction his thoughts were headed.

Forcing his gaze up, he tamped down a sigh and silently scolded his wishy-washy heart.

Curly wisps of golden hair had come untucked from the clasp gathering it in the back. Her chin jutted out, and her lips quivered, her knuckles tightly gripping the bouquet. As if she was desperately trying to hold it together.

He twisted to get a better look around the person in front of him. Not difficult since there were only five rows of chairs for the guests.

A tear trickled down the woman's ivory cheek. She swiped it away with a tissue, leaving a tiny smudge of dark makeup.

Oh, yeah. That confirmed it.

He leaned back, shock pinning him to the chair.

Jillian's eyes. Always so alluring, so enchanting with her heavy-handed application of dark shadow and mascara, under that glorious fringe of blonde hair. She'd never realized—no, *accepted*—how beautiful she was, always shrugging off his compliments with a fierce toss of her ponytail. Did she still not believe it?

The happy couple practically danced down the center aisle, love glowing from their faces as they made their way to the back of the gathering. His sister shared a secret smile with him, flicking her head toward the reception area.

He nodded and released the breath he'd been holding, filling his lungs with the wonderful aromas floating on the breeze. Roses. Cake. Coffee. Slow roasted pork.

His belly growled loud enough to earn a glare from the old bat next to him, but he ignored her.

He'd meet up with Remi in a minute. First, he planned to track down Jillian, who never once glanced in his direction as she practically flew down the aisle, hanging on to Camdon's arm and smiling up at his twin with a familiarity that unsettled him, leaving his stomach churning from more than just hunger.

He hadn't expected a hero's welcome. But he never expected to find that his high school sweetheart had fallen in love with his brother, either.

****

Thirteen years. Without one word to her, although she knew he'd called his brother plenty of times.

Did he expect that she'd just waltz into his arms now that he was back?

So not happening!

Jillian clung to Camdon's arm with her tightest firefighter grip, doing her best to sail past the long-legged man whose dark head perched higher than the rest of the guests seated in the last row, but that was proving harder than she imagined.

Especially after catching sight of him during the march to the altar. Almost like an apparition, he'd hiked onto Remi's property from the distance, his face hidden by the sun's blinding glare. Weariness dogged his steps and stooped his shoulders. Fatigue dimmed his eyes. If the tattered jeans and shabby boots were any indication, he'd walked the whole way back to Harrison.

She knew the moment he'd recognized her, after the ceremony had started. If she had her way, he wouldn't see her now. Maybe if she didn't glance in his direction, if she worked her way to the edge of the crowd, if she ignored the invisible tug that anchored her to him, she could sneak out of here unnoticed. Remi would understand.

"Well, would you look at that? He made it back." Camdon leaned down, close to her ear, pleasure deepening his voice. So much like his twin's, yet Camdon's voice never made her heart leap. Never even so much as caused a blip in her pulse.

"It'll all work out." Camdon patted her hand, acknowledging her deep intake of breath. "Come on."

"But I'm with—" She tried to tug her hand away, but the man wouldn't let go. She couldn't escape now. Not without making a scene.

Camdon led her toward the back then finally released her to yank the chair out from behind his brother. He curled a giant paw around his twin's shoulder and pulled him into a hug.

Caught off-guard, Carson swiveled. His boot tangled with the chair leg, sending him sprawling—

Oh no! She didn't have time to brace herself for impact. The breath squeezed from her lungs, and she staggered backwards, trying desperately to keep her balance. Her spiked heel snagged in the grass. Her arms flailed, windmill fashion. She closed her eyes, prepared for the pain—

A long arm snaked around her back, saving her from smacking the ground, as effortlessly as if they were professional salsa dancers performing a complicated dip. She closed her eyes and breathed deep of freshly mowed grass, thankful that Camdon had kept her upright.

She expected to smell his familiar woody fragrance, but all she took in was the scent of outdoors, of long walks in the sun, definitely masculine...

But definitely not Camdon.

Her lashes fluttered open.

"May I have this dance?" Carson's familiar face smiled down at her, tiny crinkles fanning out from those luscious emerald orbs. The brown speckled flakes seemed a bit faded with time, but they still twinkled. One arm still latched around her back. The other gripped his brother's forearm.

With extremely little effort, he hoisted her so that they both stood upright, but her head huddled close to his chest. So close that his short puffs of air tickled her cheeks.

Her pulse ratcheted up to rocket speed, and dampness blanketed the palm that gripped the bouquet. How could he still have this effect on her? She wouldn't allow it!

She wedged a sweaty palm against his chest and gave him a not-so-gentle shove, brushing his hand away in the process. Then she tugged the awkward shoes off and gripped them with two fingers, her gaze sliding to the bouquet of now-withering buds. Blades of grass pricked her bare feet, sparking her ire even further.

"I can take care of myself." She'd survived a long time without his help, and she didn't need it today. Immediately she regretted the words. Especially when he nodded, slow and uncertain, and clamped his lips together, a tic pulsing in his jaw. A lone tear trickled from his long lashes and tracked down his whisker-heavy cheek.

Her heart twisted, and her heart puddled at her feet. She sucked in a breath, warning her primary organ to behave.

He squeezed his lids closed and pressed a thumb and finger against them.

"Jillian." When his hand fell away, all traces of the moisture had disappeared, leaving his face void of emotion. Not his voice, though. The single whispered word was full of it.

"It's good to see you, Carson." As much as she might want to, she couldn't deny it. But she didn't have to like it.

"I'd have to say it's a whole lot better to see you." His eyes gleamed with appreciation. His lips quivered into a smile, and his Adam's apple bobbed up and down along his throat.

Obviously the man who stood before her now, allowing her to witness a glimpse of his vulnerable side, wasn't the same cocky guy who'd thrown away her love years ago.

Her only response was to puff her shoulders back, steeling her spine against the onslaught of good memories.

Snuggling together at high school football games. Holding hands as they walked to school. Licking from the same chocolate-covered dipped cone on Saturday nights. Sharing kisses that singed the hair on her arms.

Treasured memories that she'd stuffed deep down, and then encased them with blocks of concrete. That way his leaving couldn't hurt her so much.

Ha. As if that had worked.

She'd forgiven him a long time ago, but that didn't mean she planned to make this reunion easier for him.

"You must be Carson Lambright." A male voice broke into her thoughts, sounding hollow and far off at first, before it finally seeped into her consciousness.

Corbin Randolph.

Her date.

As if she needed the reminder that she wasn't here alone, an arm wrapped around her back, and Corbin pulled her next to his side in a possessive gesture.

She narrowed her eyes at her friend, debating how to handle this awkward situation. In a moment of weakness, she had accepted Corbin's invitation to escort her to Remi's wedding. They'd been friends for a long time, but that's all she'd ever permitted their relationship to be.

Until tonight. When she'd intended to allow their friendship to advance to the next level. A more-than-friends relationship. But she hadn't told Corbin that, yet.

Because she'd finally waved the white flag of surrender on casual dating. How many times did she want to acknowledge the hideous scars marring her body? Or decide to dress in a pair of shorts just to catch her date's reaction? Or watch a guy try to cover his horror behind a hand or turning his head?

It didn't matter which guy or how long she'd known them. They all reacted the same. With revulsion. Except Corbin, who had a morbid fascination with the medical miracle of skin grafts.

Yep. She was done with the dating scene. But, neither could she imagine a lifetime of loneliness, of pining for a man who didn't care whether she existed or not. And her heart literally ached from putting her dreams of love and children off forever.

Corbin was the logical choice for a future. They enjoyed each other's company. He made her laugh, and he was pleasant and easy enough to talk to. Her scars didn't matter to him. But the biggest reason?

He had no control over her heart.

None whatsoever.

No, her heart had only danced to the tune of the man in front of her. The man whose shoulders had suddenly stooped, as if long, backbreaking years of manual labor had aged him right before her eyes.

But he'd willingly snuffed out the music to their dance a long time ago.

Carson stared at the arm that had disappeared around her waist. The brown flecks in his gorgeous eyes widened, and a heavy eyebrow arched. A muscle ticked along his clenched jaw.

Surely he wasn't…jealous?

She considered snuggling closer to Corbin. For about one second. She'd never been one to play games, and she wasn't about to start now just because Carson showed a flicker of emotion where she was concerned.

Jerking away from Corbin's side, she stepped out of his reach, determined not to be sucked into the bitter surge of feelings threatening to drag her back out to the sea of despair that she'd almost drowned in the day she graduated high school.

The day Carson left.

She gripped the bunch of roses so tight that sharp fingernails dug into her skin. The sweet smell of cake and flowers battled with the strong scent of roasted pork, churning in her belly, threatening to expose the hamburger she'd scarfed down for lunch. She gulped it back and loosened her hold on the flowers.

"Corbin Randolph. Meet Carson Lambright, my twin. Corbin's our favorite local vet." Camdon saved her from speaking, the emotion and warring scents leaving her throat raw, her tummy unsettled.

Carson held out a hand and, after a second's hesitation, her date accepted the handshake, reluctance lining his downturned lips and firming his jaw. As if he knew Carson was a threat. Had the gossip mill already started here at the wedding? Had Corbin heard the rumors about their past? Or was her face giving something away?

She wrangled her emotions, schooling her features, and then glanced at Carson. Fatigue shadowed his face and something else. Respect? Resignation? She couldn't tell.

Camdon clapped a hand around his brother's shoulder, joy and disbelief softening the sharp edges of his usually serious expression. "I still can't believe you're back, man. When did you get in?"

"The moment Remi began her march down the aisle. Literally."

Well, technically, he'd sauntered into the yard when Jillian stumbled down the aisle, but she didn't correct him. She hid her expression by tucking some flyaway strands of hair back behind an ear.

"Did you meet Ryan?"

"Yeah. Looks like Mom and Remi both did well." His dew-glazed gaze slid back to her, and his voice dropped a notch, as did his chin. "Jillian, I—"

Light jazz came across the speakers situated strategically in Remi's yard, then a clear male voice cut in. "What a fabulous afternoon for a wedding, right, folks? Congratulations to Mr. and Mrs. Mason Mulrennan!"

The music man waited until the applause died down, then continued. "While the bride and groom take care of pictures, relax, dance, whatever floats your boat. The party's just getting started."

"That's our cue." Indecision crossed Camdon's face, not a typical expression for the unflappable and confident Deputy City Manager. "Carson, you know Remi's going to want you in the pictures."

Carson's chest lifted. His nostrils flared slightly before his lips compressed. "I'm not dressed for pictures."

His brother nodded and flicked his head toward the house. "We can fix that. Come on."

Carson allowed his brother to lead him away, but after a couple steps, he turned around, his eyes begging her for something. What? "Jillian, can we talk later?"

The wanderer wanted to talk.

She'd wanted to talk thirteen years ago. Now? Not so much. Now, she was ready to listen.

ABOUT THE AUTHOR

Dora Hiers believes that a person should love what they do or choose to do something else. She's doing exactly what makes her heart sing and considers every day a gift. When she takes a break from cranking out heartwarming romances, Dora enjoys quiet mornings sipping coffee in front of their fireplace and lazy afternoons in her hammock reading a great book. Life's too short to be stuck in traffic, to drink bad coffee, or to read books with a sad ending. Dora and her real-life hero, a retired fire chief, make their home in the mountains of North Carolina, but with a world full of amazing places to explore, that's only a landing point.

Are you a member of Dora's newsletter family? Join now and get this clean romance as a free welcome gift.

Big city attorney. Small town firefighter. A summer's love. Can these two opposites find their sweet spot of harmony?

This delicious short story ends with a happily-ever-after and a happy sigh. Subscribe https://BookHip.com/QHDTAV to download your free gift. You may unsubscribe at any time.

Books by Dora Hiers

Potter's House Series Three/Reunion Ridge
Heart's Secret
Heart's Ransom, coming June 2021
Heart's Treasure, coming October 2021
Heart's Delight, coming January 2022

Potter's House Series Two
Her Cowboy Forever
Her Christmas Cowboy
Her Covert Cowboy

Tomlinson Brothers
Summer's Reunion
Summer's Redemption
Summer's Return

Merriville Firefighter Heroes
Kissing Santa Nic
Fully Involved
Fully Committed
Fully Surrendered

Love's Time
A Time to Heal
A Time to Build
A Time to Embrace

Marshals with Heart
A Marshal's Secret
A Marshal's Promise
A Marshal's Embrace

Cider Lake
His Valentine Promise

Her Valentine Vet

Flurries of Christmas Hope
Christmas on Mistletoe Mountain
Wishes on Mistletoe Mountain

Small Town Summers
Her Small Town Firefighter

Kester Ranch Cowboys
Roping the Cowboy
Roping the Marshal
Roping the Daddy

Made in United States
Orlando, FL
14 January 2023

28665692R00139